I0659432

AN UNCONVENTIONAL COURTSHIP
Scotty Cade

Dreamspinner Press

Published by
Dreamspinner Press
5032 Capital Circle SW
Ste 2, PMB# 279
Tallahassee, FL 32305-7886
USA
http://www.dreamspinnerpress.com/

Cover Art by Reese Dante
http://www.reesedante.com

ISBN: 978-1-62380-022-2

Printed in the United States of America
First Edition
October 2012

eBook edition available
eBook ISBN: 978-1-62380-023-9

First and foremost, to Kell my heart and soul!

I would also like to dedicate this book to Paul, my dear friend, mentor, and the brains behind the plot. His financial knowledge and guidance regarding the workings of the Securities and Exchange Commission and Justice Department made this plot as real and believable as possible. Thank you, dear friend, for everything. Kell and I will be forever grateful to you and Carol for your continued support in every aspect of our lives.

Prologue

TRISTAN MOREAU strolled into his favorite coffee shop with the morning paper tucked under one arm and a loaded-down backpack over the other shoulder. He had about two hours to kill before his next class, and he thought he'd eat an early lunch, catch up on the latest news, and maybe even get in a little studying before he had to leave for his next class. He was a senior at NYU majoring in business administration and had a pretty heavy schedule. Three days a week he had back-to-back classes, but the other two days he had only one class in the morning and one in the afternoon and today was one of those lighter days. He took his place at the end of the line with his mouth watering for the first taste of his favorite mocha-flavored cappuccino.

The broad shoulders of the man in line in front of him immediately caught his attention. *I know that back. Where have I seen it before?* Continuing his summation, he followed the muscular shoulders down the natural V shape to a small waist and beautifully rounded ass. He held his gaze there a little longer than he should, savoring the view, but eventually moved back up to the sandy-brown, shoulder length hair. The package seemed so familiar, but from where? Why would someone's back be so memorable?

With nothing else to do while he waited in line, he racked his brain trying to remember where he'd seen that physique. Probably sensing Tristan's stare, the man turned around rather nervously. When their eyes met, the familiar man did a double take and held Tristan's gaze. Tristan was stunned by the depth and beauty of the rich emerald-green eyes staring back at him. Then it all clicked: Professor Scott.

Justin Scott had been his business communications professor during his sophomore year, and Tristan quickly remembered having the biggest crush on him. The professor was rumored to be bisexual, but bisexual or not, Tristan would have never gotten involved with one of his professors. So the best he'd hoped for was to attempt to sit in class and not drool. How many hours had he watched those broad shoulder muscles flexing as the professor raised his arms to write on the whiteboard? And even worse, how many times had he gotten lost in those emerald-green eyes, face-to-face with the professor just feet away from him?

"Tristan?" the man asked with a surprised look on his face.

Shocked that the professor even remembered his face, not to mention his name, Tristan's heart skipped a beat and he felt a blush cover his entire face.

"Professor Scott?"

The man stuck his hand out. "I thought it was you. It's great to see you."

Tristan shifted the papers to the other arm and nervously accepted the outstretched hand and returned the firm yet tender handshake.

"Good to see you too, Professor. I'm great, how about you?"

"Oh you know, the same ole same ole."

The barista called "Next!" and Professor Scott moved up to the counter, placed his order and gestured over his shoulder to Tristan. "And whatever he's having."

Tristan stepped up to the counter and stood next to Professor Scott. "Thank you, but you don't have to do that."

The professor laid a hand on Tristan's shoulder. "No really, I want to."

"A large mocha cappuccino with skim milk and a ham and Swiss on rye, please." Tristan turned his attention back to Professor Scott and smiled. "Thanks."

They stepped aside and exchanged a little more small talk while the barista completed their order. When the professor's name was called, he scooped up the tray of coffee cups and sandwiches and headed to a table. "Will you join me?"

Unable to say no after the professor had bought his lunch, he graciously accepted. "Sure, Professor, if you don't mind hanging out with a lowly senior."

The professor chuckled. "First, please stop calling me professor. Justin will be fine. And secondly, I'd enjoy it. Don't tell anyone, but most of the other professors are pretty boring."

Tristan smiled and twisted his fingers in front of his lips. "That will stay our little secret."

They ate their lunch while casually catching up and chatting about everything under the sun. Tristan realized that he really enjoyed the professor's company. He had a dry sense of humor, which Tristan loved, and he didn't take himself too seriously, which Tristan especially loved. And in addition to all that, he was very easy on the eyes.

With lunch long gone, and a split-second lull in the conversation, Tristan glanced at his watch. "Wow, Prof—I mean, Justin, I can't believe how quickly time has flown by. I've got to go. I have a class in fifteen minutes."

Justin also looked at his watch. "So do I. Come on, I'll walk with you."

Tristan smiled again and nodded, warmed to the heart that Justin wanted to spend a little more time with him. "That would be nice."

They both stood and Tristan took their empty tray to the trashcan while Justin took Tristan's backpack and waited for him at the front door. When they met again, Justin handed him his backpack and held the door open for him to pass through. Tristan was assaulted by a beautiful day. Although it was the end of February, they'd had a mild winter, and the temperature felt like it was in the high sixties. He was starting to see small hints of spring as they walked through Washington Square and talked. He knew after graduation, which was a little over four months away, he would surely miss the beauty of the campus, but certainly not the schedule.

"So, any prospects on a job yet?" Justin asked.

Tristan nodded. "As a matter of fact, a few, but one I'm particularly interested in."

Justin cocked his head. "Really, good for you. You want to tell me about it?"

"It's an entry-level position with an agency called Media America, one of the leading advertising agencies on Madison Avenue."

"I'm impressed," Justin replied. "I'm very familiar with them and it's not that easy to get a foot in the door."

Tristan felt a sense of pride. Justin was right; it had taken him three separate interviews just to get an interview with his potential boss. "Thanks, I am rather proud of myself."

"And rightfully so. It just so happens that I have a good friend who is in the creative department, and maybe I could put in a good word for you."

"Hey, that would be great. But please don't feel obligated."

Tristan noticed that Justin's smile faded. And was that an expression of hurt on Justin's face? Wanting that smile back Tristan added, "But look, if you're willing, I'll take all the help I can get."

Justin smiled again and Tristan felt warmed to his toes.

Justin gazed into his hazel eyes. "Then consider it done," he said, their eyes locked in a virtual embrace.

Feeling a little shy and uncomfortable, Tristan broke the connection by nervously pointing out that they had reached the building for his next class. "Here we are." And, glancing at his watch again, "And not a minute too soon. This has really been nice, and thank you so much for buying my lunch."

Justin smiled and nodded but looked as though he were contemplating something.

"Well, thanks again," Tristan said as he turned.

Justin gently laid his hand on Tristan's arm, spun him around, and again looked him in the eyes. "Would you ah... like to have dinner with me tonight?"

Tristan tried to mask the look of surprise but probably didn't do a very good job.

"I'm sorry, I shouldn't have—"

"Yes," Tristan said before thinking. It had just come out of his mouth. All his life he'd fought the mouth/brain thing. Having no filter between his brain and his mouth was really going to get him in trouble one day. "Yes, I would love to have dinner with you tonight," he repeated.

"Really? I mean... please don't feel obligated."

"No! I really enjoyed lunch and it's not like my grade depends on it or anything," Tristan teased.

Justin beamed. "Okay then, it's settled."

Tristan reached into his backpack and pulled out paper and a pencil and jotted down his address and handed it to Justin.

Justin glanced down at the paper. "Seven okay?"

Tristan stuck out his hand. "Perfect, I'll see you then."

They shook hands and Tristan bolted for his class, hoping he wouldn't be late.

Later that night, Tristan couldn't remember when he'd had such a good time. The dinner was great, the company was great and the sex afterwards, well that was simply incredible. When Justin left his apartment very early the next morning, they made plans for a second date and as the weeks passed, they became closer and closer.

They'd been dating for about three months, seeing each other a few times a week, schedule allowing, when Tristan had his epiphany. It was a week before graduation and he was sprawled out on his couch in comfortable old sweats going over some of Media America's literature in preparation for his new job. As he read page after page, thinking more about Justin than what he was reading and not really concentrating, he recognized that for the first time in his life, he was in love. He cringed when he realized that it had only been three months, and although they had never shared any thoughts about where they were headed, he'd fallen hard. He thought the only fair thing to do was to tell Justin how he felt and hope that Justin felt the same way. The next night they had plans for dinner, so Tristan invited Justin to his place and spent the entire day cooking and making a very special meal for a very romantic evening.

When Justin arrived, Tristan was flying high on pure adrenaline. He'd never told anyone he loved them before and his nerves were getting the best of him.

When they sat down for dinner, Justin looked at him with a raised brow. "You all right?"

Tristan fidgeted in his seat. "Yeah, why?"

"You just seem a little nervous."

Tristan had this terrible habit of answering a question with a question when he was nervous. "Do I?"

Justin laughed and rolled his eyes. "Yes, you do."

Tristan didn't want to spoil the surprise, so for once, he kept quiet. "I'm fine, let's eat."

After dinner, which Tristan thought was incredible, they settled on the couch. Justin removed his shoes and put his feet on the ottoman and motioned for Tristan to join him.

Tristan sat next to him and kissed his cheek. "I want to talk to you about something."

Straightening up, Justin cocked his head, looking at Tristan. "I knew you had something on your mind. I could tell the moment I walked in." Justin smiled and kissed Tristan back. "So what is it that has the normally cool and collected Tristan Moreau a nervous wreck?"

Tristan rubbed his sweaty palms on his blue jeans and felt the blood drain out of his face. *Get a grip, Tristan; you're not twelve years old.* He took a deep breath, leaned in, kissed Justin softly on the lips and whispered. "I'm in love with you."

The look on Justin's face was not at all what Tristan had expected. It was Justin's blood draining out of his face this time and he suspected it wasn't for the same reason. "But...."

Tristan pushed himself away from Justin and glared at him. "But what?"

Justin took his feet off the ottoman and planted them firmly on the floor. "I thought we were just having a good time."

Tristan jumped up and started pacing. He was breaking out in a cold sweat and he couldn't stop his heart from pounding. "A good time? That's what we're having?"

Justin looked down with an embarrassed expression on his face. "I thought we were." He stood and put both hands on Tristan's shoulders to stop him from pacing. "I'm sorry, I thought we were on the same page. Tristan, it's a well-known fact that I'm bisexual. In fact, I'm engaged to be married in a few months."

Tristan shrugged Justin's arms off. "Engaged to be married? To whom?"

"Who doesn't matter," Justin whispered.

Tristan walked back to the couch and buried his head in his hands. He finally looked up and met Justin's eyes. "How could I have not known about her? Why didn't you tell me?"

Justin held his gaze, apparently having a difficult time trying to find words. "I didn't... didn't think it mattered. She lives abroad and we currently only see each other about once a month for a day or two."

"And you're marrying someone you only see for two days a month?" Tristan asked.

"Not exactly," Justin tried to explain, pain obvious on his face. "She's moving here right after the wedding."

Getting angrier by the minute, Tristan spat out, "And when were you going to tell me this?"

Justin wiped the sweat off of his forehead with the sleeve of his shirt. "I didn't think it would affect us. She travels extensively and will be gone most of the time. We would still get to see each other as much as we do now."

Tristan forced out a dry laugh. "So you just expected me to be your squeeze on the side, a place you come to when you need a dick up your ass?"

"Tristan," Justin pleaded. "You know it's not like that."

Tristan slammed his hand on the end table. "Then tell me how it is, Professor."

Justin was silent for a few minutes. "I care for you Tristan, I really do, but I never made any promises to you about a future together."

Knowing he was never going to win this battle, Tristan sighed, leaned back, and rested his head on the back of the couch and closed his eyes "So why didn't you just tell me you were engaged and had a girlfriend?"

Justin joined Tristan on the couch and put his hand on Tristan's knee. "I guess I was afraid of losing you."

Tristan raised his head and opened his eyes. "Well guess what, Professor, your fears just came true. Now get out!"

Justin stood and started pacing. "You don't mean that. What can I do?"

Tristan reached down and picked up Justin's shoes and tossed them at the front door. "You can walk out that door and never fucking come back is what you can do." He watched as Justin picked up his shoes and opened the door.

Justin looked back over his shoulder. "Are you sure?"

Tristan glared at him and pointed to the door.

Although Justin closed the door very gently, the sound reverberated through Tristan's head like an explosion had gone off. Then there was dead silence. The only sounds he heard were his breathing and the beating of his empty heart. A tear slid down his cheek and he wiped it away with defiance. *I will not cry! Damn it, I will not cry!*

One

Seven Years Later

TRISTAN had been studying financial reports since he'd arrived at work a little after seven that morning. He blinked a couple of times in an attempt to keep the lines from running together, but it was no use. Accepting that he'd reached his limit and needed a short break, he hesitantly put down his pencil, leaned back in his chair, and closed his eyes. "I've got to get through this," he whispered to himself as he ran both hands through his thick brown hair, stopping at the base of his neck and massaging the knot that had formed between his shoulder blades.

One last squeeze to his tired muscles and he turned in his chair and poured a glass of water from the pitcher on the credenza. He glanced around his spacious office and realized the sun had set and the moon was high in the deep blue Atlanta sky. *What happened to the daylight?* He lifted his wrist and stared at his watch as if what he was seeing was somehow wrong. *Nine thirty-eight?*

Shaking his head in amazement at the time, he stared momentarily at the beautiful downtown skyline. He downed the last of his water and turned back to the work at hand. Spreadsheets and other paperwork, illuminated only by a small lamp perched on the corner of his desk, completely covered his work surface.

He remembered switching the overhead lights off when he left his office somewhere around three o'clock to grab a quick salad, but when he returned he'd heard his phone ringing from down the hall and ran for his desk to answer it, never bothering to turn the lights on again. One call led to another, and then something else urgently needed his attention, and everything led up to this moment in time. *Another Friday night working alone in my office. I've got to get a life.*

Refilling his water, he looked around again and decided that he didn't mind the dimly lit office. He'd always hated the harshness of the overhead florescent lighting universally used in every office building in the world, and he cherished the times when his coworkers were gone and he could loosen his tie, crank up his small stereo, and simply get lost in his work. He turned again to his desk and the waiting pile of financials he'd been evaluating for the upcoming board meeting, along with the smaller stack of things to do that had been continually building up since the beginning of the week. Slowly pushing away from his desk, he walked over to the bookcase on the opposite wall and scanned his stack of CDs. He settled on Etta James, and in a few seconds, her soulful sound filled his ears as she sang "Sunday Kind of Love." He kicked his shoes off and returned to his desk. Comfortably sitting cross-legged in his chair, he studied what was in front of him. He felt a twinge of anxiety realizing just how much work he still had left to do before the board meeting on Tuesday and the earnings release on Wednesday. *I've got three full days if I work through the weekend and that should be just enough time to get everything done.* He relaxed momentarily, and then looked at his to-do list again and realized he hadn't even started on the script for the conference call with the industry analysts scheduled for Wednesday afternoon. He sighed and picked up his pencil.

As he worked, the world outside of his office was silent with the exception of the distant hum of a vacuum cleaner and the muffled voices of the janitorial staff milling about emptying trashcans and exchanging polite conversation. Every single associate had left hours ago. Some early in the afternoon, excited to be heading out of town for the long Memorial Day weekend, while others who weren't leaving town opted for a three-day weekend at home. Just before five o'clock, someone down the hall had shouted "happy hour downstairs," which meant the Agency Lounge in the lobby of the Kincaid building would be hopping for the next few hours.

With no plans to go away for the weekend because of his current workload, not to mention the fact that he wasn't in the mood for happy hour, he hunkered down, resigned to a long night of burning the midnight oil. Time passed slowly as he finished one task and closed the file, sorting through the untouched pile, categorizing file folders and prioritizing what he would attempt to finish tonight and what he would work on over the long weekend. Tristan was the ultimate professional. He'd graduated at the top of his class with a degree in business administration and was very career-driven. Since taking this job, he'd kept his personal life to a minimum and didn't allow himself many distractions from his work. He was learning everything he could about mergers and acquisitions and one day hoped to head the business development group at Kincaid International. The only caveat to his picture-perfect career was that over the last two years, after fighting it tooth and nail, he'd somehow managed to fall hopelessly in love with his boss. Of course his boss didn't know Tristan was in love with him, and he never would. The pain from his first love, while no longer front and center, was still a strong enough memory after seven years to keep him from ever going down that path again. But not giving in to it didn't make it any less real. He was resigned to the fact that all he could do was love from afar while taking advantage of any opportunity to work alongside him and that would have to be enough.

With Etta James still singing in the background, he was completely lost in his work when the muffled sound of the phone buried in a mound of paperwork startled him. He glanced at his watch again, deciding on whether he wanted to answer it or just let it go to voicemail. *Its nine fifty-five on the Friday night of a holiday weekend. Who could be calling at this hour?*

He dug through the paperwork so he could read the display on the caller ID, and then a slight smile formed on his lips. He quickly reached for the phone. "Webber Kincaid's office, this is Tristan."

"Why in the hell are you still at work, Tris?" A strong familiar voice said wryly. "It's ten o'clock on Friday night."

Before he could answer, the chastising voice added, "Friday night of a holiday weekend, no less."

His smile broadened and his heart began to flutter. He shook his head in amazement as the caring voice on the phone sent the blood rushing right to his groin. *God, after all this time just hearing his voice still does this to me.* He looked at his watch again and did a quick calculation. "Good afternoon, Web," he said with a smile on his face. "How's Australia?"

Webber James Kincaid was the chairman of the board, president, and CEO of Kincaid International Corporation and just happened to be his boss and the man he was secretly in love with. KIC, as it was commonly called, was a major advertising holding company owning about 40 percent of the largest advertising agencies in the world. With Webber at the helm, it had become a major force to be reckoned with and in the past five years had grown in leaps and bounds.

Tristan's official title was chief administrative assistant, but in actuality, he was Webber's guy Friday. He'd worked by his side many long hours, innocently at first, soaking up the knowledge freely being passed on to him. But somewhere along the way, during the many hours they'd spent together, he'd fallen head over heels in love, and his job became every bit as much about spending time with Webber as it had been about learning all he could from the master. On a daily basis, he struggled to hide his feelings where his boss was concerned, and so far, to his knowledge, he'd succeeded. He didn't even know if Webber was gay, but Webber's sexual preference didn't really matter. His boss would never know how he truly felt. Sure, Tristan's career was very important to him, but the combination of his first attempt at love and the potential of damaging Webber's reputation was what kept him at arm's length. He couldn't and wouldn't risk everything he held dear for simple matters of the heart.

So day after day Tristan told himself that he was content just to be near Webber and quietly take care of him under the cloak of doing his job. He knew he was being deceitful and cowardly, but at his weakest moments, he always thought back to his first and only love before Webber and how horribly that had turned out, and thinking about that made it all too easy to justify his actions. He constantly told himself that even if Webber was madly in love with him, it could never work, and he'd spent most of his waking hours convincing himself of that. Besides, it was much easier to love a man who didn't have a clue how Tristan felt about him. No chance of getting hurt, no chance of betrayal, and never any chance of ruining his or Webber's career. On a daily basis, he imagined what the board would say to such a scandal, not to mention how that scandal could hurt Webber, KIC, and its stockholders. He could never allow his feelings to jeopardize his heart or Webber's future, so he'd kept everything on an even keel and his personal life to himself.

He'd never actually told Webber he was gay, although he'd never tried to hide it because there was really nothing to hide. Once, out of the blue, Webber had casually asked him about his social life, and since he had none, it was easy to be honest, thinking it was better for both of them not to elaborate. And after that, Webber had never asked again.

He was startled out of his thoughts by Webber's voice. "Please go home, Tris, you're making me look really bad," Webber chuckled. "How long have you worked with me now, ten years?"

Tristan laughed, "Just two."

"Are you sure it's just two years?"

"Yeah, but it does seem like forever, doesn't it?"

"How many times in the last couple of years have I preached to you about having balance in your life? All work and no play make for a very frustrating and lonely life."

Tristan smiled to himself again because he loved it when Webber called him Tris, and he thought to himself, *you have no idea*.

There was a short silence on the line when Webber spoke up again. "I hope you mean 'feels like forever' in a good way?"

Tristan laughed. "The very best, Web. I've learned so much from you; I can't begin to tell you. I'm so grateful for this opportunity."

He knew he sounded sappy, but even after all this time, the sound of Webber's voice and his concern for his happiness, in and out of his job, still sent butterflies right to the pit of his stomach. "So what can I do for you, boss?"

"You can come downstairs and have a drink with me."

Tristan furrowed his brow. "Downstairs? I thought you weren't due back from Australia until tomorrow night?"

"Yeah, well, I flew in a day early and was on the way to the office to pick up my car when the jetlag took over and I realized I wasn't the least bit sleepy. I decided to have a drink before I went home, and when I walked into the Agency, I ran into everyone still downstairs wrapping up happy hour. Hoping you were here having a little fun, I asked around, and one of the guys told me they left you at your desk hours ago, and knowing you, I thought I'd give it a shot and see if you were still there."

"Who made all the arrangements for your early return?" Tristan asked, ignoring the invitation and feeling a little jealous.

"It was late when I decided and I didn't want to bother you at home, so I called the pilot and made the arrangements myself."

Surprised and feeling a little relieved, Tristan said, "Really? It wouldn't have been a bother, Web, it's my job."

"Yes, Tris, I know it's your job, but I can do some things for myself. And besides, I know you would have done it if I asked, but you already work too hard."

Suddenly realizing how that sounded, Tristan did a little backpedaling. "I know you're not helpless and I know you're very capable of making arrangements, but hell, if you keep that up, why will you need me?"

"That's funny, Tris. Me picking up the phone to change one flight doesn't mean I can function without you. Trust me, your job is very secure. Hell, you're getting better and quicker at the mergers and acquisitions than the business development department."

Feeling a little proud and smiling again, Tris said, "Oh thank God, for a moment there I thought I might lose my job and have to start selling my body to make ends meet."

Webber laughed nervously but ignored the joke. There was an awkward silence and suddenly Tristan felt embarrassed and smacked himself in the forehead, a habit he was desperately trying to break, for making such a stupid comment. Webber must have heard the smacking noise.

"What was that?" he asked. There was a short silence on the line. "Tristan, I know you pretty well, remember. Did you just smack yourself in the forehead?"

"Guilty as charged," Tristan admitted.

"Why?" Webber asked wryly.

"Because there's no filter between my brain and my mouth."

Webber chuckled softly but apparently decided to pass on the opportunity to tease Tristan a little more. "So are you going to join me? I have something I want to talk to you about."

Relieved to be over that awkward moment and feeling the least bit curious, Tristan sighed. "Give me about fifteen minutes to finish what I'm doing and clear my desk and I'll be right down."

"Good boy. I'll see you in a few, and Tris?"

"Yes, sir?"

"Don't get lost in your work and make me call you again."

"I promise."

"See you soon."

Tristan hung up the phone and sat at his desk, starry-eyed. He thought about how he'd gotten to this place in his life. He was in the middle of the corporate ladder, steadily climbing his way up, all the while wanting to climb his way onto his boss. That mental image of him on top of Webber sent the blood rushing right to his groin again, and he shook his head, trying to clear his mind before he went downstairs and joined the man face-to-face.

A little over two short years ago, he'd been the chief administrative assistant to the president of Media America, the most successful advertising agency on Madison Avenue in New York City, which just happened to be owned by KIC. He was excellent at his job and had earned the reputation of being smart, efficient, hardworking, and most of all discreet, which was very important for a person in his position in a publicly traded company. Word of his performance had obviously traveled to KIC because he'd been sought out by the human resources department and flown to Atlanta in one of the company's private jets to meet with Mr. Webber Kincaid personally to interview for the position of his chief administrative assistant.

Although he'd been happy in New York, with a close-knit group of friends and a rising career, he'd been twenty-eight years old and single, so he thought if he was going to do something like this, now was the perfect time. He decided to at least explore the opportunity and boarded the tiny corporate jet bound for KIC headquarters in the biggest city in the South. At one point during the flight, the pilot pulled back the curtain separating the cockpit from the cabin and explained in a thick southern drawl that they were crossing the Mason-Dixon Line and would soon be entering Georgia. He couldn't help remembering the classic movie *Gone with the Wind* and laughed as he recalled Aunt Pittypat's famous quote: "Yankees in Georgia? How'd they get in?" He snickered because being born and raised on Long Island, he really would be a Yankee in Georgia.

Before his trip to Atlanta, Tristan had googled Webber James Kincaid and learned everything he could about his potential new boss. He started with his bio on Wikipedia and ended with the smallest accounts of his personal life on the various gossip sites. Of Webber Kincaid's business accomplishments, he learned that he'd graduated with an MBA from Harvard and he and his father had run The Kincaid Corporation, as it was called then, together for a period of time. After his father's untimely death, he took over the reins and five years later he'd taken the Kincaid Corporation public. It had become Kincaid International Corporation and traded as KIC on the New York Stock Exchange. At the ripe old age of thirty-four, Webber had become the youngest chairman, president and chief executive officer of a company its size in the United States. Tristan also learned that KIC continued to consistently outperform its revenue projections quarter over quarter and the industry analysts thought very highly of Webber and his capabilities, which kept KIC's stock ratings very high.

On the personal side, he learned that Webber was an only child, born on December 26, 1966, to Addison Winston Kincaid and James Michael Kincaid. His mother had died of breast cancer when he was just fourteen years old and after her death, his father had become the one constant in his life. For the next four years, they were virtually inseparable. Webber went to the office with his father every day and had been schooled by a private tutor until he went off to Harvard. The one tidbit of information that stuck with Tristan more than anything was the fact that Webber had never married, and he couldn't deny that had set his mind to wandering. Could Webber Kincaid be gay? He started looking deeper into Webber's profiles on the Internet, and the more he read, the more little snippets he found that separately, didn't amount to a hill of beans, but when all put together, might lead one to believe he could be gay. And of course, no web site had actually outed him, which made him all the more curious.

However, during the course of his research, he found many photos of Webber at special events and various fundraisers always with the same beautiful, buxom blonde on his arm. That had set off all kinds of alarms in Tristan's head, so he investigated more thoroughly. Most of the captions said "Webber Kincaid and his longtime girlfriend Deanna Lynn." But some of them fell short of calling her his girlfriend and referred to her as his longtime friend and companion. Just for kicks, he'd googled Deanna Lynn and found out that she was a very successful swimsuit model on the West Coast, and in addition to many of the same photos with Kincaid, she had a large portfolio of her own, as well as a life and a career apart from Kincaid's.

Satisfied that he'd found as much information about Deanna as was available, he went back to Kincaid's photos and studied them carefully. He appeared to be over six feet tall and extremely fit. His hair was dark brown, bordering on black, with silver streaks and silver at his temples, and he wore it fairly long on top, combed straight back, falling into a natural part. His eyes were crystal blue and his face was long and slender. In the photos where he was smiling, he had these incredible dimples that reminded Tristan of Richard Gere or a very young Tony Bennett. He especially liked the photos of Webber with his senior staff ringing the opening bell at the New York Stock Exchange. There was just something about his smile. He seemed very proud and humbled to be there, and it showed in his every expression. As he stared at the photos, Tristan had found Webber extremely handsome and was instantly attracted to him, but as he'd later found out, nothing could have prepared Tristan for the real thing.

On the day of his interview, he remembered walking into Webber's office and instantly feeling the man's presence completely encompass him, and all the fears of being a Yankee in Georgia had completely disappeared from his mind. He'd felt this immediate attraction to Webber Kincaid, and he was sure it was written all over his face and evident by the shakiness in his handshake and the rattling of his knees. "Oh man, I can see this being trouble," he'd remembered saying to himself.

After their initial introduction by the human resources representative, they were left alone, and he and Webber had talked about various aspects of the job. Tristan had done his best to impress him with all the right answers, but every time Webber spoke, Tristan had found himself hanging on his every word. And his smile melted Tristan's heart over and over again. He found himself trying to say witty things just to see that smile again. Thinking back, he realized he was smitten from the very first moment.

By the time their interview was over, he had no doubt that Webber Kincaid was sincere, confident, and caring, with no signs of being pompous or egotistical, which in Tristan's mind was genuine. He was drawn to the man both on a personal and professional level and when they shook hands at the end of the interview, he decided that if he were offered the job, he would take it in a heartbeat.

Almost two years later to the day, he turned off his stereo, stepped into his shoes, switched off the lamps, and waved to the janitor as he made his way to the elevator. On the ride down, his heart raced in anticipation of what Webber wanted to talk to him about.

Two

TRISTAN stepped into the company lounge and scanned the room looking for Webber. While he searched, he remembered just how much he liked the look and feel of the dark and cozy space. Webber had designed it himself and to Tristan, it was what he thought of as comfortable elegance. The circular bar was the focal point in the center of the room, with a large stone fireplace beyond the bar on the far wall. On the right side of the lounge were columns and half walls separating small intimate booths with seating covered in burgundy and amber velvet. On the left side, mahogany bookcases holding Webber's personal collection of antique leather-bound classics lined the wall, and a large leather sectional was positioned front and center, forming yet another seating area. In the opposite corner, a grand piano sat atop a raised platform with a small dance floor in front and little cocktail rounds for two or four scattered about. The place was well designed and had a classic nostalgic feel, which Tristan loved, but he was most impressed with the lighting. Amber pennants hung above the bar every three feet or so and over each table and booth making every seat seem intimate and personal. The tops and bottoms of the mahogany columns were illuminated, as was the small area above the dentil crown molding surrounding the room. Each time he walked in he couldn't help but wonder if this was what Webber's home looked like.

Tristan spotted Webber sitting alone at one of the booths in the corner sipping what he knew was a single malt scotch on the rocks with a squeeze of lemon. He was staring intently at his glass and looked a little uneasy and deep in thought. He wondered what was on Webber's mind that had him so focused, but figured he'd find out very shortly. On his way to the table, he looked around and saw a few coworkers at the bar and a couple of tables with some others finishing up drinks, but didn't stop, choosing to wave and nod instead.

As Tristan crossed the lounge Webber seemed to sense his approach, glancing up from his scotch, morphing his concerned look into a huge smile as he stood. Tristan approached with an outstretched hand. Looking around again he teased, "Boy, you can sure clean out a joint."

"Tell me about it," Webber replied, accepting his extended hand.

It was a joke between them because many of KIC's employees didn't know Webber on a personal level, and on the few occasions he'd gone down to have a drink with Tristan, he'd always cleared out the place. Tristan knew it bothered Webber a little, and he'd tried to explain that most KIC employees were simply intimidated by him or any person in his position and it had nothing to do with him personally. In turn, Tristan had always told every employee who would listen that although Webber was a big guy with a big personality, he was always gracious, warm, and never judgmental.

Tristan took a seat as the waiter came over to take his order. "How's the scotch?" he asked, looking at Webber.

"Pretty good."

He looked up at the waiter. "I'll have what he's having."

With the waiter on his way back to the bar, Tristan looked back at Webber. "Welcome back?"

"Thanks, it's damn good to be home."

"Was it a successful trip?"

"Yes and no," Webber admitted.

Tristan knew that Webber had accompanied Nathan Bridges, KIC's chief financial officer, to Australia to look at possible acquisitions Nathan was championing. "How so?" he asked, cocking his head to one side.

"There are just too many possibilities," Webber confessed. "The board only approved five acquisitions, and there are at least fifteen that are ripe for the picking."

"Sounds like a pretty good problem to have."

"It is, but I need to pick the best five and I don't feel like dealing with...." Webber stopped and looked down at his scotch as the waiter approached with Tristan's drink.

Tristan sensed that Webber was struggling with something and wanted to reach out and touch his arm in a show of support, but didn't dare. They'd never shared any type of personal contact with the exception of a handshake, and he wouldn't be the first to break that unspoken policy.

When the waiter was again away from the table, Tristan spoke. "Dealing with who or what, Web?"

Webber looked up and their eyes met. "Finance and Business Development," he sighed. "We've got the best damn finance and business development departments there are, but they do such a thorough analysis that it always takes so damned long and well... to be honest, I built this business on my gut instinct, and I don't want to wait another six months or a year to get the answers I know in my heart I can get in a few weeks."

Tristan looked at him. "Web, I know you pretty well after two years and—"

"Happy Anniversary, by the way," Webber offered with a smile.

Shocked and a little flattered, Tristan's mouth opened and shut and he raised an eyebrow. "Thank you? I can't believe you remembered."

"Of course I remembered. I could never forget the day you joined KIC and my life changed for the better."

But before Tristan could find the words to speak, Webber reached out and touched his arm. Tristan watched every deliberate move as if in slow motion as Webber's hand rested on his forearm and squeezed. Suddenly, his heart was beating out of control and his knees were shaking from the sheer warmth of Webber's touch.

"I mean it, Tristan," Webber continued with admiration in his voice. "You've gone above and beyond what was expected of you as my assistant and have become invaluable to me. I hope you know that."

Tristan smiled and nodded. "It's been really great working with you the last couple of years too, Web. I've learned so much from you."

"I think the actual day is tomorrow, isn't it?" Webber asked.

Tristan's smiled widened. This man never ceased to amaze him. "You're right, tomorrow *is* the actual date."

"I'm glad you're here, Tris. Happy anniversary."

Webber withdrew his hand from Tristan's forearm and held up his glass in a toast.

Although Tristan was warmed to his toes by Webber's kind words and his simple touch, he felt a sudden emptiness as Webber withdrew his hand.

He forced a smile and touched his glass to Webber's, and they each took a sip of their drinks.

"You're right, the scotch is very good," Tristan shared.

Webber smiled, still staring at his glass.

"Okay, Web," Tristan whispered. "If you don't mind me saying so, there seems to be a little more going on here than how slow the business development department is."

Webber sighed and swirled the scotch around in his glass. He cocked an eyebrow. "As usual, Tris, you're right on the money."

"So?"

Webber hesitated for a moment then sighed. "This will probably sound really stupid to you, but I've been feeling a little out of touch with my own company lately."

Webber leaned back in his chair and took a quick look around to make sure there was no one in earshot of their conversation. "We've grown so fast, you know. Tris, in the old days it was just me and my dad and we made all the decisions based on our gut instinct and the information at hand, and to be honest, that combination never steered us wrong. But lately it seems that between Business Development, Finance, and the board of directors, I can't get a damn thing done."

Webber looked down at his scotch for the umpteenth time and Tristan again fought the urge to reach over and comfort him in some way. "So what are you going to do about it?"

Webber cocked both eyebrows this time.

"Come on, Web, I know you, and when you want something, you go after it, and if you don't like something, you change it. That's just the type of man you are."

Webber smiled the smile that always made Tristan weak in the knees and leaned in on his elbows. "Okay, well you got part of that right, so I guess you do know me pretty damn well."

Tristan grinned in triumph and leaned forward in anticipation.

"As you probably know, I own a private island in the Caribbean."

Tristan nodded, having no idea where he was going with this. "The one you allow our high-end clients to utilize? Isn't it called Nectar Island or something like that?"

"Yep and yep," Webber acknowledged. "Right on both counts."

Now Webber really had his attention.

"Anyway, I checked availability on the way back from Australia and it's empty for the next three weeks."

"And…?" Tristan asked.

"I want to take all the necessary paperwork and all the information I can find on all fifteen acquisition possibilities and then eliminate them one by one until I get to the top five. Then I'll give them to Finance and let them have at it. But if I'm right and I still have it, they will come to the same conclusions I did and we'll have our top five. What do you think?"

"For starters, it sounds to me like you're all of a sudden doubting your abilities and need reassurance that you still have it and your gut feeling still works."

Webber leaned back in his chair again and smiled. "Damn, you're good."

"And secondly, it sounds like you need a vacation."

Webber's smile broadened but he didn't change position. "Guilty as charged," he added.

"So how do I play into all of this?" Tristan asked.

"I need help and I want you to go with me."

Tristan's heart dropped to the pit of his stomach and he suddenly felt light-headed. "Me?" he said as his heart bounced down to his toes and back up and then lodged in his throat.

"Yes, you. Why not you?"

"Maybe because I don't have an accounting background, and all I know about mergers and acquisitions is what I learned from you."

"Don't sell yourself short, Tris. You've got a great head on your shoulders, and you've already proven to me that you have a knack for this sort of thing."

On the outside, Tristan stayed calm and reserved, but the inside was quite another story. In his mind, he was doing backflips. Three weeks alone on a private island with Webber was something he'd never imagined. He was excited and frightened all at the same time. Trying to remain nonchalant, he shrugged. "Okay, if you want me and think I can be of some help, I'd love to go."

"Good, then it's settled. I've already told the pilot and we're scheduled to leave from Peachtree-Dekalb Regional Airport Wednesday afternoon right after the analyst call."

"There you go again doing my job and making plans."

"I was right there on the plane. It wasn't that hard to do. I didn't even have to make a phone call."

And there was that smile again. *God, if I could only wake up to that smile every day for the rest of my life.* Still in shock, Tristan nodded as his mind kicked into overload with everything that had to be done. "If we're leaving on Wednesday afternoon, I'll need to get a lot of work done over the weekend to clear both of our desks before we take off."

"Don't you worry about my desk. I'll be in tomorrow morning to take care of that, but please promise me that you'll try to enjoy some of the holiday weekend before we leave."

"I think I can manage a couple of days over the weekend to have three weeks in the Caribbean."

"If you insist," Webber chuckled. "I guess that means I'll see you in the morning then?"

"I'll be here bright and early."

"Why am I not surprised?" Webber said as he reached for his wallet and dropped a hundred-dollar bill on the table to cover the cost of the aged single malt.

Looking down at the bill on the table, Tristan added, "Man, you're a great tipper."

Webber smiled. "Not really. That single malt was thirty-five dollars a shot."

Suddenly feeling horrible for saying "I'll have what he's having," Tristan reached for his wallet. "God, Web, I'm sorry. I didn't realize you were drinking such expensive scotch."

Webber laid his hand on Tristan's arm to stop him from getting his wallet. Tristan felt another spark at the simple touch and stopped dead in his tracks.

"No, it's on me. Happy anniversary, Tristan."

Tristan started to protest but Webber held up his hand. "I won't take no for an answer." Webber stood. "I'd better get going," he shared. "Deanna is out of the country as well, and I told her I'd call when I got home."

Tristan felt his expression change at the mention of Deanna's name as old memories came flooding back, but he hoped Webber hadn't seen it. "Have a good evening, Web, and thanks for the drink and for the opportunity."

"Tris, you do so much for me, it's the least I can do for you. Besides, I think you'll enjoy it and I know I'll enjoy the company."

Webber stood there for a moment staring at him, and Tristan suddenly felt flushed. Webber laid his hand on Tristan's shoulder and whispered, "Good night, Tris."

Tristan stood. "Good night, Web." As Webber turned to walk away, Tristan added, "Drive safely," and Webber turned around and nodded with a smile.

Tristan watched, frozen in place, as Webber walked toward the doors. When Webber was out of the lounge and no longer in sight, Tristan returned to his seat and called the waiter over to settle the bill. He was half excited, half scared to death, and his mind started to go off in a million directions. *Three weeks on a private island with Webber. How am I going to handle that?*

Whoa, Tristan, slow down! What do you think is going to happen on that island, he's gonna sweep you off of your feet and profess his undying love? You better get a grip before you get on that plane. He's got Deanna, remember? Speaking of Deanna, I wonder if she's going to be there. He didn't mention her joining us, but that doesn't mean anything. He did say he would enjoy my company and that would suggest that maybe she isn't going. Stop it you fool. It doesn't matter, he's straight or at most bisexual. And you know what happened the last time you fell for a bisexual man.

Tristan sat up straight and cursed himself for going back to that horrible time in his life. But he remembered that he'd promised himself that very night he would never get involved with anyone who wasn't free to give him his entire heart and soul. And Webber was certainly not in a position to do that. He leaned back in his chair and tried to imagine how he would get through the next three weeks with Webber on a private island.

"You can do this," he whispered to himself. "Just put everything else but work out of your mind." That he could do. After all, he'd done it for the last two years, and above all, Tristan knew their working relationship was solid. From day one, they'd worked well together, and over the years they'd developed a mutual respect for one another's abilities. Tristan soaked up every bit of knowledge Webber offered and

Webber was never too tired or too busy to explain things if Tristan had questions. He was a quick study and could almost see the delight in Webber's eyes when he'd applied something he'd learned on one project to another project, making Webber smile that damn smile.

Many late nights they worked closely together on presentations to the board or quarterly earnings releases, not to mention the many mergers and acquisitions KIC did in a single year, and Tristan learned more then he'd ever imagined. But when a project was complete, Webber would break out the scotch and they would sit, sometimes for hours, talking about the various aspects of the project and what Tristan had learned and even what Webber had learned. Those were the times Tristan treasured, and it was those times that carried him through when he just didn't know if he could keep up the charade any longer.

He loved it when Webber would let his guard completely down and they would go from conversation to conversation about everything under the sun until they both realized how late it was. They would ride down the elevator still discussing one topic or the other, and Webber would always get lost in conversation and end up walking Tristan to his car. Tristan wasn't sure if he knew what he was doing or not, but he didn't care; he would take what he could get.

He took another sip of scotch and wondered if there would be time for a little fun. Probably not, but that didn't stop him from imagining Webber in a bathing suit walking along the beach, and damn if his blood didn't go right where it shouldn't.

Although he and Webber didn't socialize that much, Tristan knew that if he asked Webber to a dinner party or some type of gathering at his home, he would certainly come, but the problem was that he never entertained. On the flip side, Webber had always included Tristan in parties and charity events given at his home, but Tristan never felt quite right attending. He didn't really think he could stand to watch Deanna on Webber's arm acting as co-host, so he always made up some excuse why he couldn't attend and bowed out gracefully.

In the two years that Tristan had been in Atlanta, he'd not taken the time to make many friends. Hell, he hadn't even finished unpacking all the boxes from his move. From day one, he'd thrown himself into his job, never wanting to disappoint Webber. But as he got to know the man, he realized that he simply enjoyed his company. It got to the point that whenever Webber was in the office, Tristan made a point to be there as well. And Webber worked an awful lot.

Through fantasizing about what would never come to pass, he decided it was time to go home. He picked up his attaché and made his way to the employee parking lot. When he reached his car, he was surprised to see a note on the windshield tucked under the wiper blade. He instinctively looked around the parking garage but saw no one. He lifted the blade and removed the note. It said, "I promise we'll have some fun. Thanks for doing this and don't forget to bring a bathing suit." It was signed with a simple W.

Tristan smiled and leaned against the car, again looking around the garage for any sign of Webber. He lifted the note to his heart and held it there for a few seconds, imagining Webber writing it and slipping it under the wiper blade. He heard a car coming down the ramp from the floor above, so he folded the little piece of paper and slipped it inside his coat pocket.

AT 5:00 A.M., Tristan's alarm went off with an irritating blare. He hesitantly sneaked an arm out from the covers and groaned as he slapped the top of the alarm clock. He contemplated briefly snuggling back into the warmth of his bed, but instead he threw off the covers and shuffled his bare feet across the cold hardwood floor to the bathroom. Face washed, teeth brushed, he ran a comb through his hair as he studied his reflection in the mirror. He didn't look any different from the day before, but the smile on his face, as he remembered he'd be spending three weeks on a tropical island with Webber, was new. He liked the look. After dressing in his typical workout clothes, he packed a bag with jeans and a golf shirt for the weekend workday. Twenty minutes later, he was pulling into the garage of the Kincaid building headed for the company gym. Tristan started his workout with thirty minutes on the treadmill at a very steep incline, then a cool down of ten minutes before he hit the machines and free weights. He was in the zone, his breath a little quick, sweat forming on his brow and trickling down his temples, determined to complete the two reps left on his third set of bench presses. Suddenly there was a pair of legs and a crotch at his head.

"You think maybe you could use a spot?" Webber said, looking down at him.

Tristan smiled weakly and nodded.

He'd purposely started working out in the mornings, since he had run into Webber in the gym after work on several occasions and being so close to him, smelling the musky sweat of his skin in the air, watching those bulging and flexing muscles, made it difficult to concentrate on his own workout. Not to mention dangerous. Working out in the company gym with his sexy boss's scent in his nostrils and his shorts tented probably wasn't the smartest career move.

"Morning and thanks," Tristan hissed as Webber helped lift the weights into the rack after his last two reps.

"Morning to you too." Webber nodded his head toward Tristan's sweat-soaked T-shirt. "By the looks of it, you've been at it awhile."

"Yeah, a little over an hour," he responded, sitting up on the bench and wiping his hands on his shorts. "What about you? Don't you usually work out in the evenings?" Tristan asked, already knowing the answer to the question.

"Yeah, well, I'm still jetlagged and didn't sleep very much last night. I woke up at four o'clock, tossed and turned for an hour, and gave up on going back to sleep, so I figured I'd get an early start knowing we had a full day of work ahead of us."

Quickly realizing his workout was now over whether he liked it or not, Tristan said, "This was my last set."

He thought he saw a flash of sadness in Webber's eyes, but he wasn't sure, and he'd long stopped trying to read something into the man's every look or off-the-cuff comment.

"I ran around the grounds about thirty minutes before I came in and saw you, so I just need about thirty more to finish up and I'll meet you in my office."

"Great. That gives me enough time to shower and get upstairs to make coffee. I'll have a hot cup on your desk when you get there."

Smiling that mind-numbing smile, Webber joked, "If I ever forget why I hired you, please remind me that it was mostly for your coffee abilities."

"Oh thanks a lot," Tristan teased. "At least it wasn't because of my pretty face." He immediately regretted saying it, but again no filter between his brain and his mouth. *I've got to work on that.*

Before he could apologize, Webber smiled and said, "That too," as he turned and walked over to the next set of machines.

Tristan stood there frozen. *What did he just say?* He shook his head in an attempt to erase Webber's response and willed himself to walk in the direction of the locker room. He dialed the combination, opened his locker, and sat down on the bench to remove his shoes and socks, all the while trying to digest what Webber had just said. Then he suddenly caught himself for the hundredth time. *Stop overanalyzing every little thing he says. You're gonna make yourself crazy.*

He finished undressing, wrapped a towel around his waist, walked over to the shower, and turned on the taps. Setting the water temperature to just this side of scalding, Tristan stepped into the hot, steamy shower. He stood under the cascading water, letting the powerful flow and heat relieve the aches in his sore and overworked muscles. He also hoped the water would wake up his tired and befuddled brain. Like his boss, he hadn't slept well the night before. His mind simply wouldn't shut off and he spent the night contemplating the next three weeks, locked away with a man he was in love with, but could never have. He stood there lost in thought, or rather trying not to think, until he wiped his eyes and noticed his fingertips were becoming shriveled, so he washed quickly and turned off the taps. After grabbing his towel from a hook, he dried off quickly, wrapped the damp cloth around his waist, and stepped out of the shower. He grabbed a second towel and rubbed it against his wet hair as he stepped into the locker room, then stopped dead in his tracks. He clenched the towel in his hand. *Damn!*

Webber stood in front of his locker buck-ass naked. Tristan's mouth watered at the sight of the tight muscular ass revealed before him. Webber's broad shoulders flexed with each movement as his thick arms fumbled for something in his locker.

Gawking, Tristan snapped his mouth shut and quickly stepped back into the shower stall. He had a hard enough time controlling his libido around Webber totally clothed. With the man gloriously naked, no chance. Hoping to avoid embarrassing himself, he waited, giving Webber enough time to finish gathering up his items and cover his nakedness.

Please let him cover that temptation, he silently prayed.

Luckily, his prayers were answered, and a few seconds later, Webber came walking into the shower area just as Tristan was stepping out of his stall for the second time.

"Oh," Webber said when he saw him. "I thought you'd be upstairs by now."

"Should be, but the hot water just felt too damn good. I stayed longer than I'd planned."

Before Webber could respond, Tristan got the hell out of there, tossing over his shoulder, "See you upstairs." He made a beeline for his locker, dressed quickly, and ran out of the gym still zipping up his gym bag. During the elevator ride to the top floor, images of Webber's muscular bare ass kept flashing through his mind, and he had to stifle the moan those enticing images produced. *I can just imagine what kind of day this is going to be. Lord, help me!*

Three

THE coffee had just finished brewing, and Tristan was arranging the pastries he'd picked up on the way into the office on a small platter. The constant hum of the white noise was interrupted when he heard a familiar voice. "I sure hope those are what I think they are."

Startled, Tristan quickly turned and saw Webber leaning in the doorway of the break room looking like a million bucks in jeans and a black turtleneck, sporting a smile that warmed him to his toes. "Maybe," he teased, his heart racing at the sight in front of him. Seemingly out of his control, his mind did a quick flashback to the locker room and Webber's naked muscular backside. He felt very flushed and shook his head to get rid of an image that was apparently burned there. He regained control of his mind again and returned the smile as he grabbed two mugs from the dishwasher and proceeded to pour them each a cup of the freshly brewed coffee.

Cheese danish had been the first thing they'd realized they had in common shortly after Tristan had taken the job. It had become a friendly competition between them to find the best in the city and, always up for a challenge, Tristan had made it his mission to take the gold. As luck would have it, he'd discovered an incredible bakery on Peachtree Street in midtown and knew after only one bite that he could soon claim victory.

Tristan chuckled to himself as he remembered bringing the danish into the office proudly claiming his win and Webber rolling his eyes in an "I'll be the judge of that" gesture. But after biting into the warm, freshly baked danish, Webber had immediately admitted defeat. From that day on, Tristan had picked up the same cheese danish at least once a week and the smile on Webber's face when he savored the treat made it so worth the extra effort.

Tristan turned and handed Webber a cup of coffee and picked up the tray of danish and his cup and stood in front of Webber, who was still blocking the doorway.

"What are you smiling about," Webber asked in a teasing tone as he stepped aside and allowed Tristan to pass.

"You," he said as he looked back over his shoulder, noticing that Webber was now following closely behind him. "You look like a puppy dog after a chew toy," he said as he burst into laughter.

"Oh really," Webber said as he caught up to Tristan and in a very swift move grabbed the tray from him and made a run for his office. "Who's the puppy chasing the chew toy now?" he chuckled. The two men settled in Webber's office and ate their breakfast, laughing about the incident and chatting about the gym, Nectar Island, but mostly about the work that had to be done before they could even think about leaving.

Tristan shared that he still needed to write the earnings press release, which was scheduled to hit the newswire right after the close of the stock market on Tuesday. He also had to write the script for the conference call scheduled for Wednesday morning when Webber would discuss the earnings release with the Wall Street analysts. And finally, he had to do preliminary evaluations for three more potential acquisitions before he could give them to Webber to determine if he should present them to the board on Tuesday morning. Feeling overwhelmed and anxious, Tristan downed the last of his coffee and stood. "It's been great, Web, but I've got to get to work. I'm finishing up the first of the remaining three potential acquisitions and I'll have that on your desk by noon and the rest by end of the day tomorrow. After lunch, I'll start on the press release and have that on your desk by the end of the day today, and then I'll get started on the analyst script and hopefully have everything to you by midday on Monday."

"That's a lot to take on, but if you can do it, I'll make it work," Webber replied. "I'll call and have lunch brought in and we can stop for a quick bite about one o'clock. Will that work?"

"It's my job," Tristan said as he glanced at his watch. "But one should be fine. I'll need a break by then."

"One it is, but I'm ordering lunch. I want to try this new deli in Buckhead and it just happens that they deliver."

"But…," Tristan protested.

Webber put his hand up. "No buts," he said. And "Tris?" he asked hesitantly.

Tristan looked up. "Yeah?"

"I'll look over the acquisitions you've already put on my desk and this afternoon I'll join you and maybe we can do the press release together. That might make it go a little faster."

Tristan felt a rush of excitement and did the best he could to try to hide his emotions. "Works for me," he said with a smile. "Thanks."

Webber nodded and smiled back. "See you at lunch then," he said seeming a little nervous and shy all of a sudden.

"Till lunch," Tristan said as he left Webber's office. *What's with Webber today? He's acting a little strange.*

Comfortably seated behind his desk listening as Billie Holiday softly sang "God Bless the Child" and basking in the afterglow of sharing breakfast and coffee with Webber, he stared at the mound of paperwork in front of him, sighed, and leaned back in his chair, gazing out of the floor to ceiling windows. He loved this time of day and the way the bright morning sun reflected off the Peachtree Plaza building, casting interesting rays of yellow and gold across the downtown Atlanta skyline. He turned back to the stack of paperwork on his desk and smiled when he recalled the first time he'd shown an interest in mergers and acquisitions. Webber had quickly taken him under his wing and vowed to teach him everything he knew. Webber had spent weeks patiently tutoring him on how to review business plans, profit and loss statements, and projected sales, and how to calculate the potential returns on investment.

Once he'd become more familiar and comfortable with the way all the numbers related to one another, he'd developed a spreadsheet that enabled him to plug in all the financial data and have the spreadsheet automatically do all the calculations and produce a summary of the company's potential.

Not long after Webber had turned him loose on his first project, he used the method that Webber had taught him and also did a parallel evaluation using his new spreadsheet, and much to his delight, he'd come up with virtually the same answers. When he'd gathered the nerve to show Webber what he'd done, Webber had been delighted and amazed at how quickly he'd grasped the process and had been truly impressed at the initiative he'd taken to improve upon it. When all was said and done, he'd taken a three to four day job and reduced it to a couple of days tops with a lesser chance for error. Since that time, Webber had started running all the potential acquisitions by him to get his opinion before he forwarded them to Business Development.

TRISTAN began his routine and quickly became lost in his work. He was putting the finishing touches on his report when he was startled by a loud noise. He jumped and jerked his head toward the sound and saw Webber standing in his doorway holding two bags of potato chips between his teeth, a deli bag in one hand and two bottles of water in the other. Tristan quickly looked at his watch and couldn't believe it was already past one o'clock.

"Sorry," Webber mumbled through the chip bags hanging out of his mouth. Tristan jumped up and took the deli bag from Webber and Webber spit out the chip bags.

"I didn't mean to startle you," Webber explained. "I lightly kicked the door twice and you didn't look up. I guess I kicked it a little too hard the third time."

Tristan smiled. "No, I'm sorry. You know how I get when I'm working."

"That I do," Webber agreed. "So you ready for lunch?"

"I can't believe it's after one already."

"Yeah, time has a way of getting away from us. I'm doing pretty well on my end, how about you?"

"I'm right on schedule," Tristan shared rather proudly. "I was just verifying a few figures before I turn it over to you."

"Oh joy," Webber joked. "Turkey with Swiss with mustard and no mayo, right?" he asked as he dug in the deli bag.

Tristan cocked his head to the side, raised a brow, and couldn't hide his smile. "How do you know that? I always order lunch."

"Come on, Tristan; give me a little credit here. We've shared lunch many times, and like me, you're a creature of habit and always order the same thing."

"Yeah, but…," Tristan again protested.

"Eat your lunch, Tristan," Webber ordered.

"Okay," Tristan said, looking down at his sandwich and shaking his head.

After lunch, they took the positions they had become accustomed to whenever they worked together on a project. Tristan was behind his desk at his computer and Webber was pacing back and forth in front of Tristan's desk deciding what points he wanted to get across in the earnings press release.

"While you do your thing, I'll get started on the basic information," Tristan said as he typed and read as he went.

"Kincaid International Corporation (NYSE: KIC) today announced results for its fiscal quarter ended March 31, 2012. For this quarter, revenues grew—" He stopped and looked up at Webber.

"Oh, sorry," Webber offered. He glanced at the financials in his hands. "That would be 27 percent to $668.4 million compared to—" He flipped to the next page for the previous year's information. "—compared to $526.3 million in the prior fiscal year." Flipping back to the first page, he added, "Cash earnings per share grew 21 percent to eighty-eight cents compared to—" He again flipped to the next page.

"—seventy-three cents in the prior year, and don't forget to add the reference to schedule two for cash earnings."

"Got it. See schedule two for cash earnings," Tristan said aloud as he typed.

Webber continued rattling off numbers, flipping back and forth between pages, and Tristan typed as fast as he could trying to keep up.

"On a GAAP basis, the company reported fiscal 2012 first quarter diluted earnings per share of seventy-nine cents compared to sixty-one cents in the prior year. See schedule one for GAAP consolidated statements of income."

"Now for my quote," Webber said as he laid the financials on Tristan's desk and started pacing again.

Tristan once again started typing and reading aloud as he typed. "Chairman, President, and CEO Webber J. Kincaid stated...." He stopped and looked up to Webber who was still pacing.

Webber stopped and looked at Tristan. "We delivered strong first quarter results, driven by continued solid execution and organic growth across all of our businesses, and the January addition of five completed acquisitions. As a result of our strong performance, we are raising our earnings expectations for the year. Furthermore, based on our core performance this quarter, we now expect overall total company cash margin to greatly expand in fiscal 2012. What do you think?" Webber asked.

"Pretty damn impressive," Tristan said. "You've done an incredible job at growing this company. Bravo, Web."

"You know what I always say," Webber joked. "If you see a turtle sitting on a fence post, you know it didn't get there alone. We are all responsible, not just me."

"I think you're being modest," Tristan replied. "But in any event, I'll give it my touch, add the schedules, analyst conference call information, and corporate boilerplate, and give it back to you for a review. Then I'll forward it to the board and the legal and investor relations departments for their approvals."

Webber was now standing at the massive wall of windows in Tristan's office looking out over the sun starting to set. His office faced north, and from his windows, he had a great view of sunrise and sunset.

Tristan slipped his hands into his pockets and walked over to Webber. He stood right next to him and their shoulders brushed; Tristan shivered from the simple touch. The sun was just starting to dip below the Atlanta skyline, reflecting off the buildings and casting an eerie glow over downtown. "Beautiful, isn't it?" Tristan said.

"It is indeed," Webber admitted. "I never get tired of this city."

"I know what you mean. I've only been here for a couple of years, but it feels almost like home."

They watched as the last burning orange glow of the sun slipped behind the row of high-rises and then witnessed the evening coming to life.

"Almost?" Webber asked.

Forgetting their previous conversation and still lost in the view, Tristan said, "Almost what?"

"You said Atlanta *almost* feels like home. Why almost?"

"Oh… it just gets a little lonely at…." Tristan stopped talking and immediately regretted the words the moment he'd said them. "No, I really love it here," he quickly added.

Desperately wanting to change the topic of conversation, Tristan urged, "Hey, why don't you call it a night. I'm sure you have something better to do with your holiday weekend than spend it working with me."

"In a little while," Webber said. "Unless you have somewhere to be?"

Tristan was a little embarrassed to admit that he didn't have plans and way too shy to say that being with his boss was right where he wanted to be, so he simply shook his head and said, "Nope, nowhere to be."

"Come on, let's walk down to my office and have a scotch before we go. You game?"

Tristan said the first thing that came to his mind. "I'd love to, but I've got to finish this press release."

"Oh come on, Tris, the press release can wait until the morning," Webber insisted. "And besides, we've been at it all day. We deserve a break."

"But—"

"No buts, I won't take no for an answer, and remember I'm your boss and trust me, I will always persevere," he added with that undeniable smile.

Tristan's heart fluttered at the sight of Webber's dimples, and he was smart enough to admit the agony of defeat. Besides, the smile had already sealed the deal, so he did the only thing he could do: he conceded.

They walked through the boardroom connecting their two offices and into Webber's expansive corner office. After two years, Tristan still got goose bumps every time he entered this space. On one end of the room was a sitting area, complete with a couch, club chairs, end tables, a coffee table, and a wall-to-wall console. In the corner of the L-shaped office was a large conference table with six chairs. Opposite the conference table was Webber's massive desk and credenza, with floor to ceiling built-ins covering the wall behind his desk.

Webber walked over to the console, opened a door revealing a small icemaker and fridge, and filled two rocks glasses with ice and a lemon wedge. He retrieved a crystal decanter from a sterling silver tray on the console and poured generous shots into each glass. He handed one to Tristan, and Tristan felt a jolt of electricity as Webber's hand brushed lightly against his. He wondered if the simple touches they exchanged would ever not make him giddy as a schoolgirl. Webber took a seat on the couch, crossing one leg over the other at the knee and, as Tristan observed, seemed to be very relaxed.

Tristan sat in one of the club chairs across from the couch and watched as Webber took a sip of his scotch. Webber looked Tristan in the eyes. "You know, I try never to ask you about your personal life, right?"

Tristan nervously nodded, took a gulp of scotch, and he felt his eyes starting to water as he endured the burn of the single malt sliding down his throat. He could only imagine what must be coming next. He rested his glass on his knee to keep his hand from shaking and looked at Webber.

Webber continued, "But you started to say that you get lonely sometimes and that pains me, Tris. You're a great guy. Isn't there someone special in your life?"

His first instinct was to panic. Webber had finally said the dreaded words Tristan had been avoiding for the last two years, and he suddenly felt anxious and flushed. He took another gulp of his scotch, this time the burn a little more manageable. This was only the second time in two years Webber had asked him about his personal life. *Of course there's someone special in my life. It's you, Webber Kincaid, it's you!*

Okay calm down Tris, you can't say that, but how do I answer that honestly without giving myself away? I've never lied to Webber and I don't want to start now.

Tristan looked up, met the silvery blue eyes staring back at him, and shrugged. "Yeah, there is sort of someone, but I'm not even a blip on their radar, so it's really a nonissue." He relaxed just a bit. There, that was the truth; still too much information, but the truth.

He saw a flash of what he thought was disappointment in Webber's eyes, but whatever it was, it quickly faded and Webber stood and began to pace. "That's what I was afraid of," he said, walking back and forth in front of the couch. "So what can I do to help get you on the radar?"

Tristan opened his mouth to speak, but before he could form a word, Webber said, "Why are you so surprised that I want to help?"

"I... I don't know," Tristan said. "Maybe it's just we've never really discussed our personal lives. I mean... other than meeting Deanna a few times, talking to her on the phone, and making travel arrangements and dinner reservations for the two of you, I know nothing about your personal life, nothing that isn't public information.

And this is only the second time in two years that you've asked about mine, so I just assumed…."

"But I did try to get to know you on a more personal level shortly after you started working here. At the first mention of your personal life, you pretty much clammed up and quickly changed the subject, so I figured you didn't want that type of working relationship."

"It's not that at all," Tristan tried to explain. "I really didn't have much of a personal life then and still don't now, but when you first asked, I didn't know you very well, so I guess I was a little embarrassed about it."

Webber stopped pacing and at sat in the club chair next to Tristan. "Okay, I tell you what," he promised. "In a few days we'll be on a tropical island for a full three weeks, and you can tell me all about this special person and how I can help, and I'll tell you everything you want to know about me. What do you say to that?"

Dread filling him to the core and not really knowing what to say, Tristan simply nodded and said, "Okay."

"Then it's settled." Webber downed the rest of his scotch and put the glass on the table. "Now, let's get out of here."

Tristan stood. "You go ahead. I'm gonna try to get a jump on tomorrow."

Looking up from his chair, Webber raised an eyebrow.

Tristan quickly added, "I promise I won't stay long. I just want to finish the press release and review my notes about the analyst call script before I leave."

"Tris, it will all be here when we arrive tomorrow."

"I know it sounds stupid, but sometimes if I review my notes before I leave, what I want you to say in the script comes to me in the middle of the night. It's like my subconscious kicks in and does all the work for me."

"That's not stupid. It happens to me all the time," Webber offered. "But promise me you won't stay very long."

"I promise," Tristan replied with a wink. "Have a good night, Webber."

"You too. I'll see you in the morning," Webber said. "And thanks for everything you do. I know I don't say that near enough."

"You're welcome and for the record, you say it plenty."

Tristan walked out of Webber's office wondering what the hell had just happened. Did he just agree to share his personal life and the special person in it with Webber? *How in the hell am I going to get out of this one?*

Four

IT WAS Wednesday afternoon and despite their shaky start on Saturday, the past few days had gone exceptionally well. He and Webber had worked through the long holiday weekend and finished everything that needed to be done. The board had approved the earnings press release, and the release and the analyst call had all gone off without a hitch.

Tristan was syncing his laptop with his desktop computer and gathering what paperwork he thought he might need for the next couple of weeks, when out of the corner of his eye, he saw movement in his doorway. He frowned when he looked up and saw Nathan Bridges leaning against the doorframe with his arms folded across his chest. Tristan didn't care for Nathan Bridges and knew for a fact the feeling was mutual.

Nathan had been the CFO of The Kincaid Corporation for fifteen years when Webber took it public, and he'd stayed on in the same capacity for Kincaid International. Their troubles had begun shortly after Tristan joined Kincaid and Nathan had secretly approached him about taking another position in one of the departments under his control. Tristan had politely declined, and from that point on, Nathan had done his best to try to undermine Tristan at every turn. Most times his actions had backfired and landed right back in his own lap, so Tristan never worried. And although it had bothered him in the beginning, he eventually adjusted to Nathan's distrust of him. One day while Tristan and Webber were enjoying a drink after a long night of due diligence, Webber had finally explained the way Nathan operated. "In Nathan's mind, you are either loyal to him or loyal to someone else, in this case me, and when you declined Nathan's offer, he knew your loyalties lay with me, and that quickly added your name to his short list of enemies," Webber explained. "And to make matters worse, Nathan can't stand the fact that I value your opinions as much as Nathan's and involve you in the decision-making process regarding highly confidential investor relations and business development activities."

But Tristan wasn't alone in his issues with Nathan. Webber, too, had always had a strained relationship with him. Early on he'd explained to Tristan that Nathan's insecurities, micromanaging, and control issues were not good traits for nurturing relationships but were great traits for a CFO, and for that reason, he tolerated his behavior but kept a close eye on him and kept him on an exceptionally short leash.

"What can I do for you, Nathan?" Tristan said, looking back down at his desk and sorting through his paperwork.

"Word has it that you're traveling to the Caribbean with our chief for a while to review some possible acquisitions," Nathan said in a sarcastic tone.

Before Tristan could answer, Webber entered his office from the boardroom door wearing a Panama Jack hat and a broad smile. His leather attaché was in one hand and he was pulling his roller board with the other. "Our car is downstairs, Tris, are you about ready to go?" he said excitedly.

Tristan couldn't help but laugh at the sight of Webber in his business suit with that silly hat. "Almost," he replied, not able to hide his smile as he peered at Nathan. "But I think Nathan has something to say."

When Nathan saw Webber he straightened and unfolded his arms. Tristan watched his entire demeanor change. "No! No, it's not important." Looking at Webber, he added, "And don't worry about anything here, I'm on top of it."

"No need, Nathan, but thanks. Everyone knows what they need to do and I'll be checking in daily."

"Oh, okay, sure. How long will you guys be gone?" Nathan asked casually.

"Lots of work on the agenda, so I'm not really sure. Probably a few weeks," Webber replied. "We've got a pretty tight schedule. Come on, Tristan, we've got to go," he continued, almost bouncing from one foot to the other.

Tristan had never seen Webber so excited and the feeling was catching. He turned off his desktop computer, closed his laptop, and shoved the rest of the papers in his bag. He threw the bag over his shoulder, grabbed his luggage, and off they went. Tristan looked back and couldn't help smiling as Nathan stood in his doorway looking really annoyed, glaring at them as they walked down the hall. "Looks like we pissed somebody off," he said.

"No doubt," Webber chuckled as they stepped into the elevator.

Once they were settled in the car on the way to the airport Webber asked, "What did he want, by the way?"

"Who?" Tristan asked.

"Nathan."

"Oh, the usual. Upset that I was going with you and not him."

Webber laughed out loud. "Yeah, I figured as much. That's why I didn't give him too many details. I'm sure it's killing him."

"I think you really enjoy torturing him," Tristan teased.

"Guilty as charged," Webber added with a wink.

"You, my good man, should be ashamed of yourself," Tristan chuckled. "But... please don't ever stop!" he quickly added.

They reached Peachtree-Dekalb airport on schedule, and the driver took them right onto the tarmac and pulled up to the waiting Kincaid jet. Tristan had traveled with Webber a few times in the past; he always felt like he was on some television show and Robin Leach from *Lifestyles of the Rich and Famous* was going to step out of the plane with a television camera pointed right at him.

They boarded the plane and the flight attendant greeted them and took their bags. "Good afternoon, Mr. Kincaid. Good to see you again, Mr. Moreau."

"Ally, how many times have I asked you to call me Webber?"

The flight attendant blushed and smiled as she took their bags. "Sorry, Mr. Kincaid... I mean Webber."

"That's better," Webber joked. "I'm gonna go say hello to the pilot and the co-pilot. I'll be right back."

"Sure," Tristan said as he glanced around the company jet. It was just as impressive as he remembered, beautifully appointed with rich mahogany paneling and black leather furnishings, very plush. Near the door on one side of the cabin were four leather seats, two facing forward and two facing back, and on the other side of the cabin was a curved dining banquette that seated six. In the middle were two couches facing each other with a coffee table in the middle, and the galley and the lavatory were in the rear of the plane.

Tristan made his way in and took a seat in one of the two seats facing forward. When Webber joined him a few minutes later, much to his surprise Webber chose the seat next to him instead of across from him.

"You all buckled up?" Webber asked as he sat down.

"Getting there," Tristan said as he reached between their two seats and froze when he grabbed Webber's hand, also searching for the end of his seatbelt. Again, he felt a jolt of energy at the mere touch of Webber's skin against his. Their eyes met and Webber's face turned beet red. *Oh God, now he thinks I'm making a pass at him.*

Tristan quickly withdrew his hand and Webber turned away, but continued to dig for the end of his seatbelt. When he did get the end of a belt, it just happened to be Tristan's, so he handed it to him and Tristan buckled himself in. "All set," Tristan said with a quivering voice as the buckle clicked into place.

Trying to defuse the awkward moment, he attempted a little humor. "Since you made all these arrangements all by your lonesome,"

Tristan said sarcastically, "may I ask how you are getting us from Tortola to Nectar Island?"

"You certainly may," Webber replied, his blush now slowly disappearing. "Have you ever been in a helicopter?"

Tristan felt his eyes widen and couldn't help the broad smile that was forming on his face.

"You're not serious?"

"Of course I'm serious. There's no better way to get a bird's eye view of the US and British Virgin Islands than from a helicopter."

Tristan simply shook his head in amazement as the excitement of what was ahead of him started to build. The pilot's voice echoed through the cabin announcing they were cleared for takeoff and would be airborne momentarily, and the flight attendant came by to make sure they were buckled in. While Webber shared more pleasant conversation with her, Tristan turned his head and stared out of the window. *This is really happening.* Then his mind suddenly went from excitement to fear. Being alone with Webber for three whole weeks and not being able to be *with* him was probably going to be his demise. *This is going to be the toughest thing I've ever done.* He took a deep breath and tried to convince himself that everything would be fine. *This is going to be all you get, so you better take advantage of it and try to enjoy yourself. When it's over, it's over, and you go back to your real life.*

The engines whined as the small jet sped down the runway, quickly leaving the ground and starting its ascent through the clouds. Minutes later Tristan was snapped out of his thoughts by the sound of the "fasten seatbelts" sign being turned off. Seconds later, Ally was raising the conference table attached to the wall between the four seats and then disappearing again, returning with two glasses of scotch on the rocks with a lemon wedge, along with a fruit and cheese tray.

"I hope you don't mind, but you seemed so deep in thought, I didn't want to bother you," Webber said apologetically. "So I had her bring us both a scotch while she prepares a late lunch for us. Is that okay?"

"Ah… yeah, sure," Tristan mumbled.

"Are you okay, Tris? Is something bothering you?"

"No... no, I'm fine. You know me, mind's always working."

"Okay, look," Webber said. "We're gonna get some work done in the next three weeks, but we're gonna have some fun as well, so you better get used to it. Have you ever been to the Virgin Islands?"

"Yeah, I've spent a decent amount of time there."

"Which island?"

"St. John mostly, but once I chartered a catamaran with some friends and sailed to all the islands. In fact, I've sailed by Nectar Island a few times. I just never dreamed I'd be staying there."

"Well, all the islands are beautiful, but the British Virgin Islands, in my opinion, are the most beautiful."

"I think you're right," Tristan agreed and was about to elaborate when Ally stepped up to their seats. "Your lunch is served Mr.... Webber."

Webber laughed. "That's better... I think."

The two men moved across the plane to the banquette with Webber sliding in first and Tristan sliding in opposite him. The space was small and their knees bumped a few times; Tristan had to calm himself in each case.

They enjoyed their lunch over casual conversation about the many US and British Virgin Islands and how different each island was in what they had to offer tourist and locals alike.

"I think we'll set a goal to visit every island before we head back to Atlanta, what do you say?" Webber offered.

"I think that's a great idea," Tristan agreed, offering his hand to seal the deal.

"By the way, Nectar Island comes with a forty-foot Sea Ray Cruiser as well, and a fifty-two-foot Manta catamaran, and they're always at our disposal," Webber added.

Tristan smiled and shook his head. "Man, this is going to be fun."

Webber laughed and really seemed to be getting a kick out of Tristan's reactions to the anticipation of learning about the finer things in life.

BEFORE Tristan knew it, the pilot was announcing their descent into Tortola and telling them that the views out the right side of the plane were breathtaking.

"Come on," Webber said, tapping Tristan on the leg. Like an overgrown kid, Webber moved across the plane and kneeled on the couch, looking out one of the two side-by-side oval windows. He looked back and patted the space next to him and smiled. "What are you waiting for; come on, the view's incredible."

Tristan froze when he saw how close together the two windows were. He knew if he followed Webber, there would be some physical contact involved, and after the seatbelt incident and the bumping knees, he was a little skittish. But as he saw it, he had no real choice. He slowly crossed the plane's cabin and kneeled down on the couch next to Webber. As he suspected, his body gave in to the indention the weight of Webber's body was making on the cushion and his thigh slid right up against Webber's. Webber tensed slightly, but this time he didn't move or pull away.

In his heart of hearts, Tristan knew it was wrong to be lusting after his straight boss, but resistance was useless against the warmth flowing through him as their bodies touched in the simplest way. He took a deep breath, trying to regain some sort of control, and tried to relax the tension in his body. When he did, his hip pressed fully against Webber's, and that small sensation sent his blood speeding throughout his body and right to his groin. As Webber pointed out island after island, Tristan relaxed at the sights below. The deep water was bluer than he remembered, and the shallower water was crystal clear. The mixed colors of the reefs below seemed to leap right out of the water.

"Isn't this incredible?" Webber asked.

"Uh-huh," was all Tristan could manage.

The pilot announced that they needed to fasten their seatbelts for landing, and they quickly moved back to their seats and buckled up. Tristan immediately felt the lack of Webber's touch, which brought him right back to reality. He looked out the window and watched as Tortola rose up from the Caribbean Sea to meet them. Lost in the silence again, he began to chastise himself for allowing even the slightest inappropriate behavior. *You've spent the last two years of your life keeping your feelings under control and in one day, God, not even a day, you've got a hard-on for your boss because your legs touched. You'd better get a grip, or the next three weeks are going to be over before they even start.*

As the plane was taxiing over to the gate, Tristan was startled out of his thoughts by Ally asking for their passports so the pilot could get them cleared through customs. While they waited, Ally brought their attachés back to them, and the co-pilot unloaded their luggage and loaded it into the awaiting sedan. The pilot quickly returned with their approved immigration forms and passports, and just like that, they were cleared and on their way. The sedan rapidly took them across the airport to the helicopter waiting to take them the rest of the way to Nectar Island.

Approaching and entering the helicopter with its large rotors spinning quickly overhead was a little intimidating, and Tristan instinctively hesitated and ducked his head to avoid getting decapitated.

"It's okay, Tris!" Webber yelled over the loud roar of the spinning blades. Tristan realized that Webber must have sensed his hesitation because he felt Webber's hand in the small of his back guiding him to the open door of the helicopter. "The rotors are over eight feet off the ground," he yelled. "I promise you won't lose a hair on that pretty little head." Surprise surged through Tristan's mind. *Did he just say pretty little head?*

Seated side by side in the backseat, Webber and Tristan were buckled in by the ground crew and given headsets to communicate with the pilot and each other during the flight. The attendant closed and secured the door and then walked around to the front of the helicopter and stood about twenty feet away. Through his headset, Tristan heard the ground crew give the "all clear" for takeoff and the adrenaline rush was almost unbearable. If he thought getting in the helicopter was intimidating, that was nothing compared to leaving the ground.

The pilot increased the engine power and the helicopter began to vibrate as the spinning rotors above and the tail rotors in the rear spun faster and faster in opposite directions. Tristan thought the feeling could be likened to being locked in a pod in the center of two equally powerful windstorms. The sheer sense of raw powers fighting against one another was exhilarating and more than enough to justify the heart palpitations he was experiencing. But when the helicopter actually left the ground and quickly banked hard to the left, the sensation of falling through the opposite door was enough to make his palpitating heart leap right out of his chest.

In an attempt to ground himself and to try to steady his equilibrium, he grabbed the arms of his seat and held on tight until the helicopter leveled out. As they climbed higher and higher, he started to get accustomed to the sensation of the alternate forces keeping the helicopter in the air and soon began to relax and take in the beauty of his surroundings. As usual, Webber had been right; there was no better way to see the Virgin Islands than from a helicopter. The lush green islands, surrounded by white sandy beaches and reefs of coral, pink and green, looked like emeralds floating in the deep cobalt-blue waters; the vistas were simply breathtaking.

There was so much to see, Tristan's head was spinning around like a barnyard owl trying to make sure he didn't miss anything. "Look," he pointed out. "There's Norman Island."

"And there's Willie T's anchored in The Bight," Webber added.

"Ah, the William Thornton," Tristan said as if reminiscing. "Have you ever been there?" he asked.

"Many times," Webber acknowledged.

Looking over his shoulder and pointing off into the distance, Webber said, "There's Jost Van Dyke, and that thatched roof in the white sand is Foxy's. And look over there in the distance, that's Virgin Gorda."

Tristan had never seen Webber this excited. It was like he was suddenly two different people. At the office he was all corporate.

Although down-to-earth and funny sometimes, he was never like this. He couldn't help but stare at the man he thought he knew inside and out. Webber must have sensed his stare, and turned. Tristan was suddenly lost in Webber's eyes. They were sparkling, as azure as the waters below, and the sun was reflecting off the silver streaks in his hair. He looked more handsome than Tristan had ever seen him. Webber held his gaze for what seemed like an eternity, and then the pilot announced that they would be touching down on Nectar Island in three to five minutes and the spell was broken. When Webber looked away, Tristan did the same. *Oh fuck, did that just really happen? What did I just see in Webber's eyes?* Tristan recovered quickly. *Nothing you idiot, you didn't see anything.* "Just stop it," he mumbled a little too loudly to the annoying voice in his head.

"Stop what?" Webber asked.

Tristan panicked. *Oh my God, I said that out loud.* "Ah... nothing," he said nervously. "So where's Nectar Island?" he quickly added, trying to change the subject.

Webber pointed out of his side of the helicopter. "There she is."

Tristan leaned over a little to get a better look and Webber threw his arm around Tristan's shoulder and rested it there. "Can you see it now? It's that nickel-size green spot in the water off in the distance. This is going to be so much fun, Tris."

Tristan's heart was suddenly lodged somewhere in the top of his throat and he couldn't breathe, so he attempted a weak smile. *Breathe in and breathe out, Tristan, you can do it.* Webber was now so close that Tristan could feel his warm breath against the back of his neck, switching Tristan's emotions to overload. Suddenly a nervous chuckle escaped and he bit his tongue to try to stop any additional outbursts. Not wanting to move, but knowing he had to, he straightened in his seat, but Webber didn't remove his arm from around Tristan's shoulder. Tristan's excitement was building by the second and he was enjoying the touch way too much. *Maybe I'm not imagining this. Either way, at least I know the fear of physical contact is behind us.*

Tristan tried to focus on what was ahead of him and switched his attention to the island slowly growing larger and larger as they approached. From the air, he had a view of the entire island. It appeared to be a few miles long and maybe a mile wide. In the distance, he could just make out the massive estate perched on the highest peak. As they got closer, he could see several bungalow-type buildings surrounding the larger building and a winding road that led down the mountain to a huge cabana and dock with a catamaran and a powerboat standing ready. Other than those structures, the island appeared to be all natural woodlands surrounded by white sandy beaches.

For days Tristan had been scared to death thinking about how he was going to handle being alone with Webber for three weeks, but now that he was flying over the island with Webber's arm resting on his shoulders, he could hardly wait to get there.

As they approached the helipad, Tristan's heart pounded with anticipation. His mind was doing backflips with eagerness of what the next few weeks might bring. Webber slipped his arm from around Tristan's shoulder and started pointing. "Look, there's Deanna!"

Everything switched to slow motion. *I couldn't have heard him right... wait.* "What?" Tristan asked as he turned his head in the direction Webber was pointing.

"Deanna! Look, she's on the helipad," Webber repeated.

When Tristan looked, there was Deanna standing on the edge of the helipad in a white suit, her blonde hair glowing in the bright sunshine. She was waving, jumping up and down, and although Tristan waved back, he felt like someone had knocked the wind out of him. His stomach dropped and his smile quickly faded. *Stupid! Stupid! Stupid! Did you really think he was bringing you here to seduce you?*

After they were on the ground, the pilot came around and opened the door. Tristan watched from his seat as Webber jumped out of the helicopter and ran to Deanna, kissed her, and wrapped his arms around her for a long embrace. He cursed himself again for even thinking for one second that Webber was the least bit interested in him. When he saw that Webber was walking back toward him, Tristan plastered on the best fake smile he could muster and unbuckled his seatbelt. He stepped out of the helicopter in a daze, so much in a daze that when he walked under the spinning rotors above, he didn't even duck his head. He stood tall, not really caring, in fact hoping the blades above would slice his fool head right off and save him the embarrassment of the next three weeks with Webber and Deanna. *Just hold it together for a little while longer and you can pretend to be sick and stay in your room for the rest of the trip.* He walked up to Deanna, smiled and stuck his hand out. "Nice to see you again," he yelled over the sound of the swirling rotors.

"You too," she responded, her voice barely audible over the roar of the helicopter as she took his hand.

Webber walked up with their bags, and the three of them turned to wave as the helicopter lifted up and headed for Tortola.

"Let's get up to the house so we can unpack and relax," Webber suggested. "It's been a long day and I'm sure it's five o'clock somewhere."

Deanna smiled and linked her arm in Webber's.

Arm-in-arm, they started up the walkway to the main house with Tristan following. In Tristan's mind, this parade said it all: Webber and Deanna together and him as the third wheel, for three whole weeks. He felt like running back to the helipad and begging the pilot to come back and get him, but what was he actually expecting? This was his job and he'd made a commitment that he needed to stick to.

When they reached the main house, Tristan turned his attention to the impressive structure. It was more incredible than he could have imagined. The house was a poster child for bringing the outdoors in. The great room had huge glass accordion doors that nested into columns, giving the illusion that there were no walls at all. The room had open-air cathedral ceilings that allowed for the Caribbean breezes to circulate throughout, and all the furniture was arranged in the middle of the massive room to allow for views in every direction.

Two marbled stairways, one on each end of the room, led down to where Tristan assumed were the sleeping quarters and kitchen. A wrap-around porch circled the entire structure with little vignettes of seating spread here and there, and of course, the view. The view was among the best he'd ever seen.

Webber dropped their bags in the foyer and walked over to the bar, and Deanna walked out onto the terrace. But before Webber could pour them a drink, a tall, thin, and very distinctive older gentleman with mocha-colored skin appeared out of nowhere. Tristan could tell by his domestic uniform that he was probably one of the staff.

"Ah, Mr. Webber, good to have you back, sir," the gentleman said in a heavy island accent. "Please allow me to do that."

Webber grabbed the man in a warm embrace. "Good to be back and so good to see you Kenton, how is Amani?"

"She's just fine, sir, thanks for asking."

"And Kit?"

"She too is doing very well. In fact, she's here on break from university."

"Splendid," Webber replied. "Tell them to come up when they get a minute."

"I'll tell them, sir. They're downstairs prepping for dinner, but I'm sure you'll see them soon enough."

Kenton poured Webber his usual and looked at Tristan. "And you, sir?"

Before Tristan could answer, Webber said, "The same and forgive me, where are my manners?"

Just then Deanna walked up to the bar. "Kenton, you remember Deanna?" Webber asked.

"Of course, good to see you, ma'am."

Deanna kissed Kenton on the cheek. "Nice to see you too, Kenton, and please call me Deanna."

"Yes, ma'am," Kenton replied shyly.

Webber continued, "Tristan Moreau, meet Kenton Reynolds."

"Pleased to meet you, sir," Kenton said with a nod in Tristan's direction.

"My pleasure," Tristan replied.

"Kenton, his wife Amani, and their daughter Kit have been with us since I was ten years old," Webber explained. "Well, not Kit, she was born after they joined us, but she's grown up here and they are practically family."

Kenton handed Tristan his scotch and poured Deanna a drink.

"I think I'll skip the drink right now," Deanna said rubbing her stomach. "I'm a little queasy from my flight. Do you have any club soda or ginger ale, Kenton?"

"Yes ma'am, right away."

"Now don't forget to send the girls up," Webber reminded Kenton as he motioned for Tristan and Deanna to follow him out onto the terrace. As they reached the railing, Tristan saw that directly below on the next level down was an enormous infinity pool with a whirlpool spa attached. The grandeur of the home left him speechless.

Webber looked out over the Caribbean. "Well, what do you think?" he asked, Tristan following his gaze.

"Simply amazing" was all Tristan could say.

"I'm glad you like it," Webber said proudly. "In case you're wondering, there are six bedrooms on the level below us, all with the best views the Caribbean has to offer, as well as a chef's kitchen and a fitness center. On the lower level down, there is a home theater complete with a concession stand and a bowling alley. In addition to the main house, there are three bungalows for guests who prefer a little more privacy. I hope you'll try to take advantage of everything this house has to offer. Where do you think you might like to stay?" Webber asked nonchalantly.

"I'll give you and Deanna some privacy and stay out in one of the bungalows," Tristan responded quickly. No way did he need it thrown in his face what Webber and Deanna had, what he could never have.

Tristan again thought he saw a flash of disappointment on Webber's face, but he was through with all the speculation. The truth was in front of him in living color.

Webber simply said, "Wherever you'll be the most comfortable."

"Thanks," Tristan replied and downed the rest of his scotch. "It's been a long day. If you'll show me to my bungalow, I'll go unpack and give you guys some time alone."

Tristan was sure he saw a quick frown on Webber's face, but at this point, he no longer trusted his own eyes.

"Come on, I'll show you to your room," Webber said as he motioned to one of the marbled stairways. As they stepped inside the great room, a portly woman as round as she was tall with the same beautiful mocha skin as Kenton stood with her hands on her hips staring at Webber. She looked to be near the same age as Kenton, and Tristan quickly thought how odd she and Kenton would look standing next to one another, he being so tall and thin and she being so short and round.

"Mr. Webber, you sure are looking well," the portly woman said. "Now come over here and give Amani her due."

Webber ran to her and threw his arms around her neck and kissed her cheek. She lifted him completely off the ground and spun him around like he weighed fifteen pounds. Webber roared with laughter and Tristan's heart melted just a bit more to see this side of Webber and the relationship he had with these people.

When Webber regained his footing, he looked back and held out his arm. "Amani, you remember Deanna."

"Of course, good to see you, ma'am," and the two women shared an embrace.

Webber continued, "Amani, this is Tristan Moreau. He'll be staying with us while we try to get some work done."

"Oh, Mr. Webber, you already work way too hard. I sure hope you folks can get some fun in while you're here," she said, glancing back and forth between the three of them.

"We'll do our best," Webber insisted.

Tristan shook Amani's hand, but before he could say anything, a thin and very attractive young girl ran into the room and jumped into Webbers arms. "Webberrr!" she screamed. He spun her around like Amani had done to him and she squealed with laughter.

Webber put her down; she straightened her clothes and hugged him again. "It's so good to see you."

"You too, sweetie, how's university?"

"Good. Three point nine grade point average," she boasted with a smile.

"Good girl. I knew you'd make us proud."

"She sure has," Amani added.

"Kit, this is Tristan Moreau, and of course you already know Deanna."

"Good to meet you, Mr. Moreau." She nodded in his direction before turning her attention to Deanna and adding, "And always good to see you, Deanna. I hope you can find the time to give me some good supermodel gossip to bring back the girls at university."

Before Deanna could answer, looking a little embarrassed, Amani chimed in. "Come on Kit, let's get back to work and give these good folks some time to unwind."

She looked at Tristan. "Welcome, Mr. Tristan, and if you need anything at all, just ask. You too, Miss Deanna."

"I will, Amani, and thank you," Deanna said as she winked and squeezed Kit's hand. "We'll talk later," she added. Kit's eyes lit up and she almost bounced out of the room, led by her mother.

"I'm sorry, Tristan. I was about to show you to your bungalow before all of the commotion. Deanna, would you like to walk with us?"

"No thanks," she said. "I think I'll take this opportunity to rest and freshen up a little. This humidity does horrible things to my hair and makeup."

Webber and Tristan both smiled. Webber looked at Deanna. "See you in a bit?"

She simply nodded.

Webber kissed her cheek before leading Tristan down the stairs to the lower level. As they made their way down the hall, Webber stopped and opened one side of a double swinging door. "Here's the kitchen if you need anything. You'll find that it's very well stocked."

"Thanks, but I'm pretty low maintenance," Tristan shared.

"Well if you do need anything, don't hesitate to ask, and most of all, please make yourself at home."

"I will," Tristan replied.

Webber continued, "FYI—Kenton, Amani, and Kit live on the lower level and are always here, but you almost never see or hear them unless you want something. They'll prepare all of our meals and do all of the housekeeping, but they really do fade into the background. It seems I have to always go looking for them if I just want to visit and catch up."

"They seem awful fond of you," Tristan observed.

"And I of them," Webber admitted. "Kenton and Amani are like my adoptive parents and Kit, well she's like the little sister I never had."

"You're all very lucky to have one another."

"We are indeed."

They continued down the hall and Webber pointed to the left. "Deanna and I will be staying in the main house bedrooms in that direction and the gym is to the right. Again, make yourself at home and use it anytime."

"This is really nice, Webber. Thanks so much for having me."

"My pleasure," Webber said through a smile.

Webber seemed nervous all of a sudden and it threw Tristan off a bit. He'd known him for two years and Webber Kincaid was always calm, cool, and collected. What could he be nervous about?

They continued down the long hallway that ran the length of the house and when the hall ended, a great room appeared that opened to the massive pool area. The great room was almost as large as the room above, but a little more casual. There was a variety of gaming tables on one side of the room, a pool table on the other, and several arcade-type video games lining the far wall.

They walked out to the pool deck and Tristan stopped dead in his tracks. The view from this side of the island was just as incredible as the other. "Breathtaking," he murmured.

"That's the same way I felt when my father first bought this place. I've always felt more at home here than anywhere else on earth."

"I know what you mean," Tristan shared. "I've only been to the Caribbean a few times, but it's one of the only places I can unwind and relax. It takes me a few days, but it's so worth it."

Tristan was looking out over the water, but he felt Webber's stare. He turned and their eyes met again. Webber held his gaze this time and Tristan was sure he saw something hiding behind Webber's silvery blues. Webber opened his mouth to speak. "Tris, I...." Then suddenly he hesitated and looked away. "Your bungalow is just around the corner to the left. You should be very comfortable, but if you don't like the accommodations, we have plenty more from which to choose."

"Oh, I'm sure it will be perfect," Tristan assured him. "When do you want me for dinner?"

Webber smiled and quickly looked down at his feet. When he looked back up, their eyes met again. "Oh, how about cocktails around seven?"

"Seven it is," Tristan said, running his hand through his hair.

"Tristan, is everything all right?"

"Sure, why?"

"You just seem ill at ease, a little nervous."

"Oh, I'm fine, just tired. It's been a busy few days."

"I know what you mean, but hopefully you'll get some much deserved downtime in the coming weeks."

Tristan wanted to scream, *You mean the coming weeks with you and Deanna?*

But he took a deep breath and did the appropriate thing. Tristan always did the appropriate thing. He stuck his hand out to Webber. "I can't thank you enough for inviting me along."

Webber accepted Tristan's outstretched hand and they shook. In a move that surprised Tristan, Webber covered their joined hands with his free hand and said, "The pleasure is all mine, Tris. See you at dinner."

Tristan picked up his luggage and started walking in the direction of his bungalow. He felt Webber's eyes following him until he was around the corner and wondered what in the hell just happened. Webber looked like he had something to say, but stopped midthought. *I think this has been the weirdest day of my life.*

He found his bungalow right where Webber said it would be, and it was glorious to say the least. It was very spacious but had the feeling of being warm and cozy. To the left was a sitting area, with a couch and two club chairs situated around a fireplace with a large flat screen television hanging over the mantel. In the center of the room was a large, canopied king-size bed surrounded by mosquito netting. To the right was a massive bathroom with a jetted tub looking out over the Caribbean Sea. There was a glass-enclosed steam shower large enough for ten people and an enormous walk-in closet. Tristan left his bags in the closet and walked back into the bedroom and over to the bed. He kicked off his shoes and pushed the netting aside enough to crawl in. He put his hands behind his head, closed his eyes, and let his mind wander over the events of the day.

Why am I suddenly reading something into everything Webber says? Am I looking for something that just isn't there? Of course you are, you idiot. Webber has never expressed any personal interest in you, so why are you looking for something now? Is it because he asked you along on this trip? It's a work trip and he needs your help, that's all. Besides, if he had the least bit interest in you, why would he bring his girlfriend along?

God, I'm so lame. He rolled over on his side and pulled the pillow over his head, hoping to make the entire day go away.

Five

WEBBER walked into Deanna's bedroom, where she was sprawled across the bed nonchalantly flipping through a magazine. He cleared his throat and she looked up with a hesitant smile. "Well?"

"He doesn't know I'm alive," Webber said with a defeated tone. He plopped down on the foot of the bed and rested his head in his hands. Deanna sighed and closed her magazine. She scooted down to the foot of the bed and sat next to him.

"So did you tell him?"

"Tell him what?"

"Did you tell him you're alive?"

Webber ran his fingers through his hair, the frustration mounting with each second. "How can I do that, D? As I told you the other night, he said there was someone he cared for."

"But you also told me that he said he wasn't even a blip on that person's radar. What if he's talking about you, Webber?" Deanna questioned.

"I can't believe I'm the person. He's never given me any reason to believe that he has any interest in me outside of our working relationship."

"Yeah, but from everything you've told me, he's the ultimate professional."

"I know. I mean... he is the ultimate professional, but I think I would have gotten some sort of vibe from the guy."

"So tell him already," Deanna pleaded.

"Kiddo... if I tell him how I feel and he isn't interested, he could sue me for sexual harassment. Not to mention if he went public with this I could be caught in the middle of a scandal that could really hurt the company my father founded, not to mention ruin me and my career."

"Come on, Webber, you have more money than you could ever spend in your lifetime, and besides, you know Tristan. You've worked closely with him for two years and you've been in love with him for a majority of that time. Even if he isn't gay and he has no desire to take a trip on the wild side, do you really think he would call foul and use it against you in a court of law?"

"No. I guess you're right."

"So...?"

"I'm trying, okay," Webber insisted. "I thought if we got away and had some time together outside of the office, I could get a better sense for where his head is." Webber stomped his foot. "Damn it, D, I don't even know for sure that he's gay."

"Come on, Webber, I've only met him a few times, but even on those few occasions, I could see the way he looks at you."

Webber stood up and started pacing. "Then why can't I see it? Why can't I be sure?"

"Because you're too close to it," she tried to explain. "You're his boss. Look at this from his point of view. What if he has feelings for you and he confesses those feelings and you're not interested. *He* could lose his job. Maybe you're both just caught up in the what-ifs."

"So what in the hell do I do?"

"If you really love him, you try to find a way to make this happen. You don't have to seduce him, just start by trying to get him to open up to you. And you open up to him as well."

Webber stopped and looked at Deanna. "You know, kiddo, there were times today during our trip when I thought I saw something in his eyes, like we connected on some level. Then when we landed it was gone as quick as it came."

Webber walked over to the balcony and stood at the rail. A few seconds later he felt Deanna step up behind him and slip her arms around his waist and lay her head on his back.

"I'm sorry," she whispered. "But do you really think my being here is helping? He was gracious when we saw each other, but I saw the disappointment in his eyes. You really need to tell him that we are just best friends."

"I know, but I want to be sure he's interested because if he's not and it's gets ugly, you're here as my beard."

"God, I hate that term," Deanna chuckled. "Do you really think it will turn ugly?"

"God, I hope not," Webber admitted. "I know this will really sound stupid to you," he confessed, "but today on the jet, Tristan and I were both reaching for our seatbelt at the same time and his hand brushed against mine, and I swear my body tingled for the next ten minutes. Then a little later, in all the excitement of his first helicopter ride, our eyes met and we held each other's gaze for what seemed like eternity."

"Then what?" Deanna asked.

"The damned pilot announced our approach to the island and interrupted whatever was happening. I know I felt something and I think he did too. But… what if I'm wrong, D? I could lose everything."

Deanna turned Webber around, took both of his hands in hers, and looked him in the eyes. "Sweetie, you're scared. You've known Tristan for two years. From what you've told me, I can't believe that he would do anything to hurt you."

Webber sighed and rested his forehead against hers. "I know you're right. But God, if we're wrong, I could lose…."

Deanna released his hands and put her finger on Webber's lips to quiet him. "And if we're right, look what you could gain," she whispered. "I guess you just need to decide what's more important, what you stand to lose, or what you stand to gain. It's now or never."

Webber took Deanna's hands, brought them to his mouth, and gently kissed them. "You're the best friend, beard, and fag hag a guy ever had."

Deanna took a swat at Webber's chest and turned away from him with folded arms and pouty lips. "God, I hate fag hag too. Can't you come up with some better terminology?" Then she quickly turned back to him and smiled. "Fruit fly, maybe. Yeah, fruit fly, I like that better." She giggled.

Webber laughed, turned her around again, and smacked her on the butt. "Now you go and freshen up and I'll go and make myself presentable so I can sweep one Tristan Moreau off his feet."

"Now that's the Webber Kincaid I know and love," Deanna teased. "Always confident and in control. Go get 'em, tiger."

TRISTAN lazily turned over and stretched. He opened his eyes and suddenly realized where he was. He looked at his watch. *Six thirty-five. Shit! I must have dozed off.* He threw his head back on the pillow in frustration. With no time to waste, he sat up and frantically searched for an opening in his enclosed cocoon. Finding where the netting overlapped, he slipped through and in the process, got his foot caught in the puddled fabric and went down with a thump, landing flat on his face. He didn't know why, but after everything that had happened that day, this struck him as funny. He rolled over and stared at the ceiling, roaring with laughter.

When he was able to compose himself, he got to his feet and ran to the closet to grab his suitcase, stopping only to turn on the steam shower. He rummaged around in his bag until he found a pair of white linen slacks and an emerald green polo shirt. He spread his clothes out on one of the club chairs and ran back into the bathroom, stripped and hopped into the shower. Fifteen minutes later he'd showered, brushed his teeth, dried his hair, and was spraying on a little Dolce and Gabbana cologne. He dressed, slipped on a pair of canvas loafers, and looked at his watch. *Damn, I'm good, five minutes to spare.*

Wanting to be fashionably late, he had a few minutes to kill, so he meandered around the grounds admiring the lush gardens and how well they were manicured. When he realized it was after seven, he walked around to the pool area, stopping to again take in the magnificent view. He rested his elbows on the rail, gazing out at the orange ball of fire hovering just above the horizon. *I could certainly get used to this. Maybe I should dump corporate America and become a beach bum. I'm sure I could sell T-shirts at Foxy's or something.*

He was startled out of his fantasy by a familiar voice. "Looks like it's going to be an incredible sunset."

Tristan spun around and looked up to see Webber standing on the balcony looking down at him. Webber was wearing tan slacks and an open-collared, short-sleeved white linen shirt that hugged every inch of his muscular chest. Tristan's mind started wandering. *Who needs a sunset with a view like this? You just can't help being gorgeous can you? What a god.*

Tristan shook his head, knowing he had to concentrate on forming words. "I think it already is," he said when was able to gather the composure to speak.

"Come on up, I've got a drink waiting for you."

"Be right there," Tristan choked out.

He made his way through the game room, past the kitchen and up the staircase to the upper level. When Tristan reached the top of the stairs, Webber motioned for him to come over to the bar where Kenton was pouring them drinks. When he reached the bar, he was instantly consumed with a sweet, woodsy, very masculine smell. Tristan smiled as Webber handed him his drink. *He even smells like a god.* "Thanks."

Tristan quickly scanned the room. "Where's Deanna?"

"Oh, she's still primping. You know the supermodel type. Uh, about Deanna…."

"Actually I don't," Tristan confessed. "But she seems really nice."

"Yeah, she's a doll."

"What about Deanna?" Tristan asked.

But before Webber could answer, he heard the click clack of high heels against the marble floor. "I better be the doll you're talking about, mister," Deanna said, sashaying over in a little lime-green sleeveless dress with silver high-heeled sandals, looking every bit the supermodel.

"How about a glass of wine?" Webber asked walking over to Kenton.

"I'll pass," she said. "Dear Lord, look at that sunset."

"You'll pass?" Webber chuckled. "Since when?"

"Oh stop it, you. Take a look at that sunset."

Webber and Tristan turned just in time to see the breathtaking contrast of the orange, pink, and yellow hues against the pale blue sky and the deep azure water.

They stared in silence until the last of the sun had slipped below the water's edge, leaving the warm glow hovering over the horizon.

Webber turned to Tristan. "We don't get many sunsets like this in Atlanta, do we?"

"Not like this we don't," Tristan confessed. "I'm not sure many people do."

"Oh, come now, boys," Deanna interjected. "You're landlocked there in Atlanta. You need to come out to the West Coast. We get these sunsets every night."

Before he or Webber could respond, Amani walked onto the terrace and held a silver tray in front of them. "Butter-poached lobster on Asian spoons," she said. "One of my specialties."

They each took a ceramic spoon off the tray, and Amani handed them each a linen cocktail napkin.

Tristan was the first to sample the island favorite. "Wow, Amani, this melts in your mouth," he said, putting the ceramic spoon back on the tray and taking another. "I have to have one more."

"I have more where that came from," Amani said, smiling proudly. "And thank you, sir."

"No, thank you," Tristan responded. "And please stop calling me sir."

Amani giggled and nodded her head.

Deanna and Webber both sampled the lobster and gave their kudos to Amani, who seemed to be floating on air from the compliments. "I'll be right back with Mr. Webber's favorite, my homemade conch fritters."

Webber's eyes lit up. "You're too good to me, Amani."

"No such thing, Mr. Web," Amani insisted. "Mr. Tristan, I'll bet you didn't know that the senior Mr. Kincaid paid for Kit to have a tutor so we could live here on the island and take care of this place. And when she grew up, Mr. Webber paid for her entire university education."

Tristan smiled warmly at Webber, his heart melting again. "I didn't know that."

"Where are those conch fritters you've been promising?" Webber asked in an obvious attempt to change the subject.

Amani turned and headed for the stairs. She stopped and looked over her shoulder. "He doesn't like me talking about how generous he is," she shared. "But sometimes I just can't help it. He makes my heart swell with pride."

"Enough already," Webber exclaimed with a wave of a hand, his face turning several shades of red. "Now get my fritters."

They heard Amani chuckling all the way down the stairs.

"That was very generous of you, Webber," Tristan offered genuinely. "And it seems like the money wasn't wasted."

"Kit's a great girl and she deserves every break she can get in this life," he explained. "Kenton and Amani gave up a normal life to live on this island and take care of this place and our family, and it was the least we could do. In fact, my parents made sure they were well provided for in the event we ever sold this place or worse, lost it."

"Your parents sound like they were great people," Tristan concluded.

"They were great people, and I really miss them," Webber confessed. "Even more so when I'm here, they loved this place so much."

They fell silent. Tristan watched as Deanna laid her hand on Webber's arm in a show of support and secretly wished it was him comforting Webber.

The awkward silence was broken when Amani popped out onto the terrace with a tray of her famous conch fritters.

"Now that's what I'm talking about," Webber proclaimed as he eyed the delectable treats.

Webber took a bite and savored every second. After he swallowed, he turned to Tristan. "I've been crazy about conch since I was a kid, but I don't think I enjoyed it as much then as I do now. There's something about Amani's perfect combination of secret herbs and spices that just blows me away, and she never fails to deliver the goods."

Everyone enjoyed the fritters over light conversation. They covered the Virgin Islands, KIC stuff, and Deanna's modeling career, to name a few. They were lost in conversation about the baths at Virgin Gorda when Kenton interrupted, "Dinner is served, Mr. Webber."

"Oh my God, I'm still stuffed from the poached lobster and fritters," Deanna whined.

"Me too," Tristan agreed.

"What's wrong with you two," Webber teased. "We're on vacation and what do you do on vacation? You eat, drink, play, and maybe work a little," he added winking at Tristan.

"If I may, sir," Kenton asked.

"Certainly," Webber acknowledged.

"Amani assumed that you'd probably be tired from your day of travel, so she prepared a light mixed grill with sea scallops, shrimp, and mahi-mahi over couscous with a green salad," Kenton explained. "Will that be acceptable, sir?"

Webber looked around the table and everyone nodded their approval.

"Absolutely," Webber said. "Please thank Amani for her thoughtfulness."

"Sir," Kenton added. "She did say to please be sure to save your appetites for tomorrow's dinner as she has something special planned."

Webber looked between Deanna and Tristan, smiling like a kid at Christmas. "That woman knows how to tease me unmercifully," he said.

"That she does, sir," Kenton agreed. "Right this way."

Kenton escorted them to the beautifully set table on the opposite end of the terrace, and he pulled out Deanna's chair before Webber could get to her. Tristan and Webber waited to take their seats until they were sure Deanna was comfortably seated.

During dinner, the nervousness between Tristan and Webber seemed to melt away more with each additional glass of wine. Relaxed conversation flowed freely, and there were never those awkward silences that often accompany a situation such as this. Tristan decided no matter how secretly disappointed he was that Deanna had been included in their getaway, it was very hard to dislike her. She was witty, charming, and beautiful, but most of all she seemed to genuinely care for Webber. And from Webber's standpoint, he could quickly see why he was attracted to her. He recalled the research he'd done on Webber before he took the job at Kincaid and knew that they'd been an item for over a decade, but he often wondered why they'd never married.

"Gentlemen," Deanna proclaimed placing her dinner napkin on the table in front of her and winking at Webber. "This has been delightful, but I'm exhausted and the good Lord knows I need my beauty rest. Tristan, I hope you won't be offended if I turn in a little early."

Tristan stood, "Not at all. It's been a pleasure finally getting to know you."

Deanna stood and came around the table and kissed him on the cheek. "The pleasure has been all mine. See you in the morning."

She turned to Webber, who was now standing behind his chair. "Enjoy the rest of your evening, sweetie," she whispered as she kissed him on the cheek.

"Tris, I'll have Kenton bring a bottle of port down to the pool area, if you're up for a swim?"

A chill ran down Tristan's spine. Oh Jesus, the alcohol, the night, the pool, and Webber were not good combinations. *What in the hell am I gonna do?*

Webber was staring at him waiting for an answer. "Uh, sure, I'll head back to my bungalow, change, and meet you down there."

Tristan went weak in the knees for the tenth time that day when Webber's lips formed that smile that he'd become so famous for, at least in Tristan's eyes.

"Perfect," he said looking then to Deanna. "I'll walk with you and change into my swimsuit."

"That would be lovely," she said with another wink. "Good night, Tristan."

"Good night."

Tristan's mind wandered as he watched Webber take Deanna's hand and lead her to their bedroom. *If I'm gonna spend the next three weeks with these guys, I better learn how to deal with seeing them together. And Christ, what about the pool? And how do I get used to seeing Webber running around half naked? This will surely be a test of wills for me. If I can make it through this, I can make it through anything.*

He was so deep in thought he didn't see or hear Kenton come up and start clearing the table.

When Kenton spoke, Tristan jumped from the mere sound of another's voice. "Sorry, Mr. Moreau, I didn't mean to startle you."

"No problem. I didn't hear you come out," Tristan admitted. "And please call me Tristan."

Kenton nodded. "I hope dinner was to your liking, sir."

Tristan smiled. "It was delicious. Please give my compliments to the chef."

"Can I get you anything else, sir, before I take the port down to the pool?"

"Not a thing, Kenton, you've been great. I'm gonna head back to my bungalow and change into my swim trunks."

"Certainly, sir. I'll have fresh towels awaiting your arrival."

"Wow, I see why Webber can't live without you and Amani."

"Thank you, sir…."

It looked to Tristan like Kenton was going to say something else and then he hesitated.

"May I speak freely?"

"By all means," Tristan said.

"Mr. Webber is a very good man, and he and his family have been really good to Amani, Kit, and me, but we worry about him."

"How so?" Tristan asked.

"Well, sir, for starters, he works too much. He loves this place, and we see him maybe three or four times a year. And when he does visit, he's always working. Amani and me, well, we just wish he had more of a life."

"What about Deanna? Doesn't she come with him?"

"Sure, she visits, but not all the time," Kenton shared.

That really surprised Tristan. "Why do you think that is?"

Kenton hesitated again. "I… I'm sorry, sir, I think I said too much already."

"Kenton, I promise you that whatever you say to me stays between us, and I know it's out of concern."

Kenton seemed to relax just a little. "The only reason I say anything at all is because he is like a son to us, and Miss Deanna has her own career and they can't always get away together, and you are the first person Mr. Webber has brought here other than Miss Deanna."

"Really? Have you ever spoken to her about this?"

"Not really, sir. It didn't seem appropriate, especially if they were, well, together."

Tristan couldn't help the next question. "And are they together?"

"I thought you would know, sir."

"Webber and I have worked very closely together for the last two years, and although I've met Deanna on a few occasions, I've only just had a chance to get to know her tonight."

"And she is a really nice lady," Kenton added. "But they've known each other for a long time, and Mr. Webber has never mentioned marriage or settling down."

"Kenton, it's obvious that you and your family love Webber a great deal, and it appears to me that he feels the same way about you, but he's a big boy. You've got to trust that he'll find his way and settle down when he's ready."

"Yes, sir, I guess you're right."

Tristan stuck his hand out. "But… I'll make you a deal."

Kenton took Tristan's extended hand, looking a little unsure.

"I promise if you take good care of him when he's here, I'll try my best to see that he's taken care of when he's not."

Kenton smiled. "That would be great, sir, and this will stay between us?"

"You have my word," Tristan promised.

"Thank you, sir."

"Now I better go back to my bungalow and get changed before Webber gets back and catches us talking about him."

"Indeed, sir."

Tristan stood and made his way to his bungalow in deep thought.

WEBBER was deep in thought as he walked Deanna back to her bedroom. She couldn't take it any longer and finally broke the silence. "Do you wanna share?"

"Share what?" Webber replied absentmindedly.

"What's on your mind," Deanna chuckled. "Like I really need to ask."

Webber elbowed her in the ribs lightly.

"Heeey," she protested. "That hurt."

"You're such a girl," he teased.

She rolled her fingers into a fist and punched him right in the stomach.

A grunt escaped his throat and Deanna professed in triumph, "Who's the girl now?"

"Okay, okay. I give."

Deanna touched his arm, "Look, sweetie, he seems like a really good man."

Webber smiled weakly. "Am I that obvious?"

"Of course you are," Deanna replied. "To me anyway."

"He's a good guy, D, at least what I know about him."

"After spending some time with him, I think he's definitely interested in you," Deanna concluded. "Do you not see the way his eyes light up when you mention his name, or the way he looks at you when you're telling a story. Come on, Webber, he hangs on your every word. I can see it, and I'm just a girl, remember."

Webber laughed out loud this time. "Yeah, but what does all that mean?"

"I think it means that he wants more from you. But you need to think the same thing."

"What should I do?"

Deanna didn't answer right away. They approached her bedroom door and she turned to him and cupped his face with both her hands. "As I said before, sweetie, you need to decide if the chance of a possible relationship with him and all that goes with that is more important to you than a life without him. But... I can't make that choice for you. The choice has to be yours."

She opened her bedroom door and motioned for him to follow. Looking over her shoulder, she said, "Remember, I'll support you either way, but if it were me, I'd go for it."

Webber smiled. "You would, huh?"

"Yes, I would."

Deanna kicked off her shoes and threw herself on her bed patting the spot next to her.

"Come and sit. I want to talk to you about something."

Webber sat on the bed next to her and waited for her to speak.

She rolled over on her back and stared at the ceiling but didn't say anything.

"What is it, D?" Webber asked. "Is something wrong?"

"I'm pregnant, Webber."

"What!" Webber jumped off the bed and stood staring down at her.

"Sit back down, you goofball."

"Deanna! Who? When? How? I mean, I know how, but *how*?" he stuttered.

"Do I really need to go into detail?" she asked.

"Yuck, no! But…." He watched as Deanna's concerned look turned to a smile.

"Oh, stop stressing. I'm twelve weeks along, and I've had a lot of time to get used to the idea."

"Ooookay, twelve weeks. I think that means you're past your first trimester, and that's good, right? And that's why you're not drinking?"

"Yep and yep," Deanna replied. "Very good."

"Okay, with that out of the way," Webber said, "here comes the real question. Who in the hell is the father?"

Deanna rolled back onto her stomach. "Does it really matter?"

"It matters to me," Webber said.

"If you must know, it's Sebastian. You remember, the guy I was dating from France. We're over and he's back in France, but he left me this little gift."

Webber finally sat back down on the bed and rubbed Deanna's back. "Are you happy about it?"

"Very," she said. "I mean. I always thought I would have your baby one day, but this just happened and, well, I'm happy it did."

"Does Sebastian know?"

"Yeah, I told him, but he wants nothing to do with the baby."

"Bastard," Webber cursed under his breath.

"No, it's better this way, Web. The baby will have me and you and maybe Tristan if things work out the way you want them to."

Webber smiled and leaned down and kissed Deanna on the temple. "This child will be the luckiest baby ever."

"Thanks, Web," Deanna said, sitting up and taking Webber's hand in hers. "But please do me a favor and keep this under wraps for a little while. I'm just now starting to sport a little baby bump, so I'd say I've got a couple of weeks before I make the announcement. Besides, my lawyers have contracts to sort through and deal with. No one wants a pregnant supermodel."

Webber chuckled. "Got it," he said, locking his lips with a mock key. "Wow, a baby!"

"Yep, ole Deanna is going to be a mom. And in all actuality, you're sort of going to be a father."

"I think I like the idea of that."

"Okay," Deanna said. "I'm ready for bed. Boy, do I get tired easily these days."

"That's my cue," Webber said, kissing Deanna on the top of the head. "Good night, Deanna. You know you can count on me, right?"

"Good night, sweetie, and of course I do. And... good luck tonight."

Webber smiled shyly as he opened the door, crossed the hall to his bedroom, and began undressing. *A baby! That girl is full of surprises.*

He started searching his closet and came up with a pair of short black spandex swimmer's trunks. *Damn, are these the only trunks I have here?* He rummaged through more drawers and came up empty-handed.

He sighed and shook his head. He slipped the trunks on and looked in the mirror. "Oh boy, a little formfitting but I guess these will have to do. Why in the hell didn't I bring another pair?" *'Cause you're always here alone and no one ever sees you in a bathing suit but you.*

He turned in front of the mirror and looked at his butt. "I guess I don't look that bad for a forty-five-year-old man. I sure hope Tristan agrees."

TRISTAN walked into the bathroom, took his clothes off, and dug through his suitcase as if on autopilot. After stepping into his surfer trunks, he slipped a T-shirt over his head and put on his flip-flops. He stood in front of the mirror and sighed. The anticipation was building and he had no idea how he was going to handle being in the pool with Webber in a swimsuit. The more he thought about it, the more scared he became. For the last two years he'd secretly hoped, maybe even said a few prayers, to spend some time with Webber outside the office, anything that didn't have to do with KIC, but this? Never in his wildest dreams had he imagined it would be this.

He stepped out of the door to the bungalow and stopped. Putting his hand on the doorjamb, he took a deep breath and counted to ten to get his emotions in check. He put one foot in front of the other and slowly made his way down the lighted path to the pool area. When he turned the corner, he froze and swallowed a gasp. Webber was at the other end of the swimming pool, standing on the edge with his arms over his head, about to dive into it. The silver streaks in his hair were reflecting off the lighted surface of the pool, and his long, slender, but muscular body looked incredible in the hottest black bathing suit Tristan had ever seen. It was a picture he wanted to burn into his memory and keep tucked away for the rest of his life.

The sound of Webber's body hitting the water brought Tristan back to the land of the living, and he started walking toward the pool. Just as he reached the edge, Webber popped up out of the water, ran his fingers through his hair, and wiped his eyes. "There you are. I thought I was going to have to send a posse after you."

Tristan was speechless. Webber was treading water at the deep end of the pool, looking up at him with those crystal-blue eyes sparkling against the sapphire-blue of the water. Another vision Tristan never wanted to forget. *Say something you idiot.* "Oh, sorry I'm late. I couldn't find my bathing suit."

"I know the feeling," Webber said. "This is the only one I have here, so I'm sorry if it's a little too, well, you know, skimpy."

"Not at all, it looks great," Tristan said before he could stop himself. *Brain to lips, you stupid ass! When are you ever going to learn?*

Webber flashed that sexy smile, and Tristan's stomach fell, his heart fluttered, and his blood pressure flew off the charts. Suddenly he was overcome with a million emotions, but only one that he could identify. His brain was telling him to run. *Run away as fast as you can.*

"Well?" Webber said. "Are you going to stand there all night or are you going to join me?"

Tristan didn't run. Instead he kicked off his flip-flops, pulled his T-shirt over his head—all the while never taking his eyes off Webber—and dove right into the deep end, literally and figuratively.

Six

THE moment Tristan's fingertips hit the sparkling water and the rest of his body disappeared under the surface, he felt like he was wrapped in a warm embrace. He instinctively arched his back, stretched his hands toward the surface, and started kicking. On his way up, he stopped momentarily and watched Webber's taut stomach muscles flex as he slowly kicked back and forth, treading water. Tristan started kicking again, broke the surface, and found himself face-to-face with Webber.

As their arms and legs slowly moved through the tepid water, their eyes found one another's and Tristan was suddenly lost in an indigo trance. They were so close he could feel Webber's warm breath on his face, and in that very moment, everything but the two of them disappeared. *This can't happen*, Tristan told himself over and over again. But Webber's gaze was too strong to fight. There was no KIC to worry about. No board of directors. What career? What reputation? It was just the two of them locked in a mental and visual embrace. Nothing else mattered to Tristan except that he was here with Webber.

Lost in Webber's gaze, Tristan didn't think it was possible, but Webber's incredible eyes were bluer than he remembered. And his hair—the silver streaks running through his dark hair glistened like diamonds off the rippling water. He felt like he was having an out-of-body experience, that every second of his life had led to this very moment in time, here with Webber where he belonged.

Closing his eyes, Tristan shook his head, trying to clear the mental fog, and when he opened them again, Webber was still smiling that mind-numbing smile. Tristan's heart began to beat faster and faster, and for an instant, he was afraid if he didn't do something soon, it would leap right out of his chest. All he could think to do was talk to Webber and try to convince him that this was a bad idea. He remembered Webber was going to tell him something about Deanna before she interrupted them, so he went in that direction. Never breaking eye contact with Webber, and in a shaky voice, he asked, "Earlier, you were going to tell me something about Deanna."

Before he could get an answer, he saw as much as felt Webber leaning in closer to him until their lips were a couple of inches apart.

"Forget Deanna," Webber whispered as their lips met.

Without conscious thought, Tristan grabbed Webber behind the neck and drew him in closer as he savored the kiss he'd fantasized about every night for the last two years. With one hand keeping him afloat and the other behind Webber's neck, Tristan came completely unglued.

Webber was ravishing his mouth, tasting and exploring, the sensation almost too much to handle. Every nerve ending was on fire as he dangled by his fingertips on the edge of an emotional cliff. He surrendered and allowed his body to take over as they moved slowly through the water. He felt Webber's tongue pressing against his lips and Tristan opened for him. That's all it took and he plummeted, slowly falling through the abyss. Bright bursts of light were exploding behind his eyelids, and he vaguely felt Webber's arms wrap around him as they both sank below the surface. While their lips were sealed tightly against one another's, Webber's tongue gently explored Tristan's as they hovered just below the surface, slowly sinking. When their feet touched the bottom, they instinctively pushed back up and broke the surface, still locked in their embrace. Something about breaking the surface and their lips coming apart brought Tristan back to reality. *Holy shit, what about Deanna! What in the hell did we just do?*

Out of breath and flushed, Tristan pushed away from Webber and swam to the side of the pool.

"What in the hell, Web?" *We can't—you're with Deanna. What in God's name was I thinking?*

Out of the corner of his eye, he saw Webber swimming toward him and he vaguely heard him say something, but before Webber could reach him, he lifted himself out of the pool, grabbed his clothes, and started running back to his bungalow. *Fuck, fuck, fuck! I guess you learned nothing from Justin Scott?*

When Tristan reached his room, he slammed the door shut behind him and dropped onto the couch, distraught and disillusioned. He was so disappointed in Webber. How could he have said "forget Deanna" when she was waiting for him in his bedroom? Did his infatuation with Webber block him seeing the real man? How could he love a man who could do that to someone he was involved with? Webber was no better than Justin Scott. Webber's indiscretion was bad enough, but if Tristan was being honest, he was more disappointed in himself. How could he forget everything that happened seven years ago, everything he believed in? He'd kissed Webber, and just after having spent an evening getting to know Deanna and finding out that he really liked her. Tristan smacked himself in the forehead. *God, I knew it was a bad idea to come to this fucking island. I should have listened to my better judgment.* He felt a tear slide down his cheek and brushed it away with the back of his hand. "I will not cry," he said as he ran his fingers through his hair and leaned his head back and rested it on the couch. *How could I have been so blind?* He raised his head and the room started to close in on him. *I've got to get out of here.* He pulled his T-shirt over his head, slipped his flip-flops on, and headed for the door.

"TRISTAN, wait," Webber yelled as Tristan disappeared around the corner, heading in the direction of his bungalow. "God damn it, shit," he cursed rather loudly. He slapped the water repeatedly as he spun around in a circle kicking himself in the ass for his actions. *How could I make my move before telling him about Deanna and me? What the fuck is wrong with me? I know him well enough to know his strong principles would never allow him to get involved with me if he thought I was with Deanna! Damn it all to hell!*

He anxiously climbed out of the pool, not remembering where he'd left his shoes, shirt, and towel, and scanned the patio frantically.

After locating his clothing, he slipped into his shoes, grabbed his T-shirt and towel, and started drying himself off as he headed to Tristan's bungalow. He had to try to repair the damage he'd done, hoping it wasn't too late. He walked slowly, trying to decide what to say, but nothing seemed right to him. All he could do was throw himself on the mercy of the court and take what he was given. When he reached Tristan's bungalow, he knocked gently on the door and softly called Tristan's name. After a few minutes with no answer, he knocked again and slowly opened the door, determined to talk to him before this went any further. Tristan was nowhere in sight. "Shit," Webber mumbled under his breath. "Where could he be?" *He couldn't have gone that far. I'll search this entire island until I find him.*

TRISTAN was deep in thought as he hesitantly made his way down the lighted path winding its way along the mountain. He wasn't really paying much attention to what he was doing or where he was going, which was evident by his frequent stumbles. He decided he'd better pay a little more attention before he bit the dust and found himself hanging off the edge of a cliff. When the path ended, he stepped onto the boat dock at the water's edge and stopped to listen as the waves crashed onto the white sandy beach below his feet. The nearly full moon was high in the sky, casting a beautiful soft glow against the cobalt-blue water. At the end of the dock, as Webber had told him, were two very handsome boats, one powerboat and one catamaran. They flanked the dock, bobbing gently in the rolling waves, acting almost as sentinels welcoming him. *Oh God, Webber?* he mused. *What am I going to do about Webber?*

He walked out to the end of the dock, sat with his legs dangling over the edge, and contemplated his next move. The events of the night began to flood back into his mind. He started to shake uncontrollably and instinctively wrapped his arms around his shoulders and rocked as the surf gently caressed the shore. He felt more alone than he'd ever felt, and for the first time, he was at a crossroads in both his personal and professional lives. How could he go on working for Webber, knowing what he knew now? His mind went back to what he and

Webber had done. The kiss was incredible, as soft and tender as he always imagined it would be. He pressed a finger against his lips, remembering the feeling of Webber's pressed to his. "How could something so wonderful be so wrong?" he whispered.

"It wasn't wrong," Webber said softly as he stepped up and placed a hand on Tristan's shoulder. Tristan flinched at the touch and realized he'd been so lost in his thoughts that he hadn't even heard Webber walk onto the dock.

"Can I talk to you?" Webber asked in a hushed tone.

Tristan hesitated for a second and then said, "It's your island."

He saw Webber flinch this time, and his heart ached for him, but at the moment he couldn't drop his armor or he might just forgive him and run into his arms.

"Technically yes, but...," Webber responded.

"Whatever," Tristan said with the wave of his hand.

"Look, Tris, you have every right to be upset with me," Webber pleaded. "What I did was wrong."

Tristan just stared off into the horizon trying to breathe, ignoring the overwhelming pain seeping into his heart.

"No, that's not what I mean. What I mean is the kiss wasn't wrong. I'll never forget that kiss, and you will never ever hear me say that it was wrong. But the way I handled it was so wrong."

"Webber," Tristan said as he turned his tear-filled eyes to meet Webber's. "I'm turning in my resignation effective immediately."

Tristan saw Webber's legs start to shake, and he looked like he was having trouble staying on his feet. Tristan's heart was breaking because of something Webber did, but yet all he could do was think about how he was hurting Webber. How could their lives have gone from hope and respect to fear and devastation in less than twenty-four hours? He felt like Webber had sucker-punched him.

"Tris, no, please."

"My mind's made up." He hadn't really made up his mind, but as the words came out, he knew it was the right thing to do. "I can't work for a man I can't trust. And you proved to me tonight that you can't be trusted."

"Tris, you've got it all wrong. Please let me explain."

"Webber, unfortunately there's nothing you can say that will change my mind."

Tristan got to his feet and watched Webber take a few steps back. Tristan straightened his shoulders, gathered up every bit of strength he could muster, and tried to walk as tall and proud as he possibly could.

When he reached Webber he stopped. "Tomorrow morning I'll make arrangements to get back to Atlanta and my office will be cleared out by the time you return. Good night, Webber."

"Tris, please wait."

Tristan closed his eyes as tears ran down his cheeks, but he kept on walking. When he reached the first overlook, he saw Webber on his knees with his hands covering his face. His shoulders were visibly shaking as if he were sobbing. It took everything Tristan had not to run back and scoop him up in his arms and tell him it was all going to be okay, but something in him would not allow it. He'd let himself down and his trust in Webber had been terribly shaken, and he was sure he would never be able to get it back. He turned away and started walking up the path back to his lonely bungalow. He realized that this was going to be the longest night of his life.

Seven

WEBBER stayed on his knees, sobbing until he had no tears left. He'd only cried this hard twice in his life. Once as a teenager when his mother died, and then later when he'd lost his father. He felt like he'd lost Tristan just as he'd lost his parents, but this time the person he'd lost was still living and breathing, and rejecting him. He realized he must have hurt Tristan really badly for him to not even hear him out and give him a chance to explain.

He somehow gathered up the strength to stand and started making his way back up the path to the house. He walked by Tristan's bungalow hoping to catch a glimpse of him and maybe get another chance to explain, but the bungalow was in total darkness. He walked back to his room but stopped in front of Deanna's door. He stood there for a long moment before he got the nerve to knock. In a couple of minutes, Deanna opened the door and Webber fell into her arms and started sobbing again.

She held him and stroked his back and hair until he stopped crying. "Web, what happened?"

"I kissed him in the pool," was all he was able to get out.

"And...?" she asked.

He tried to get his breathing under control long enough to get a sentence out. "D, I know there's something there. The kiss was incredible. He was just as into it as I was."

"So what's the problem?" she asked with a confused look on her face.

"I never got a chance to tell him about our relationship," Webber replied painfully.

"Oh" was all Deanna could say.

"He thinks I was cheating on you with him," Webber explained. "And now he says he can never trust me again. He resigned his position at KIC and is leaving tomorrow."

Deanna took Webber in her arms again. "Oh Web, I'm so sorry. Did you try to explain?"

"It's too late, what's done is done," Webber admitted. "I tried to tell him earlier this evening, and you walked up so I stopped, knowing I would have time later to explain everything."

"Oh my God, Web, this is my fault." Deanna sighed.

"No, no, I didn't mean it like that. I had another opportunity, and I got so caught up in Tristan that what I said and what I meant to say were two very different things. I told him to forget about you right before I kissed him."

Webber saw the moment the scene became clear in Deanna's mind. She took him into her arms. "I'm so sorry, baby. I love you and you know I always will, right?"

Webber nodded as he buried his face in the crook of Deanna's neck and stayed there.

TRISTAN didn't go back to his bungalow right away. He walked around the villa lost in his thoughts. He went to the bar and poured himself a scotch, and looking down at the glass, he longed for Webber. Scotch was Webber's drink. Tristan had only started drinking it because Webber loved it so much, and he soon found that he'd developed a taste for the easy burn and had been drinking it ever since. He downed the first shot and poured another. When he finished the second shot, he poured a third and put the decanter away. He walked over to the balcony and tried to make sense out of everything that had happened, replaying the series of events over and over. He remembered that Webber had been trying to tell him something about Deanna earlier in the evening, but what could that have been? As the scotch took the edge off and softened his heart, he kept seeing Webber on his knees sobbing uncontrollably, and his heart broke again with every sob.

Maybe I should have given him a chance to explain. Could anything he might say to me change my mind? Tristan slowly started talking himself into going back to see Webber. *I owe the guy that much after everything he's done for me.*

The scotch now doing his thinking, Tristan walked toward Webber's bedroom. He didn't know exactly which room it was, but he would knock on every door until he found him. He rounded the corner and stopped dead in his tracks when he saw Webber wrapped in Deanna's arms. He backed up and leaned against the wall. He heard Deanna say, "I love you and you know I always will, right?"

Webber, no! This can't be happening, please, no. Painful memories assaulted him again, now intensified by the scotch. His heart broke for the second time in one night, but Webber hammered the last nail in the coffin when he nodded and buried his face in the crook of Deanna's neck. He cheated on Deanna with Tristan earlier in the night, then came after him, and when he was rejected, he went right back to Deanna. Tristan felt the pain in every ounce of his being. It took all he had not to start sobbing himself, but he couldn't let that happen. There would be time for that later, but not tonight. Somehow Tristan found the energy to put one foot in front of the other, and he made his retreat. When he got back to his pitch-black bungalow, physically and mentally exhausted, he collapsed onto his bed, not bothering to undress, and closed his eyes.

THE next time Tristan opened his eyes, it was to sunshine creeping in through the plantation blinds and a constant knocking sound. His head was pounding from the scotch and the sun, and the knocking wasn't helping. He looked at the clock and saw it was just past seven o'clock, and still there was that knocking sound. It took him another second to realize that the sound was coming from the door. Someone was knocking at the door. He got out of bed, still in his swimsuit, and answered it. He cringed in pain when the blinding sun hit him, and he struggled while his eyes adjusted to the intrusion. When he could finally see, he realized it was Deanna. She was wearing a bright yellow sundress with her hair piled up on top of her head. He knew it was the last thing he should be thinking about, but she looked like a supermodel even at 7:00 a.m.

"Deanna," he said with surprise. Was she here to give him a piece of her mind for trying to take her man? If so, he'd stand up and take it like a man. After all, he deserved everything she could throw at him.

"Can I come in?" she asked in a very calm voice.

"Sure," Tristan said as he opened the door enough for her to step inside.

"You look like shit, honey," she said with a slight smile.

"Thanks a lot," he responded as he walked to the bathroom to get some water and take some aspirin. "Long night," he added.

"So I've heard," Deanna agreed.

When Tristan came back from the bathroom, Deanna was staring out the window.

Tristan walked up behind her. "Look, Deanna, I deserve everything you think I do. I'm so sorry," he explained apologetically. "I resigned and I'm leaving today, so you'll never have to see me again."

She turned to look at him. "You'll do nothing of the sort," she snapped. "Look," she said. "There's been a huge misunderstanding and I need to help fix it."

Tristan raised a brow and cocked his head to one side. "How so?" he asked.

"Tristan," Deanna continued, "Webber is gay and he's in love with you."

Tristan's heart almost stopped. He felt certain he looked like the proverbial deer in the headlights. "What did you say?"

"I said, Webber is gay, and he's been in love with you for almost two years."

"But...," Tristan said, his heart now racing.

"But nothing," Deanna said as she put up her hand to stop him. "Honey, Webber and I have never been anything more than great friends, and that's all we will ever be. He's so in love with you, he can hardly stand it."

Tristan felt his knees go weak and he reached for something to steady himself. He eventually fell into one of the club chairs and dropped his head to his knees. "But I saw you two last night in an embrace, and I heard you tell him that you loved him and you always will."

"Honey, you heard me consoling him after you dumped him," she tried to explain. "Baby, he had no idea if you were even gay, but he felt this connection to you, a strong enough connection to go out on a limb for you. He was so scared that if he was wrong you might hate him, maybe even sue him for sexual harassment or something, so he brought me along to hide behind, so to speak."

Tristan looked up and met Deanna's gaze. "But why didn't he tell me?" he asked, still not sure he was hearing correctly.

"He tried to tell you earlier in the night, but I interrupted him, so I feel like most of this is my fault."

Tristan brought his fingers to his lips and held them there remembering the kiss. A light bulb went off in his head. "That's what he was trying to tell me."

Deanna nodded. "Then he got so carried away with you in the pool that it came out all wrong. Listen, the fact that you could push him away because you thought he was cheating on me just magnifies your strong sense of right and wrong—"

Tristan waved his hand in the air, motioning for her to stop. "No! No, it wasn't just that." He explained to Deanna about his relationship with Justin Scott, and he saw the look in her eyes the moment she got it, all of it.

"Oh Tristan! I'm so sorry, honey, but this explains so much." She pulled him into a tight embrace. "Don't sell yourself short. You still came to my defense and I will never forget that. But you two belong together."

Tristan sighed against her shoulder and finally let the tears flow freely. *Webber didn't betray anyone.*

Tristan wiped his face with the back of his hand. "Where is he?"

"I guess he's still sleeping."

"Take me to him, please," he begged.

"Okay, let's go," Deanna said, walking to the door.

"Wait," Tristan yelled. "I need to brush my teeth."

Deanna laughed heartily and sat down and waited patiently.

Three minutes later, Deanna was leading Tristan to Webber's bedroom. When they reached the door, Tristan's hand was shaking uncontrollably.

"You'll be fine, honey, just be honest with him about everything. He'll understand," Deanna urged. "Do you have any feelings for him?"

"Deanna, I have loved him for almost as long as I've known him, but I couldn't come between you two and I couldn't give my heart to someone who couldn't give his back."

Deanna smiled happily and gave him a hug. "And now you can. Go tell him how you feel."

Tristan put his hand on the doorknob, turned it hesitantly, and slowly pushed it open.

The bed was still made up and looked like it hadn't been slept in. Tristan swallowed hard. "Webber?"

No answer. He walked over to the large bathroom and peeked inside. "Webber?" Still no answer.

Tristan's heart sank and panic filled every fiber of his tall frame. He literally felt the blood draining out of his face. "Deanna!" he yelled.

She must not have gone too far because she was by his side in moments, fear and worry written all over her face. "What's wrong?" she asked, her voice cracking.

"He's gone." Tristan pointed to the bed. "He didn't sleep here, and he's not in the bathroom."

Deanna took him by the hand. "He can't be far. We're on an island, remember."

"Never underestimate Webber Kincaid," Tristan said, feeling weak enough in the knees to need Deanna for support. She must have sensed his weakness and slipped her arm through his and steadied him enough for him to slow his heart rate and try to think.

"Maybe he's taking a swim," Deanna offered.

Tristan's mind was doing backflips. *I'm not going to let him get away. I've got to find Webber.*

"Okay," he said, suddenly feeling stronger. He took Deanna by the hand. "Let's split up. We can cover more ground that way. If you find him, sit on him and don't let him move. Start yelling like a banshee until I get there."

He gave Deanna's hand a squeeze and she smiled at him. "We'll find him, honey. Everything's going to be all right."

Tristan wanted to believe her and he appreciated her support, so he gave her a faint smile. "Okay, you take the pool and the lower levels, then search the rest of the main house and the bungalows. I'll go down to the beach and check the dock, and if I don't find him, I'll meet you back in the main house."

Deanna nodded and Tristan took off running as fast as he could. Other than the beach and dock, he had no idea where he was going, but he was determined to cover every inch of that damn island until he found Webber.

The path down to the dock seemed a little more manageable in the daylight, but he was in such a hurry, he stumbled as many times as he had the night before. Again, he wondered how things could change so drastically in such a short time, but he had to put that on the back burner and concentrate on finding Webber. He reached the dock and followed it until the end. No Webber. He checked the beach on either side of the dock and still nothing. He turned to leave and saw that the companionway door was open on the powerboat. He didn't remember it being open last night, so he cautiously stepped onto the boat and walked to the open door. Peering into the cabin, he saw nothing but an empty salon and galley. He stepped farther down the stairs and stopped dead in his tracks, taking a deep breath of relief when he saw Webber lying on the berth in the forward stateroom, curled up in the fetal position. He was still wearing his swimsuit and T-shirt from last night and had a pained look on his face, even in slumber.

Tristan tiptoed into the cabin and sat alongside Webber on the berth. He brushed Webber's dark hair out of his eyes and gently laid his hand on Webber's shoulder.

WEBBER stirred and slowly opened his eyes. He blinked several times in surprise, not believing what he was seeing.

"Tristan?" he said in a hushed tone, reaching out to touch Tristan's leg just to make sure it wasn't some cruel nightmare.

"It's me, Web," Tristan said softly, continuing to stroke his hair.

"But...," Webber protested.

"Shhhh," Tristan whispered. "I was wrong, Webber. Deanna explained everything. I'm so sorry."

"No!" Webber rose up on one elbow. "It's all my fault. I should have told you about Deanna and me sooner. I was just... scared. I love you, Tristan. I have for as long as I can remember."

Tristan smiled. "If you only knew how much I've longed to hear those words, and now that you're was actually saying them, I'm not totally convinced I'm really hearing them. Say them again," he begged.

Webber smiled. "I love you, Tristan."

Tristan leaned in until their lips touched ever so lightly. A shot of pure voltage ran through Webber from his head to his toes. When

Tristan pulled away, his eyes were full of love and need and it warmed Webber to the core of his being.

"I love you too, Webber, since the day we met."

Webber couldn't help the broad smile that consumed his face. Tristan was actually here, kissing him, professing his love. He thought he could die a happy man right here and now.

Then Webber saw the smile on Tristan's face turn to one of concern. "What's wrong, baby?"

Tristan stood and started pacing in the tiny cabin. "Web, I'm so sorry about the way I reacted in the pool last night."

Webber sat up and scooted to the edge of the bed. "You thought I was cheating on Deanna with you. I get that. I would have probably had the same reaction if the situation were reversed. I mean… how could you ever trust me?"

Tristan continued pacing, looking like he was trying to find the words to say something very important. He stopped and looked at Webber. "Yeah, that's a really big part of it, but there's so much more."

Webber suddenly felt anxious and it quickly spread throughout his body. He leaned back on his elbows, trying not to overreact, and waited for Tristan to find the words. "You can tell me anything, you know that, right?"

Tristan nodded. He sat down next to Webber and rested his hand on Webber's knee. "For starters, you have to understand, I had no idea if you were gay or straight. You weren't married, and when I googled you, every picture I found showed you and Deanna. She was always referred to as your longtime girlfriend or longtime companion. So, I just assumed that you were straight. But when we finally met for the interview, I was immediately attracted to you, and damn if that attraction didn't continue to grow until I was hopelessly in love with you. So, here I was in love with a straight man I could never have, just like…."

Webber tilted his head and waited. When Tristan didn't speak, Webber whispered, "Just like what, baby?"

Tristan sighed and closed his eyes. "Just like my first and only love until you."

Webber sat up straight and waited again. But before he could encourage Tristan to tell him what was on his mind, Tristan started his story.

He told Webber about Justin Scott and their love affair and how it ended, and the scars he'd been carrying around with him since that time.

Suddenly it all made complete sense to Webber. He'd had no way of knowing what was going on with Tristan, but that didn't make him feel any better. "Oh Tris, I'm so sorry. I don't know what to say. I can't imagine what you've been going through."

Tristan turned and burrowed his face in Webber's neck, his head resting on Web's shoulder. "There is nothing to say. I just couldn't go through that again, and when you kissed me, knowing that Deanna was so near, I just freaked out. It was Justin all over again."

Webber wrapped his arms around Tristan and held him tight. "You know that's not the case now, right? Deanna and me, well, we're...."

Tristan broke the embrace and finished Webber's sentence as a tear slid down his cheek. "Just friends. Yeah, I know that now, but that doesn't change much."

Surprised but not able to keep his hands off Tristan, he reached up to brush the tear away. "How so?"

"Despite the way I feel about you and despite the fact that you were straight, I told myself over and over again even if you were gay and in the closet, I could never get involved with you."

Webber tensed. "Why?"

"Because of your career. I could never be the one to bring a scandal to your doorstep. I mean what about KIC, the board, the shareholders, not to mention your reputation? How can we ever explain how this happened? They don't even know you're gay."

"Tristan," Webber whispered as he stroked Tristan's face with the back of his hand. "We'll make it work. I won't lose you, and I don't want to lose KIC, but if I do, so be it. You are so much more important to me than any company."

"Your company! Your father's legacy. One you both built, one step at a time from the ground up. I could never be the cause of you losing that."

Webber sighed. "Tris, how can I make you understand how I feel about you?" He stood up and took Tristan with him. Taking both Tristan's hands in his, he looked him in the eye. "Don't get me wrong, I will fight for my company, but not at the expense of losing you. I love you so much, and I thought I'd completely screwed it up and now that I have a second chance, I'm never giving you up."

Webber watched as Tristan listened intently to everything he was saying. "But—" Tristan protested.

"No buts," Webber said as he placed his index finger over Tristan's lips to silence him. "Not another word about KIC. We'll deal with that as it comes along, together."

"Webber, I'm scared for you and your company," Tristan tried to explain. "I could never live with myself if I was the cause of you losing KIC."

"Look, Tris," Webber reassured him. "If I lose my position at KIC, I lose it. But I don't think that's going to happen. I'm a major stockholder in the company, and I own 51 percent of the stock, giving us controlling interest. If my relationship with you has any negative impact on KIC, I will resign for the good of the company, but I will not give you up. Is that understood?"

Tristan burrowed into Webber's open arms and kissed him over and over again. When Tristan nibbled at Webber's bottom lip, Webber reveled in the touch and then panicked. He placed his hands on Tristan's chest and pushed him away gently. Tristan had an immediate look of concern.

Webber smiled. "I need to brush my teeth."

Tristan's concern faded away and his smile reappeared. He opened his mouth to speak but before anything came out, he cocked his head to the side and listened. Following his lead, Webber did the same. They heard the faint sounds of a helicopter in the distance getting closer and closer. Webber caught Tristan's gaze and he saw the wheels already turning, so before Tristan could jump to conclusions, Webber clarified, "Must be Deanna's ride."

"Oh my God! Deanna!" Tristan exclaimed.

"What about Deanna?" Webber asked with concern.

"We split up to look for you. I went to your bedroom and you weren't there and I panicked. She came running to my rescue and offered to help me find you. She's probably still looking."

"Well, then," Webber teased. "We'd better go and find her."

Webber stole another short kiss and jumped to his feet, bringing Tristan with him. He took Tristan in a tight embrace and whispered, "Remember what I said. We're in this together. Whatever happens, we deal with it together. Promise me you won't bolt, Tris?"

Tristan nodded, burying his face in Webber's neck. "Together," he promised.

Tristan pulled away and looked Webber in the eyes. "Why is Deanna leaving?"

Webber held his stare. "She'd always planned on leaving today," he explained.

"Really?" Tristan asked with a tilt of his head.

"Really!" Webber confirmed. "Look, I've been planning this trip for quite some time, and I've been racking my brain trying to find a way to tell you how I felt without really telling you, in case you weren't gay, or even worse, you were gay, but not interested. She was here mostly for moral support, but also in case you rejected me and I was being faced with some type of sexual harassment issues."

Tristan glared at Webber with suspicion in his eyes but didn't say anything.

"Yeah, I know," Webber said. "But Tris, you remember, I am the chairman, president, and CEO of a publicly traded company. Human Resources would have my head if they knew what was going on. I just wanted to cover as many bases as I could."

Tristan's expression softened, and Webber knew the instant he realized what Webber had put on the line for him.

Webber again took Tristan in his arms and held him tight. "But now that's no longer a concern, let's go find Deanna and give her the news." He took Tristan's hand and together they walked up to the main house.

THEY didn't have to search for too long because when they rounded the corner, Tristan spotted Deanna near the pool, frantically pacing back and forth. He squeezed Webber's hand and motioned in her direction. When she saw them, she froze with a concerned look on her face. Webber held up their joined hands and a huge smile spread across her face as she ran to them with open arms, almost knocking them over from the sheer force of her embrace. "Where have you been?" she asked, pulling back, glaring at Webber, and smacking him on the chest. "We were worried sick and looking everywhere for you."

"It's okay, D," Webber said in a reassuring tone, trying to calm her down. "I was down at the dock and everything is going to be just fine," he added as he kissed her cheek. "Thanks to you."

She threw herself in his arms again, at the same time reaching a hand out to grab Tristan.

"Webber, I want to know everything, but my helicopter's here," Deanna said glancing up at the helipad.

"He'll wait, honey. He works for us, remember?" Webber teased.

Hand in hand Webber and Tristan explained what had transpired since she and Tristan had taken off in search of Webber.

She listened intently, looking back and forth between them. "Are you sure everything's okay?"

"It's more than okay, D, it's perfect, and I'm gonna make sure it stays that way."

Tristan saw a little of the tension drain out of Deanna's beautiful face, and it looked like she was starting to relax.

She took both their hands in hers. "I'm so happy for both of you. And I hate to leave like this, but I've got to be in New York for a shoot tomorrow morning. And besides"—she winked—"I think you two could use some much-needed time alone. I'm just gonna run and get my bags."

Tristan put his hand up. "No, let me. It'll give you guys a chance to chat and say good-bye."

Deanna flashed Tristan that supermodel smile, and then turned to Webber. "I knew I liked this man."

Webber smiled. "Me too."

"Don't forget my purse," Deanna yelled as Tristan turned and headed for her bedroom.

DEANNA shifted her weight and rested on one foot, crossed her arms over her chest, and waited. "Well?"

Webber tilted his head and smiled. "It really is going to be all right, D."

Deanna smiled. "You better treat him right, Webber Kincaid."

Webber returned the smile as Tristan rounded the corner with Deanna's luggage and her purse. "Oh thank God," Webber teased. "You're just in time to save me from the 'you better take care of Tristan' speech."

Deanna glared at him as she slapped him on the arm, but broke into a broad smile. "What am I going to do with you?"

Tristan stopped in front of them, looking a little confused. "Save you from what?"

Webber moved behind Tristan and stuck his head out around Tristan's shoulder. "Supermodel D. She can be deadly."

"Tristan, did you know you're in love with a wannabe comedian?"

Tristan chuckled and winked at Deanna. "No, I wasn't aware of that."

Webber stepped out from behind Tristan and put one hand on his hip. "So, is this how it's gonna be? Two against one?"

Before Tristan could answer, Deanna chimed in. "Probably, but if you both walk me to my ride, I may have to reconsider."

"Deal," they said simultaneously.

They walked Deanna to the helipad and exchanged embraces and promises to stay in touch and see each other again soon. Just before she climbed into the helicopter, Webber patted her stomach. "Take care of you know who."

She smiled. "I will."

"Can I tell Tristan?" he whispered.

Her smile broadened, and she looked at Tristan, who was taking it all in. "Sure."

She stepped into her seat and the pilot strapped her in, closed her door, and went around and climbed into his seat. Tristan and Webber backed away and stood on the walkway as the helicopter rotors started spinning faster and faster until the helicopter slowly lifted off the ground, turned, and off she went. They stood waving until it was out of sight.

TRISTAN slipped his arm around Webber's waist. "What was that all about?"

"She's pregnant," Webber said through a huge smile.

"Pregnant?" Tristan responded.

"Yep, pregnant."

Tristan was sure he must have been a sight with his mouth wide open and his eyes big saucers.

Webber filled Tristan in on the entire story as they walked back up to the main house. Every few feet Webber would stop talking, wrap his arms around Tristan, and place gentle kisses on his cheeks, neck, forehead, and lips. When they reached the balcony, Webber turned, took Tristan's face in his hands, and gently brought their lips together in a slow, zealous kiss. The moment was interrupted by the sound of someone's throat clearing. They both froze and then turned to see Amani standing just inside the house with both hands on her hips glaring at them. Tristan felt Webber tense, so he released his hold and waited for some type of signal from Webber as to what he should do.

Before Webber could say anything, Amani's face broke into the biggest smile and she waved them inside. Tristan felt Webber relax and he slipped his arm around Tristan's waist, and they walked arm in arm until they reached Amani. Tristan stepped back and Amani threw her arms around Webber's neck. "Are you happy, Mr. Webber?" she asked.

"Yes, thank you, Amani, very happy."

"Then I'm happy. It's so good to see you caring for someone after all these years."

She then turned her attention to Tristan. "You best take care of this man or you'll have Amani to answer to, you hear me?"

She smiled while she was saying it, but Tristan knew he'd have her to deal with if he screwed this up. "Yes, ma'am," he promised.

She wrapped him in a warm embrace and kissed his cheek. "How about some breakfast?"

Webber smiled. "That sounds perfect."

Amani turned in a flash and high-stepped down the stairs, very light on her feet for a big woman.

Webber turned to Tristan. "Why don't we freshen up and meet back here in fifteen minutes."

"Oh good, I could really use a shower," Tristan said.

Webber lifted his arm and took a sniff of his armpit. "Me too," he proclaimed, smiling. Tristan gave him a peck on the cheek and tried to leave, but it appeared that Webber didn't want to let him go and that warmed his heart. He hung on for a few more seconds and finally spoke. "You promise you're coming back. No more running, right?"

Tristan leaned and placed a gentle kiss on Webber's lips. "I promise." He cupped Webber's face in his hand. "Not to say that I'm not still worried about KIC and how this is all going to play out, but I gave you my word and I always keep my promises."

Webber placed both his hands on top of Tristan's. "I feel like we can get through anything, as long as we do it together."

Tristan dropped his hands and stepped away. "I hope you're right, Web. God, I want you to be right."

"Do you love me, Tristan?

"God, yes," Tristan whispered.

"And I love you, and as far as I'm concerned, that's all we need." Webber kissed him again. "Now go get that shower."

Eight

TRISTAN walked back to his bungalow as if he were floating on air. The thought of Webber loving him, making love to him, sent his heart into overdrive. His pulse was racing, he had goose bumps, and his hands were shaking. *If just thinking about Webber loving me makes me this excited, what's gonna happen when we actually do make love? When we make love!* He liked the way that sounded in his head. Two days ago he would have never said those words. They would have seemed ridiculous and unattainable to him, but now it was actually going to happen.

But as happy as he was, he was still uneasy about what would happen when they returned to the real world. How would this all play out? Would they come forward with their relationship? Fess up to the board? Would Webber expect him to stay in the closet, and if so, for how long? That part didn't matter to him; he would stay in the closet as long as Webber wanted him to, or as long as it took for them to decide on a plan of action. He would not be Webber's downfall; he loved him too much for that. In the closet wasn't where he wanted to be, but he'd damned well stay there if it meant Webber could keep his company.

When he got back to the bungalow, he showered and changed his clothes, all the while thinking about the potential for Webber to lose his company over a scandal like this. How could they be together without the press finding out about their relationship? Webber was very visible in the press and considered sort of a playboy, but his reputation was about to change. Tristan could see the caption on a photograph:

"Former Playboy Webber Kincaid and his Homosexual Lover." He cringed at the thought and tried to block it out of his mind. He would go to the ends of the earth to protect Webber from a scandal, but he wouldn't leave him. He'd promised Webber that much, and he'd never break that promise. They would have to find a way to get through anything and everything together. He was in all the way up to his eyeballs, and as he second-guessed his decision mentally, physically he was already halfway back to the main house. He smiled to himself. *I guess my body and my brain are on two separate schedules.*

Webber was already there and looking as handsome as ever. He was wearing tan shorts and a black linen short-sleeved shirt, which made the silver in his damp hair stand out and the blue of his eyes sparkle like sapphires. *God, he's gorgeous.* Tristan stepped into Webber's open arms, slipping his own arms around Webber's waist. Webber rewarded him with a moan when their lips met. Tristan felt the warmth of Webber's lips pressing against his, Webber's tongue begging for entry. He opened to him and they explored each other as they had done in the pool the night before. He felt the blood drain out of his face and right to his groin and wondered how he was ever going to get enough of this man. He'd dreamt of a moment like this for the last two years and just the thought of it actually happening made him achingly hard. When the kiss ended, Tristan buried his face in Webber's neck and inhaled deeply. Webber's scent assaulted his senses again and again as he tasted and licked his way up and down Webber's neck. He was rewarded with another moan and a sound that Tristan could only identify as a whimper. *I'm making Webber Kincaid whimper.*

Webber whispered sweet words of encouragement. "God, Tris, you feel so good. How could I have allowed two years to pass by without doing this?"

"We may have lost two years, but we have a lifetime to make up for it."

Webber smiled, gently cupped the back of Tristan's head with his hand, and drew him in for another kiss. This time instead of a clearing of the throat, they heard a giggle and both looked up to see Kit standing there with a platter of eggs, bacon, sausage, and potatoes.

Webber smiled. "Sorry, Kit, we didn't know anyone was here."

Kit giggled again. "Obviously," she said. "I just got here and don't mind me. I'll be gone in a flash."

Webber took the tray from her, placed it on the table, and turned back to her. "Wait, Kit, I want to explain."

Kit took both his hands in hers. "No explanation needed. Momma told me and I couldn't be happier for you guys. All we've ever wanted was for you to be happy."

The sight of the two of them standing there, with such admiration between them and their eyes watering, was more than Tristan could take. He felt his own eyes start to water and had to look away. When he looked back, Kit was on her tiptoes and wrapped inside Webber's large arms. She stepped back, wiped her eyes, and ran over to Tristan, placed a kiss on his cheek and wrapped her arms around him. When she released him, without a word, she was gone as fast as she came, and Webber was standing there smiling at him. Webber offered his hand and Tristan walked over and accepted it. He led Tristan to the table and pulled out his chair. "So far, this is all going much better than I would have expected," Webber confessed.

Tristan was about to sit, but stopped. He looked at Webber curiously. "Which part?" he asked. "'Cause I'm not sure I agree with that statement. For me it was pretty touch and go for a while."

Webber dropped his head. "Yeah, I did almost ruin everything," he mumbled, almost into his chest.

Tristan brought his finger up, placed it under Webber's chin, and raised his head until their eyes met. He placed a gentle kiss on his lips and was rewarded with another one of those whimpers that he was already getting so used to.

When the kiss ended, Webber whispered, "But we're good, right?"

"We're better than good," Tristan assured him. "We're great."

Webber wiped his hand across his forehead and shook it off. "That's a relief, but when I said things went well, I was mainly referring to the Amani and Kit part."

"Oh yeah, that part I agree with. Even I can tell, after just meeting them, how much they love you and only want the best for you. You do know that, right?"

"Yeah, I just didn't really expect to be dealing with them finding out so soon. I was kind of hoping I didn't have to share you with anyone. Just for a little while anyway."

Tristan studied Webber's face. "Web, you realize people are going to find out."

"Wait, wait, Tris," Webber protested. "I didn't mean it like that. I'm not some closet case trying to hide you away. Hell, I want everyone to know how proud I am of the man I'm in love with."

Tristan felt very conflicted. "But… you never came out. You always sort of hid behind Deanna."

Webber had a painful look on his face. "Tris, it wasn't like that. I never hid behind Deanna. She was and is my best friend and so when I had engagements to attend, I asked her along. If the press got the wrong idea, it presented fewer questions, but I never hid behind her or alluded to any relationship."

Tristan had to admit he felt a little better. "Thanks for clarifying all that."

Webber took both of Tristan's hands in his. "Look, baby, you're right, I've never come out to the press, but I never tried to hide it either. I've just never found anyone worth coming out for, until now."

Tristan smiled. He was no longer just feeling better, he was flying high.

"One step at a time, big guy," he teased. "We'll cross the 'coming out' bridge when we get to it."

Webber's expression turned from one of relief to one of concern. "Tris, I'm certainly not kidding myself into believing that all of this is going to be easy, but we agreed to take it all as it comes, together. Right?"

Tristan tried to look reassuring as he smiled and nodded. He threw his arms around Webber's neck and whispered, "Right, together."

"God, that food smells incredible, and I need some serious nutrition before the next emotional moment sneaks up on me. Can we eat?" Webber laughed as he turned and started loading food onto a plate for Tristan and then for himself. When they were both seated and enjoying their breakfast, he looked at Tristan with a sly grin. "So, what do you want to do today?"

Tristan knew the answer to that question without even thinking about it. Stopping his fork midway to his mouth, he smiled at Webber coyly. Suddenly a mental image of Webber bent over a couch popped into his mind and he felt himself starting to blush. He shook his head trying to dislodge the image, cleared his throat, and took his bite. After he swallowed his food, he cleared his throat again and admitted, "I guess we do need to get some work done."

Webber raised an eyebrow and chuckled. "Tris, I can read you like a book, and after the look on your face just now, that was the last thing I expected to hear."

Tristan felt himself blushing again. "Why, I don't know what you're talking about, Mr. Kincaid."

"Tris, what did I tell you about all work and no play. We'll have plenty of time for work later. It's play time!"

Tristan perked up immediately and he felt warm and fuzzy all over. He must have seemed a little too anxious because Webber put his fork down and eyed Tristan with amusement. "Whoa, boy, as much as I want to spend the entire day ravishing you, I want our first time to be perfect. I had a little chat with Amani while you were changing, and we've got something very special planned, so you're going to have to spend all day with me without any chance of either of us jumping the other's bones."

Tristan swallowed hard and lifted his hand in a mock gesture to close his mouth, which he was sure was hanging wide open. "All day, huh?"

Webber howled with laughter. He reached over, grabbed Tristan's hand, and squeezed. "Yes, all day, and don't try anything 'cause I'll send Amani after you."

JUST when they were finishing up with their breakfast, Amani magically appeared to clear the table. Tristan thought, *They sure do come and go quickly and quietly around here.* He watched as she and Webber exchanged a few whispers and chuckles, looking back at him, Webber's crystal-blue eyes twinkling with mischief. The sight warmed his heart more than he could ever have imagined. He reached over and pinched his own arm just to make sure he wasn't dreaming. Webber walked up behind him and put both hands on his shoulders and kissed his neck lightly.

Tristan instantly felt chills run up and down his spine, and he instinctively brought a hand up and rested it on top of Webber's. Webber kissed the top of his head and squeezed his shoulders before he withdrew one hand and let the other slide down Tristan's arm. He stooped down next to Tristan's chair and looked up at him. "So, have you thought about what you want to do today?"

Tristan shook his head. "I haven't thought about anything except how happy I am to be here with you."

Webber leaned in and kissed him again. "Good, because I have an idea."

"Do tell, Mr. Kincaid."

"Okay, how's this sound? Since we just ate breakfast, I'll get Amani to pack us a lunch for later on and some wine and cheese for sunset. So far so good?" Webber asked.

Tristan nodded but didn't say anything.

Webber continued. "Then we take the boat to Virgin Gorda, spend a little time on the beach, walk around the famous baths, then maybe go over to Jost Van Dyke and have a drink at Foxy's. After that, we anchor in the spit at Norman Island for sunset and be back in plenty enough time for our special evening?"

"Sounds perfect," Tristan said. "What do I need to do?"

Webber looked up at the sky seemingly in thought, then back down at Tristan. "You grab your bathing suit and a change of dry clothes. Then get a couple of bath sheets from the bathhouse and maybe pack some sunscreen and whatever else you think we might need. I'll get Amani going on the food, grab my suit and a change of clothes, and then I'll get the golf cart and meet you at your bungalow." He placed a quick kiss on Tristan's lips, pointed him in the direction of his bungalow, smacked him on the butt, and disappeared into the house.

Tristan stood there with the stupidest smile on his face, rubbing his stinging butt and loving every minute of it.

WEBBER took the stairs two at a time and burst through the kitchen doors. He stopped just inches before he ran into poor Kenton, who was standing just inside the doors with a stack of baking pans apparently waiting for instruction from Amani. She and Kit were buzzing around the kitchen like bees around a hive, hopefully preparing a feast for later. Kenton smiled a knowing smile and Webber felt himself blush. "What can we do for you, Mr. Web?"

Kit and Amani stopped what they were doing and all three of them smiled at him like the cats that ate the canary. "Okay, okay, you've made your point. I'm in love and I'm happy and I can now see that you're happy for me, so can we get back to normal?"

They all nodded but kept the stupid grins on their faces. "Oh good Lord." Webber snorted. "Stop smiling at me."

They nodded again but still didn't lose the smiles.

"Oh, forget about it," Webber huffed through a smile of his own. "Amani, I hate to do this to you, because I know you're busy getting ready for tonight, but can you throw together a picnic basket of lunch and some apps for sunset?"

"Yes, sir," she said in a teasing tone. "Going somewhere?"

Webber moved from one foot to the other, wanting to get this over and move on to his next chore. The sooner he covered his responsibilities, the sooner he and Tristan could be out on the water. "Yep," he responded. "We're going to head off for the rest of the day, but we'll be back in plenty of time for dinner."

"Give me fifteen minutes, and Kit and I will have you all fixed up," Amani promised.

Webber headed for the doors, but stopped and looked back at the three of them again. "Now everyone knows what they need to do tonight, right? I want this evening to be perfect."

There were those stupid smiles again. "Yesss, Web," Kit said.

"Got you covered, Mr. Web," Kenton added. And Amani just stood there smiling.

He bolted from the kitchen and ran for his bedroom, where he grabbed the same black bathing suit and rummaged through his closet for another pair of shorts, a shirt, and some underwear. He threw everything in a bag. then searched the bathroom for anything they might need. *Where did I put the damn sunscreen?* He opened every drawer in the bathroom, stopping only when he saw the bottle of lube and condoms. He'd packed them hoping this trip would go the way he wanted it to, and now that it had, he was damn glad he'd planned ahead. Smiling, he removed the items, walked into the bedroom, and placed them in the drawer of the bedside table. He knew he must look like a schoolkid, but he didn't care. Tristan was here and in love with him and that was all that mattered.

He went back into the bathroom, opening the rest of the drawers until he found several SPF levels of sunscreen. Not knowing what Tristan preferred, he threw them all in the bag, glanced around one more time, and threw in a bottle of cologne, his toothbrush, and some toothpaste just for good measure. He grabbed his Panama hat from the closet and off he went.

When he made it back to the kitchen, Kit was waiting for him with a basket and a small cooler. He was a man on a mission, so he didn't even stop, just grabbed them both and kept going, kissing her on the cheek as they did the handoff. A little out of breath, he reached the outside where Kenton had the golf cart all ready to go. Webber looked at him questioningly and Kenton simply smiled. "I figured you'd need this, sir."

"Good man," Webber responded.

He threw the cooler and basket of food, along with his bag, in the back and hopped into the driver's seat. "See you this evening," he yelled to Kenton as he drove off. "And don't forget, everything has to be perfect."

Kenton nodded and winked.

When Webber reached the bungalow, Tristan was sitting on the porch in a rocking chair, sipping a beer. Tristan stood, grabbed his bag and a second beer, and slid in next to him on the small seat. "I hope that's for me," Webber said with a crooked grin.

"Who else would it be for?" Tristan teased as he twisted the top off and handed it to Webber. "Gotta love a minibar full of cold beer," he said with a grin.

Webber happily accepted the long neck, hit the pedal, and began to maneuver the electric golf cart down the winding path. He slowed when they reached the water's edge and pulled the cart right up onto the dock. He continued down and parked right in between the two vessels. He and Tristan transferred their cargo to the boat, and Tristan took everything down below. Webber started the engines and uncovered all the electronics, turned on the GPS, depth finder, autopilot, and VHF radio. He checked all the levels on the gauges, and when he was satisfied that everything was in good working condition, he went down below in search of Tristan. When he reached the companionway, Tristan was unloading the contents of the cooler into the refrigerator. He walked up behind him and wrapped his arms around Tristan's waist. "All looks good topside, Tris, you ready to get this show on the road?"

Tristan nodded as he closed the refrigerator door and turned in Webber's arms. "All secure down below, Captain. Did you see the feast Amani packed for us?"

"No, I didn't get a chance to look. Is it good?"

Tristan looked up like he was going over a mental checklist in his head. "For lunch there's smoked turkey sandwiches, a green salad, vegetables, chips, hummus, and chocolate cookies. For apps we have all kinds of cheeses, summer sausage, tapenade, pâté, and a variety of crackers and flatbreads. Oh and three bottles of wine: one chardonnay, a pinot noir, and a cabernet."

Webber dropped his head until his forehead was resting against Tristan's. "Like you," he said, "Amani never disappoints."

Tristan smiled then gently pressed his lips against Webber's. "You haven't even had me yet. How do you know if I'll disappoint or not?" he said against Webber's mouth.

Webber slowly pressed his tongue against Tristan's slightly parted lips and deepened the kiss. He was in heaven again when Tristan slipped his hand behind Webber's head and drew him in closer. When the kiss ended, Webber felt flushed and well-kissed. "That's why," he teased.

Tristan put both his hands on Webber's shoulders, shoved him back against the banquette, and headed up the companionway. "That will have to wait, remember?" he said wryly. "Besides, I thought you said something about getting this show on the road."

Webber, stunned by how fast Tristan could move for a big guy, gathered his composure and took off after him. "Why, you little shit," he yelled. "The captain says when we get this show on the road."

TRISTAN had spent enough time on boats as a teenager to know what his role as first mate entailed, so he jumped onto the dock and started untying lines while Webber prepared the helm to pull away. With all the lines on board, he hopped back onto the boat, gave Webber the "all clear," and felt the boat inching away from the dock. He had no doubt that Webber would be a very competent captain, because as far as Tristan was concerned, Webber was good at everything he set his mind to, but he was genuinely impressed at just how good he was. He plotted a course to Virgin Gorda on the navigational system and steadily increased the boat's speed until they were on top of the water, engines whining as they cut through the azure-blue waters of the Caribbean. Tristan couldn't take his eyes off Webber at the helm of this beautiful boat in this incredible location. He couldn't remember when he'd been so happy. Webber smiled and patted the spot next to him on the seat, and Tristan happily joined him. They sat side by side, holding hands, fingers entwined, and Tristan could feel the stupid grin on his lips, but he could have cared less what he looked like—he was in heaven.

A little over an hour later, Webber docked the boat at Virgin Gorda, and while Tristan secured the lines, Webber paid for the dockage. They changed into their bathing suits, threw towels and sunscreen in one of the bags, and grabbed the cooler and the lunch Amani'd prepared for them. Together they walked along the beach to the famous baths until they found a secluded spot deep within the rock formations, far away from prying eyes. Tristan kneeled and spread their towels on the white sand and placed their bags on top. He stood up and looked around, amazed at what he saw. He'd been to the baths several times over the years but was in awe every time he came back. The natural baths at Virgin Gorda were enormous boulder formations at the water's edge, offering exotic pools and grottos with hidden rooms displaying incredible rays of streaming sunlight and natural caves with coral heads for snorkeling. In many cases, the water surged up from the beach and trapped warm Caribbean water in some of the formations, thereby creating the natural baths for which the British Virgin Islands were so well known.

Webber stepped up and pulled him close, and Tristan felt a surge of excitement run through his body at the sheer intimacy. Their muscular chests were touching and they were gazing into each other's eyes. Tristan almost fell to his knees when Webber's lips touched his and warmth spread and overtook his entire body. He wrapped one hand around Webber's waist and the other around the back of Webber's head and pulled him even closer. He opened his mouth and Webber's warm tongue slipped inside, igniting a spark from the top of his head to the tip of his toes. Webber pulled back and smiled, and Tristan was again lost in those crystal-blue eyes. Webber looked around at the enormous boulders. "You wanna take a walk before we eat?"

"Sure," Tristan said, bringing Webber's hand to his lips and gently kissing his fingers. "Let's go have some fun." Like a kid, he took Webber by the hand and dragged him off into the wonders of the baths. After exploring and frolicking for a couple of hours, they returned, ate their lunch, and spent the rest of the afternoon swimming, sunning, and just enjoying being together. When it was time to go, they packed everything up and walked back to the boat hand in hand, not paying any attention or even caring if anyone had a problem with their public display of affection.

Their next stop was a very secluded cove on Trunk Bay near St. Thomas, where Webber pointed the bow of the boat into a slight westerly breeze and dropped the anchor. Tristan was instructed to stay put and look pretty while Webber busied himself opening wine and arranging appetizers on a silver tray. When it looked like he was about finished, Webber handed him a bottle of wine and two glasses and motioned for Tristan to follow him. Together they walked out onto the bow of the boat, with Webber balancing a tray of food and a basket of crackers. They dropped down onto the padded sundeck, and Webber placed the food between them and poured them each a glass of chardonnay. In Tristan's mind, the scene was postcard perfect. The crystal clear sapphire-blue waters sparkled against the bright green foliage and white sandy beaches as the sun set low in the sky, signaling the day's end. Tristan and Webber lay on the bow leaning on opposite elbows, gently kissing each other and whispering tender words between bites of appetizers and sips of wine. The faded hues of orange, red, and purple signaled the impending sunset, adding to the joy of the moment. Tristan was certain he would never forget this moment as long as he lived and reveled in it. The closeness of Webber, the beauty surrounding them, and the love he was feeling were almost more than he could have hoped for. He didn't think he would ever lose the smile that was plastered across his face and that thought made the smile even bigger.

Webber looked at Tristan and cocked his head to one side seemingly appraising his expression. "I hope that smile is some indication that I'm doing okay in the 'sweeping you off your feet' department."

Tristan raised his glass for a toast. "You're doing so much more than okay, Mr. Kincaid."

Webber touched his glass to Tristan's and took a sip of his wine, never breaking eye contact, and certainly not able to hide the smile forming on his face.

Tristan fiddled with the platter of food and then lifted a cracker with cheese to Webber's mouth. He opened and took it into his mouth in one bite and mumbled a thank you. When Tristan turned to make another, he gasped when he caught the sight of the sun hitting the water's edge. "Web, look! It's amazing."

Without turning away from Tristan, Webber said in almost a whisper, "You're amazing." He then leaned over and placed a kiss on Tristan's cheek before turning to enjoy the view.

Tristan reached out and took Webber's hand as the entire sky lit up in a palette of peach, pink, and purple. As the sun started to fall below the distant horizon, the colors melded into swirls until the orange ball of fire could no longer be seen.

Tristan sighed then looked over at Webber. "That was probably one of the most beautiful things I've ever seen."

Webber downed the last of his wine and turned to Tristan. "I have to agree, Tris, but it pales in comparison to what I'm looking at right now."

The look of sincerity in Webber's eyes was so captivating that Tristan couldn't hide the smile that formed on his lips. "Web, I don't think I've ever been this happy."

"And it looks good on you, baby," Webber said, stealing another kiss. "I hate to do this, but I think we need to start heading back. But have no fear; this day is far from over. I have some serious plans for you, remember?"

Tristan raised an eyebrow and smiled. "Oh, I remember."

TRISTAN secured the last line to the cleat while Webber placed the basket and cooler, along with their damp towels, on the dock and closed the companionway door. Webber had been whispering on the phone the entire time they were securing the boat, and although Tristan was curious, he didn't ask with whom. But Webber must have noticed Tristan watching him and simply blushed as he disconnected the call. "Just Kenton," he volunteered without Tristan having to ask.

They loaded the golf cart and made their way back up the winding path, and Webber pulled the cart up to Tristan's bungalow. Webber turned to him, looked into his eyes, and then gently kissed him. When the kiss ended, he took both of Tristan's hands in his and again looked into his eyes. It's a good thing Tristan was seated in the cart because his knees went weak when those piercing blue eyes met his. It was like Webber was looking into his soul, and he suddenly felt bare and exposed. "Everything you'll need is in your bungalow."

Tristan's head was whirling and he was full of questions. He opened his mouth to speak, but before he could get a word out, Webber placed a finger on his lips to stop him. "It's all there, Tris. I'll see you shortly." He kissed him again. "I love you, baby."

Tristan smiled, but his brow furrowed with confusion. Webber placed another gentle kiss on his lips and whispered, "Trust me."

He reminded himself that he did trust Webber, implicitly, and with that thought, the nervousness drained from his body and was replaced with sheer anticipation. He stepped out of the cart but leaned back in, smiling, and placed a quick, gentle kiss on Webber's lips. He gazed into those crystal-blue eyes seeing nothing but love. "I love you and I do trust you."

He stepped away from the cart, his smile broadening, as he grabbed his bag and almost ran to his bungalow. He was almost giddy with excitement, and as he put his hand on the doorknob, he heard a roar of laughter from Webber as the golf cart pulled away.

When Tristan stepped into his bungalow, he stopped dead in his tracks. Lying on the bed was a tuxedo with a white dinner jacket, white shirt, suspenders, cummerbund, bowtie, and black socks and shoes. Next to the tuxedo were a black velvet box and an envelope that simply said "My dearest Tris."

Tristan felt the hair stand up on the back of his neck as goose bumps covered his body. He lifted the envelope with unsteady hands, opened it, and slid out the contents. It was a handwritten note on Webber's personal stationary. Tristan read the note out loud.

I can only imagine how handsome you're going to look in this. Meet me at the pool in one hour.

Love, Web

P.S. The black velvet box is a little something from me to you. I hope you like the gift!

Tristan's legs felt so shaky that he dropped to the edge of the bed, never taking his eyes off the velvet box. He reached out and brushed the top with a finger, not quite ready to open it, but dying to see what was inside. Seconds later, curiosity got the best of him and he finally picked it up. He started to open it, then stopped and clenched it tightly in his palm. A few seconds later, he brought the box to his heart and held it there until he finally found the courage to open it.

He swallowed a gasp as he stared in disbelief at a pair of emerald-cut diamond cufflinks and four matching diamond studs. Against the black velvet, they were sparkling like the brightest stars he'd ever seen. *Oh man, they're beautiful!* He put the box down, tearing his eyes away from its contents, and ran his fingers along the silk lapel of the white dinner jacket. He opened the coat and checked inside the breast pocket for the size. Forty-four long. He checked the size for the shirt, pants, and shoes and everything was dead on. *How did he know my size?*

Tristan glanced down at his watch and started to freak out just a little. He'd spent twenty minutes checking out his new outfit and now had only forty minutes to shower and change. He stood and backed away from his bed, never taking his eyes off the incredible gift Webber had bestowed on him until they were no longer in sight. When he reached the shower, he stuck his hand in and turned on the water. He ran for the closet, stripping as he went, returning to find the shower hot and steamy. He showered, taking a little extra time to enjoy the heat of the water enveloping his body as his mind wandered in anticipation of his evening with Webber. They'd both waited so long for this night to come, and obviously Webber had gone out of his way to make everything perfect. Tristan only wished he had something special to give Webber in return for his generosity, but that would have to wait until they got home.

He stepped out of the shower, draped himself with one of the luxurious bath sheets, dried from head to toe, and wrapped the towel around his waist. He went through his usual routine, taking a little extra time to make sure he looked his best, and with fifteen minutes to spare, stepped back into his bedroom to dress. The Armani tuxedo was simply incredible, and as he slipped on the slacks, they seemed to be tailor-made for him. He put on the black silk socks, shoes, and lightly starched white shirt and they, too, all fit perfectly. He added the suspenders and cummerbund and picked up the black velvet box. Tristan removed the diamond cufflinks from the box and put them on one by one, admiring them as he went. He fed the studs through the buttonholes on the shirt and then tied the bowtie, slipped the white dinner jacket over his shoulders, and looked at himself in the mirror. He couldn't believe it was his reflection. For the first time in his life, he felt like a prince. He swallowed down the lump in his throat, smoothed the front of his coat, and looked at his watch. *Right on time.* He headed for the door with a smile plastered across his face and feeling like he'd died and gone to heaven. *I'm all yours, Webber Kincaid, and I always will be.*

TRISTAN strolled along the beautifully manicured walkways leading to the pool area, his spirit soaring in anticipation of seeing Webber. When he rounded the corner, not the least bit prepared for what he saw, he stopped dead in his tracks. Webber was leaning against the deck railing, sipping what he knew was a single malt scotch, looking like he'd just stepped out of *Gentlemen's Quarterly* magazine. His shiny dark hair was slicked back, accentuating the silver streaks that adorned the wavy curls atop his head, and his cerulean eyes sparkled in the candlelight. He was wearing a perfectly tailored black tuxedo that hugged every bit of his six-foot-three-inch frame, with a black pleated shirt, a black silk vest, and matching necktie. Eyeing Webber up and down, it took all his reserves of strength to keep from running to him, tackling him on the spot, and taking him right where they stood. He stared, in complete awe of the man he could now call his, and the only words he could come up with to describe the object of his desires was "perfectly stunning."

Taking his eyes off Webber for a moment, Tristan took in the almost magical scene before him. There were endless hurricane lanterns lining the deck railing, surrounding the pool, and hanging in the trees. The candlelight danced in the gentle breeze coming off the ocean and the soft sound of Caribbean-style music filled his ears. When he turned in the direction of the music, he saw a steel drum band with three handsome dark-skinned men in gauzy white, loosely fitting clothing tapping lightly on the steel drums, creating a sensual rhythm that seemed to encompass him. The pool was adorned with little vessels floating lazily on the surface, each holding a hurricane lantern with flickering candlelight skipping across the water. The table was set formally with what appeared to be platinum-rimmed china and a large silver candelabra was centered on the table. Before Tristan could move, Kenton appeared, also dressed in black, and approached Webber with a silver tray containing a decanter and another rocks glass. Webber looked directly at Tristan and smiled that delicious smile that always made Tristan weak in the knees. Their eyes met and held each other's gaze for what felt like eternity, as it seemed that neither one of them wanted to move. Tristan certainly didn't for fear that everything in front of him would vanish and he would wake up in his bed, all of this a dream. The thought sent shivers up and down Tristan's spine, and he felt the blood drain out of his face. He felt as much as saw Webber moving toward him, and he wanted to move, but his legs wouldn't cooperate. When Webber reached him, he seemed concerned. "Tris, are you okay?"

No, he wasn't okay. *Could all this be a dream? Could life be this cruel?* He could feel each beat of his heart as painful stabs in his gut. But when Webber reached out and touched his cheek, he threw himself into his arms and held on tight, feeling Webber's secure embrace.

He turned his face into Webber's neck and whispered, "Is this real, Webber? Please tell me I'm not dreaming."

Webber pulled back just a little until he could look into Tristan's eyes. He cocked his head to one side. "I'm here, baby, and you're here and this is real. If we're dreaming, I don't ever want to wake up."

Tristan again buried his face in Webber's neck and sighed. He felt his color coming back and his knees getting a little stronger. "I'm being silly," he whispered. "I just can't believe all this is really happening for us."

"Tris, this is really happening. I'm never letting you go, and you know I never go back on my word."

Tristan relaxed in Webber's arms and kissed him gently on the neck before pulling away and flattening the front of his tuxedo, feeling a little embarrassed.

Webber stepped back, keeping both hands on his shoulders, and eyed him seductively. "You look absolutely gorgeous. I knew that tuxedo would be perfect on you."

Tristan smiled and felt himself blushing, but he couldn't take his eyes off Webber. "When I rounded the corner and saw you, the only word that came to mind was 'stunning', Webber Kincaid. You look stunning."

Tristan brought the same blush to Webber's face, and that made him smile even more. "Thank you," Webber whispered as he offered his hand. Tristan gladly accepted and felt himself being led over to where Kenton had left the silver tray. Webber handed him a rocks glass and picked up his own, and they continued hand in hand to the balcony's edge. Tristan sipped his scotch and took in the velvety midnight-blue waters of the Caribbean for a few seconds before turning to Webber and bringing one hand up to caress his studs, which made his cufflinks visible. "Web, these are amazing. You really shouldn't have."

Webber eyed him intently. "And why not?"

Tristan took another sip of his drink, contemplating the question. "First of all, they're too extravagant. And secondly, I didn't bring anything for you."

"Oh, Tris," Webber teased. "Nothing is too extravagant for you. You've given me the last two years of your life. The way I see it, I have a lot more giving to do, just to catch up."

Tristan was warmed down to his toes. He brushed his lips across Webber's and whispered, "Thank you."

"It was my pleasure, and they look incredible on you," Webber proclaimed. "And while we're talking about this, you'd better get used to accepting gifts as I plan to shower you with them every chance I get."

Tristan felt himself blushing again, but simply smiled and nodded. "How did you know my size?" he asked.

"Well, I didn't exactly, but Kenton did. Before he came to work for me, he was a tailor, and he sized you up for the dinner jacket and checked your bungalow for the rest of the sizes. He called a friend and had everything tailored and sent over earlier today."

Tristan could feel the shocked look on his face, but couldn't help it. "That's amazing" was all he could say. "And all of this?" he asked, gesturing to the pool area.

Webber looked around as if he were seeing it for the first time himself. "Amani and Kit. Didn't they do a great job?"

"Everything looks amazing," Tristan agreed. "I can see why you love them so much, and if you ever had any doubts about how they feel about you, I think you can put that behind you."

Webber grinned and raised his glass to Tristan. "I think you're right about that."

Tristan lightly touched their two glasses together and winked.

Webber reached over and cupped Tristan's chin, bringing his face in just close enough for Webber to momentarily brush his own lips lightly against Tristan's. The electricity between them was unmistakable as the hair stood up on the back of Tristan's neck. Webber pulled back and licked his lips lazily several times, as if tasting the lingering flavor of Tristan resting there. He turned to the band and nodded, removed Tristan's glass from his hand, and placed their glasses on the dinner table. Tristan followed his gaze and watched as a beautiful woman with mocha-colored skin, wearing a long black sequined dress slit up to her waist and a large white flower stuck in her slicked-back hair, stepped out of the house, accompanied by a guitarist and saxophone player. She walked out in front of the band and nodded. Tristan heard the soft, steady rumble of the three steel drums as the saxophone joined in and the woman sang, "At last... my love has come along." The guitarist joined in and Webber offered his hand to Tristan. "Dance with me, Tris."

Tristan's eyes were now glistening and tears were starting to stream down his face. "Webber, how did you…? Etta James. This is my favorite song."

"You're not the only one who pays attention around here," he teased. "I heard this music coming out of your office so many times, I'd be an idiot if I failed to pick up on your favorite music. Come dance with me," Webber repeated quietly as he offered his hand.

Tristan's heart almost leaped out of his chest as he took a few unsteady steps and followed Webber to a spot in front of the band, his hand curling into Webber's as they walked.

"Can you follow?" Webber whispered nervously.

Tristan couldn't answer right away. He wondered if he looked as shocked as he felt. *Webber Kincaid is asking me to dance.*

"Tris?" Webber repeated in a hushed tone.

"Oh sorry, I suppose I can try to follow," Tristan said with a rush of unexpected nerves, wiping the tears from his face. "I've never done it before, but how hard can it be?"

Webber laughed. "Oh good. Because I've never followed before either," he admitted. "In fact, this is the first time I've ever danced with a man."

Tristan stepped back and looked at Webber. "Ever?"

"Well, no, not really, but never a slow dance."

Tristan raised his left hand out of habit, then dropped it again and raised his right, both of them grinning about how to hold each other. Then Tristan brought his left hand over Webber's shoulder, cupped the back of his neck, and pulled him close. Webber stepped in and slid his other arm around Tristan's waist. Tristan could feel Webber's strength and confidence in his stance and wondered how many times he'd done this with women. As they tightened their hold, Tristan could feel Webber's breath, warm and sensual, on his neck. He reveled in the sensation, inhaling the sweet smell of his spicy cologne mixed with his natural scent. Suddenly Webber's hand tightened in his and he started moving. Hesitant at first, he quickly found a rhythm and stuck with it.

Tristan held on and did his best to anticipate Webber's next moves, quickly starting to feel the music in his head. *This isn't so bad. In fact, I think I like it.* As Tristan relaxed into the dance, he let the music slide down into his soul, and with Webber holding him so tightly, he closed his eyes and relaxed, knowing he was safe and in good hands. After a quick turn, Webber brought their joined hands between them and held them to his chest as they swayed gently.

Tristan's pulse accelerated as he gave himself over to Webber and drifted with the music. Webber's chin now rested at Tristan's temple where he placed gentle kisses every so often. Then Tristan raised his head and their cheeks met in a slow, natural movement. That's how they stayed until the song ended. It was the most romantic thing Tristan had ever done, and he wanted to do it again. The song ended but Webber didn't let go, and Tristan certainly didn't want to move. But before Tristan could be upset that the song was over, the singer took a deep breath and when she opened her mouth, Tristan was in heaven. "I… want a Sunday kind of love."

Tristan felt Webber tighten his embrace and he snuggled in closer, enjoying the feel of Webber's strong body pressed against his. The two of them swayed to the music like they had been dancing together all their lives. Dancing with someone he loved was a totally new sensation for Tristan. It was the most erotic thing he'd ever done out of bed, and God, he could get used to this. He had never slow danced with Justin, the only other person he'd ever loved, but now he was so glad he hadn't. This was something new between him and Webber, and he smiled against Webber's cheek as the corners of their mouths touched, not quite a kiss, but as sensual as any kiss Tristan had ever shared. When the music ended, Webber pulled his head back and gazed into Tristan's eyes. He tilted his head to one side and leaned in, pressing their lips together. Tristan closed his eyes as warm, insistent lips assaulted his. He instinctively opened to Webber and their tongues danced as easily and as sensually as their bodies had just done. They seemed to be lost in each other, and Tristan didn't care if he was ever found. He had no idea how long they'd been kissing when someone cleared his throat. The kiss interrupted, they both looked up. The music had stopped and there was silence surrounding them as Kenton stood, hands folded behind his back, looking a little embarrassed.

"Sorry to disturb you, sir, but you asked me to alert you when it was just before nine o'clock."

Webber gave Kenton a warm smile. "I did indeed, and thank you, Kenton."

He stole one more quick kiss from Tristan and then took him by the hand and led him to the edge of the deck, stopping briefly to get their drinks from the table.

The moment they reached the railing the first boom sounded in the distance and Tristan, a little startled, looked out over the Caribbean. The horizon immediately lit up with flashes of blues and silvers, and before the sky could settle, the second blasts sounded a little louder and reds, oranges, and greens joined the blues and silvers. The night started rumbling and the deep blue sky was quickly filled with booms, blasts, and flashes of beautiful, vibrant colors.

Not wanting to turn away, but desperate to gaze into Webber's eyes, Tristan turned his head and caught Webber's stare. He saw the fireworks reflected in Webber's crystal-blue eyes, but he also saw something that could be identified as nothing else but desire. His heart raced and suddenly, he was overcome with emotions, some of which he could identify as sheer joy, excitement, love, and amazement, but so many others that were so new to him that he wouldn't dare try to put words to them. He realized that he'd never felt what he was feeling right now. He'd never really been in love—maybe he thought he had been in love with Justin, but Justin was barely a small flicker in comparison to the emotions he was feeling now.

Webber took both Tristan's hands in his. "This is all for you, baby," he whispered.

Webber kissed him with a desperation he could feel and totally understand. He'd never been kissed like this, and he felt hopelessly and helplessly lost in it, in Webber. When the kiss ended, Webber put his arm over Tristan's shoulder, and together they turned to watch the mesmerizing colors dancing in front of the full moon. Suddenly the sky went dark and silence filled their ears. Tristan thought it was all over, but as quickly as it had ended, the sky blossomed into mushrooms of yellow, blues, greens, and reds. In rapid succession, booms, blasts, and explosions colored the sky once again. Streamers of lavender and purple floated through the darkened sky as explosions of every color mixed with the previous display, and the sky was overcome with color and sounds until there was again silence. But just as Tristan was about to turn to Webber, the sky again filled with one lone explosion. The eruption burst into a million twinkles that formed one large red heart.

The air was sucked right out of Tristan's lungs, and he thought for a second he might just pass out from lack of oxygen, but damned if he would miss any of this. It was the most spectacular thing he had ever experienced. Then just as quickly as it had lit up, the sky went dark as the red heart faded away and silence reigned again. As if on cue, the steel drum band started playing again softly in the background, and Tristan's heart became so full it took all he had to not start bawling like a little baby. *When did I turn into a silly teenaged schoolgirl?*

He smiled and gazed into Webber's eyes, and a multitude of unspoken words passed between them, each sure they knew what the other was thinking, but not quite willing to share just yet. Webber pulled him in for a long, desperate kiss that sent sparks down to his toes. Tristan ran his hands through Webber's wavy hair, now dry and a little stiff from the gel he must have applied earlier to get that GQ look, and cupped the back of his head. He held Webber's lips against his, not wanting the kiss to ever be over, exploring his mouth as their tongues fought for dominance. The kiss finally ended and Tristan laid his cheek against Webber's and simply held him there. "I love you."

"I love you too, Tris. More than you will ever know," Webber said breathlessly. "Let's eat dinner, so we can get to dessert."

Tristan shivered in anticipation and chuckled nervously. "Can we skip dinner?"

Webber looked around at the setting. "I'd love nothing more," he whispered, "but Amani, Kit, and Kenton have been working all day to make this dinner perfect. I can't disappoint them."

Tristan followed Webber's gaze and took in his surroundings. "That was so selfish of me," he admitted. "They've done an incredible job. I'm sorry for even suggesting we pass."

Webber smiled. "Thanks for understanding."

Tristan squeezed Webber's hand and they turned to find Kenton, Kit, and Amani standing arm in arm just inside the house with large smiles spread across their faces. "It looks like everyone enjoyed the fireworks," Tristan chuckled.

"Looks that way," Webber said. "But it's my fault. I told them to make sure they didn't miss it."

Waving them over, Tristan said, "I'm glad. They are your family."

"Our family."

"Right, our family," Tristan corrected himself. "Our family, and I want them to be a part of our lives."

Webber placed a kiss on his cheek as he too motioned for their extended family to join them. The five of them embraced, Kit and Amani teary eyed and Kenton smiling broadly.

"We're going to get dinner served," Amani said as she wiped her tears away and took Kit by the hand, leading her down to the kitchen.

Kenton motioned for them to be seated as he poured a small amount of a 2007 Haut-Brion Blanc into a crystal wine glass. Webber swirled the wine around in the glass several times, stuck his nose into the opening of the glass and inhaled slowly, and then finally took a sip.

Kenton raised an eyebrow waiting for Webber's summation of the wine.

Webber looked up at Kenton. "Perfect. Thanks, Kenton."

Kenton smiled as he filled Tristan's glass three-quarters full and then did the same to Webber's. "I'm glad you like it, sir. Your first course will be out shortly."

"Thank you, Kenton."

Webber held up his wine glass and Tristan did the same. "To us," he whispered.

"To us," Tristan agreed as he touched his glass to Webber's. He took a sip of the wine and let it remain in his mouth for a few moments before swallowing. "This is incredible."

"It was one of my father's favorites, and I always keep it in the wine cellar," Webber explained.

Tristan stared at his wine glass, swirling the wine around gently. "I wish I could have known your father," he said shyly.

Webber reached out and took Tristan's hand. "He would have loved you, Tris. You remind me of him sometimes."

Surprised and flattered, Tristan raised a brow and cocked his head to one side with a slight smile. "Really? How so?"

"For starters, the way your face scrunches and you chew on your bottom lip when you're trying to solve a problem. My dad did the same thing."

Webber paused and studied Tristan with his head bent to one side. "But mostly it's your crooked smile when you finally get it. That smile has pulled at my heartstrings since day one."

Before Tristan could reply, Kenton walked up with the first course. He placed a large bowl in front of him and then Webber. "Gentlemen, your first course is a chilled cucumber soup with grilled shrimp, fresh parsley, scallions, and dill. Enjoy."

"Wow," Tristan said, "this looks incredible." He held his glass up this time. "To the most magical night of my life."

Raising his glass and touching it to Tristan's, Webber nodded. "And to many more just like this one."

They both took sips of their wine and put their glasses down before sampling the soup. Of course, it was the best chilled soup Tristan had ever tasted, but the first course had nothing on the rest of the meal. The soup was followed by a caramelized pear and endive salad with maple vinaigrette, and the entrée was a wok-fried Caribbean lobster over crème fraiche-enriched orzo. Everything about the meal was spectacular, right down to the sorbet Kenton had served between courses to cleanse the palate. But the most spectacular thing on the menu was Webber Kincaid. Tristan spent the entire meal mesmerized by him: the way his lips glistened when the slightest bit of wine still lingered, the way he chewed and swallowed, his throat contracting and his Adam's apple moving up and down, and the way he wiped the corners of his mouth with his linen napkin. All of these things were daily occurrences, but on Webber, they were the most sensual things he'd ever experienced. Joy consumed him when it suddenly occurred to him that he was going to be able to look at Webber eat for the rest of his life.

Trying to stop the rush of blood to his groin, he struggled to think of something else. He made a mental note to make sure to tell Amani and Kenton just how wonderful they were and how spectacular the meal was when he saw them tomorrow. He also needed to thank Amani about just how right the portions were. He wasn't overly full, but adequately sated, and he smiled shyly as the blood started to rush south again. *Don't want to look fat or feel stuffed for my first night with Webber.*

"Care to share?" Webber asked, obviously watching Tristan intently.

"Maybe later," he replied with a full-on blush, knowing he'd been caught thinking naughty thoughts.

Webber raised a brow and gave him a questioning look but didn't push him.

Kenton reappeared tableside and smiled down at Webber and winked. "All is ready, sir."

"Thank you, Kenton. For everything," Webber said smiling as he stuck his hand out. Kenton accepted it and they shook with Webber placing his other hand over their joined hands and winking at Kenton. When they released, Kenton was once again gone.

Tristan cocked his head to one side, wondering what knowledge had passed between them, but said nothing.

"Patience, my dear Tris," Webber whispered with a chuckle, obviously aware that he had picked up on the exchange.

"I haven't said a word," Tristan teased, leaning back in his chair, resting one arm on the back and sipping his wine.

"You don't have to," Webber admitted, pushing back in his chair and crossing his legs, never breaking eye contact with him. "I've learned to read you quite well over the last two years while I've been pining away for you."

"Is that so?" Tristan said, lifting his brow.

Webber simply nodded as he topped off their wine glasses and then stood, offering his hand to Tristan. "Shall we?"

"I thought you'd never ask," Tristan replied as he too stood, accepting Webber's outstretched hand.

He allowed Webber to take the lead as they walked hand in hand around the pool, stopping to toast, sip, and steal little kisses every few steps. The sound of the band was still floating on the soft, gentle breezes of the Caribbean, filling the quiet night with romance and promise. Tristan felt as if he'd died and gone to heaven. Finally, Webber took Tristan's empty wine glass and set it down along with his own and then slipped his arm around Tristan's waist and guided them toward the main house. The anticipation built as they walked silently past the pool and the band, through the house, and down the stairs to the lower level. When they reached Webber's bedroom door, Tristan's nerve endings were on fire as a million tiny butterflies fluttered in his stomach. Webber turned him and backed him up to the closed door and gently kissed him. Tristan watched as he hesitantly placed a hand on the doorknob, then stopped. He looked back up at Tristan shyly, seemingly for some sort of approval, and waited.

He smiled when Tristan nodded and placed a gentle kiss on his cheek. Tristan smiled back. *This is it. Once I walk through this door, there is no turning back. Hell, I don't want to turn back. I want to crawl into Webber's arms and stay there forever.*

Tristan felt the back of Webber's fingers brush against his cheek, which sent shivers up and down his spine. He reached up and took Webber's hand and brought it to his lips, gently kissing his fingers one by one, never breaking eye contact.

"Close your eyes," Webber said as he slowly turned the knob on the door and pushed it open, his eyes still locked on Tristan's. He backed Tristan into the room and kicked the door shut with his foot, closing them off from the rest of the world. Before Webber could say anything, Tristan smiled when he heard Dinah Washington's soft voice in the background. Webber turned him around and slipped his arms around his waist. "Okay, you can open your eyes now," he whispered, burying his head in Tristan's neck.

When Tristan opened his eyes, the air was once again sucked out of his lungs. The entire room was aglow from the flickering candlelight, just as the pool area had been. On the balcony overlooking the Caribbean was a small table for two covered with a white tablecloth. On the table were two long-stemmed champagne flutes and a silver tray of bite-size desserts. Standing next to the table was a footed cooler chilling a bottle of champagne. The bed was turned down, exposing shiny silken sheets, and two bathrobes lay across the foot of the bed.

Webber turned Tristan around again to face him. "Let me make you a little more comfortable," he said as he grabbed the lapels of Tristan's tuxedo jacket, slid it over his shoulders, and tossed it on the chaise lounge in the corner. Staring into his eyes, Webber slowly reached up, took both ends of Tristan's bowtie and tugged on them until the knot gave way and he was able to slip it from underneath Tristan's collar and toss it aside. He then unbuttoned the top button of his shirt and removed the diamond studs and placed them on the dresser. "That's better," Webber whispered. "Not where I ultimately want you, but better."

Tristan followed suit and slipped Webber's jacket over his shoulders and tossed it on the chaise as well. He deliberately took his time unbuttoning each of the black silk buttons on Webber's vest and then slipped it, too, over his shoulders and tossed it where it joined their coats. Still gazing into the other man's sensual blue eyes, Tristan slid his hands up and loosened the black silk tie around Webber's neck and slipped it off, unbuttoning the top button as he went.

Tristan pressed his lips to Webber's in a deep, gentle kiss as he started to sway to the music, not quite dancing, but enjoying feeling Webber's body so close. The slow kiss warmed him to his toes and they stayed like that, swaying easily to the music as a warm buzz filled Tristan's head, telling him this was right where he needed to be. He worked his way down Webber's cheek to his neck and buried his head there, nibbling and kissing. He unbuttoned another button on Webber's black shirt and gently kissed his chest, burying his face in the small patch of trimmed chest hair, inhaling Webber's scent. He felt Webber throw his head back and whimper as Tristan continued his tender assault.

"Trissss," Webber pleaded as he ran his fingers through Tristan's dark brown locks. Tristan could feel Webber's arousal meeting his own, and he was so turned on, he was very close to his worst nightmare. He worked his way back up to Webber's neck, dropping kisses along the way, and finally looked up to find Webber's eyes closed and his head thrown back in the most sensual pose he'd ever seen. Webber must have sensed him staring because he opened his eyes and took Tristan's lips again fast and furiously.

Tristan smiled through the kiss and Webber must have felt it and backed off. "Web, I need to pee," Tristan chuckled.

"Oh thank God," Webber huffed. "I thought you were laughing at me."

"Never," Tris said breathlessly. "But I do have to pee really badly."

Webber turned Tristan in the direction of the bathroom, stealing a kiss as he did so, and slapped him on the ass as he urged him forward. "It's in there."

WEBBER watched as Tristan sauntered toward the bathroom in the way that only Tristan Moreau could do and licked his lips as he watched that round, muscular ass disappear through the open doorway. He turned and walked out onto the balcony and looked out over the Caribbean. He'd been dreaming about this moment for the last two years, and his heart raced as he realized that it was finally here. His hands started to shake with the implications. *What if Tris doesn't find me attractive? What if I'm no good in bed? I haven't been with that many men in my life and none since I met Tris.* He closed his eyes to try to calm himself down. *I need a drink.* He reached for the champagne and looked at the label, a 1995 Krug Clos d'Ambonnay. *Good man, Kenton.*

He started unwrapping the foil from the top of the bottle and was about to pop the cork when he felt Tristan's arms slip around his waist. "Hey, baby," Tristan whispered as he melded his body against Webber's.

"Hey yourself," Webber answered. "Did you find everything okay?"

Tristan squeezed him tighter. "Yep. And all my things as well."

Webber felt the blush come on and turned in Tristan's arms. "I hope you don't mind, I had Kenton move your things in here during dinner."

"Pretty presumptuous of you."

Webber felt the blush disappear and dread fill his being. "I'm sorry, it was really forward of me. I can have it all moved back in a few minutes."

Tristan's eyes got wider. "No!" he said. "Web, I was only kidding."

Webber sighed in relief. Tristan stepped back and looked him in the eye. "Webber, what's going on? Talk to me."

Webber popped the champagne and poured two glasses, not looking at Tristan as he handed him one, his hands noticeably shaking.

Tristan took Webber's trembling hand and held it tightly in his own. "Web, you're starting to worry me."

He looked into Tristan's eyes before he spoke. "Tris, I'm just nervous."

"Web, it's me," Tristan whispered. "There's nothing to be nervous about."

Webber broke eye contact and stared out over the ocean.

"Web?"

Webber's heart raced and there was an unfamiliar tightness in his chest. He could suddenly feel the nerves coursing through his body, and he bit the inside of his mouth to try to calm himself. "Tris, I've not been with that many men in my life, and there's been no one in the last couple of years," he admitted in a shaky voice.

He watched the surprised look on Tristan's face turn into a smile and then into an outright chuckle.

"Are you laughing at me? Again?" Webber asked in a semi-annoyed tone.

"Oh my God, Web, I'm laughing because I felt the same way when I was in the bathroom. Are we pathetic or what?"

Webber cocked his head to one side. "What do you mean, you felt the same way?"

"Web, I've only ever been with Justin and one other man, and certainly no one since I moved to Atlanta to work for you."

Webber's lips curled into a smile. Then his smile faded. "I'm so afraid of disappointing you."

Tristan took the champagne flute out of Webber's hand and put both of them on the table. Webber felt Tristan's embrace surround him and some of the tension drained out of his body as he threw his arms around Tristan's neck and held on for dear life.

He felt Tristan's warm breath on his ear right before he spoke. "I love you, Webber Kincaid, and nothing short of you being engaged, married, or cheating on me is going to change that."

Webber buried his face in Tristan's neck and released the rest of the tension he'd been carrying. "I think I'm pretty damn safe then."

"Good," Tristan mumbled as he released Webber and turned for their champagne.

Webber wanted Tristan's arms back around him, but it could wait. He knew now that it was going to be okay, which relaxed him considerably. He took the offered flute and sipped the full-bodied effervescence of the nicely aged champagne.

Tristan raised the glass to his lips and sipped slowly. "This stuff is extraordinary," he proclaimed.

"Isn't it, though?" Webber agreed. "You can thank Kenton. He brought it up from the wine cellar this morning and had it chilling all day."

Tristan nodded. "I'll do that," he said, taking another sip.

Tristan smiled at Webber and then turned to glance at the desserts on the silver platter. Webber watched as Tristan perused the selections, settling on something that appeared to have cream cheese icing. *Man does he know me.*

When he raised his selection to Webber's lips, he gladly opened and let the delectable treat slide onto his tongue. He savored the flavor and realized that it was Amani's carrot cake. Tristan was suddenly smiling at him and before he could ask why, the other man moved in and licked something off the corner of Webber's mouth. He licked his lips. "Icing," he said through a chuckle.

Webber felt a smile grow from deep within his soul and took Tristan in his arms. He lifted him off the ground and spun him around, champagne flying everywhere. Tristan howled with laughter, which only made Webber go faster. When he stopped, Tristan melted into his arms, both of them now covered in champagne and a little dizzy.

After they'd caught their breath and the dizziness had subsided, Tristan started unbuttoning Webber's shirt. "Let's get you out of these wet clothes."

Webber felt a jolt of lust run through him and shivered at the mere suggestion of where the act would ultimately lead. He stared into Tristan's hazel eyes and the flecks that were now sparkling like gold dust with a look of desire Webber had only seen in his dreams. As if in a trance, he felt Tristan finish unbuttoning his shirt and lift each arm slowly to remove his cufflinks while placing gentle kisses on his hands and fingers. Tristan's eyes were focused and his gaze deliberate as he completed his mission, and Webber was caught somewhere between ecstasy and bliss. Never breaking eye contact, Tristan slid Webber's shirt over his shoulders and let it drop to the balcony floor. Tristan's warm hands began caressing Webber's chest, and without conscious thought, a whimper escaped Webber's lips as his soon-to-be lover's hand brushed across his now erect nipples. Moving up his body, Tristan left a trail of open-mouthed kisses that made Webber shudder. Once

Tristan had paid attention to his left nipple for a few moments, he worked his way across Webber's chest to the right one and did the same. The low rumbling tone of his voice filled Webber's ears as he whispered, "you're amazing," over and over again, sending him into a tailspin. Dragging his lips slowly and sensually across Webber's chest, Tristan continued his litany of praise. When Tristan ran his tongue over his left nipple again and circled it several times, his knees buckled and he reached for the small table to steady himself. Tristan must have sensed his shakiness and wrapped both arms around his waist. "I've got you," he whispered, holding Webber tightly to steady him.

Webber regained his footing and wrapped his arms around Tristan's neck and kissed him tenderly. When the kiss ended, he nuzzled against the warm skin of Tristan's neck. "Thanks for catching me," he said in a soft tone.

"Always," Tristan answered. "Web?"

"Yeah?"

"Let's go inside before I strip you right here on the balcony."

Webber raised his head and gave him a sly smile. "Afraid to put on a show for the entire Caribbean?"

Tristan, with a defiant look in his eyes, reached down and slipped a hand into the waistband of Webber tuxedo pants.

"Okay stop! You win, I was just teasing."

"I figured you'd see it my way."

Smiling victoriously Tristan took him by the hand and led him into the bedroom. The candles flickered as Dinah sang "I wanna be loved" as if she were singing it just for them. They stood at the side of the bed, Tristan looking hungrily into his eyes with something that could only be described as primal need. He brought his lips so close to Webber's ear that Webber could feel his warm breath. "I want you desperately, Webber Kincaid," he whispered in that low growl that made Webber's toes curl. "I've wanted you for so long, I can't remember a time when I didn't."

Webber sighed contently. "You've had me from the day you walked into my office. And like it or not, you'll have me until the day I die."

Tristan shook his head. "Not long enough," he protested as he pressed his lips against Webber's eagerly while slowly guiding him back toward the bed. Webber stopped when the backs of his legs hit the side of the bed and sat when he felt Tristan apply a light pressure to his bare shoulders.

Desperately needing Tristan out of his clothes but not wanting to break their kiss, Webber reached behind him and unfastened his cummerbund, letting it drop to the floor. He yanked Tristan's shirt out of his pants and slowly fumbled with the buttons. When his shaking hands failed to execute the simple task, Webber used both hands and pulled Tristan's shirt apart, the sound of buttons popping and hitting the wall sending shivers down his spine. Tristan didn't flinch and continued the assault on Webber's welcoming lips, then broke the kiss and dropped to one knee. He slowly untied one of Webber's shoes and then the other. He slipped them off and lifted Webber's legs around and placed them on the bed. Webber was now leaning against the headboard with his legs stretched out in front of him. Tristan stood and slid his shirt off and let it join his cummerbund on the floor at his feet. He toed out of his shoes and climbed on the bed placing his knees on either side of Webber, straddling him. In a slow and deliberate move, Webber took Tristan by the shoulders and maneuvered him so that he was lying at his side. He looked into Tristan's eyes where he saw the stars, the moon, the universe, and the heavens all mixed into one. He saw his life from here on out with Tristan. "I love you."

Without waiting for a response, he straddled Tristan and stared down at him. He admired the muscular chest beneath him and let his gaze drift down to the rippled stomach and the little patch of dark hair disappearing into his waistband. He leaned down and ran his tongue over Tristan's chest, his soft, sweet skin attacking Webber's senses. His scent was a raw combination of manliness and sweetness, and Webber wondered how many times he'd thought about what Tristan would taste like, smell like, and how the other man would feel under him as they moved in unison loving one another. The reality of the man was even better than any fantasy he could have ever conjured up. The warm, soft skin against his lips, the taste of his lover on his tongue, sent the blood rushing to his groin and consumed him as he slid down a little farther to Tristan's knees. He slipped his hand into the waistband on Tristan's pants and slowly unfastened them, sliding the zipper over his now obvious erection. Webber allowed his hand to linger long enough to feel Tristan's reaction to his touch. The sudden pulse under his fingers was almost enough to send him over the edge way too soon, so he retreated.

In one continuous movement, he slid down to the foot of the bed taking Tristan's trousers with him and tossing them onto the floor. He removed Tristan's socks and stood admiring his soon-to-be lover, lying before him in black boxer briefs and looking sexier than any Calvin Klein underwear model. Tristan's licentious look was enough to finish him, but he held his gaze and began to unfasten his own trousers, allowing them to drop and puddle on the floor around his ankles before stepping out of them and removing his own socks.

Tristan reached a hand out to him, urging him onto the bed, and he gladly accepted, easing himself down on top of Tristan. He could feel Tristan's excitement as their groins collided and desire coursed through Webber's veins. He placed gentle kisses on Tristan's forehead, nose, cheeks, and neck, nipping and kissing his way down Tristan's chest, and then farther down to his stomach and ultimately his groin. When his face was lined up with Tristan's groin, he inhaled deeply as his senses honed in on the man's scent through his cotton briefs. Tristan's rock hard erection strained against the fabric of his underwear and Webber gently dragged his teeth along its length, nipping as he went. His efforts were rewarded with a gasp as Tristan fisted the sheets on either side of him, his eyes closed and his head moving from side to side.

Aroused beyond anything he thought possible, Webber continued his onslaught. He slipped his finger into the waistband of Tristan's briefs and pulled them down just enough to hook the elastic band under his perfectly shaped balls, exposing his gorgeous cock, totally erect and straining upward toward his stomach. Tristan was a sight to behold fully clothed, but naked, he was an Adonis. He was perfectly proportioned from his broad chest down to his small waist, slim hips, and long muscular but slender legs. His circumcised cock was long and thick, but not too bulky, and the perfect mushroom at the head was red from the blood pulsing there. Webber was looking down at the most beautiful human being he'd ever seen and reveling in the thought that Tristan wanted him and only him. Unable to form a complete thought, he leaned forward and licked a long line up Tristan's inner thigh. When he came back up, he allowed his five o'clock shadow to lightly brush Tristan's cock.

Tristan's body tensed and something escaped his lips: a hiss, a whimper, a growl, Webber couldn't tell, but he knew he loved hearing it. Encouraged yet again, Webber repeated the same movement on the other side, this time going all the way down to Tristan's foot. He gently kissed the top of the foot and worked his way back up, hearing Tristan's breath catch as his cheek once again brushed his length. Butterflies danced in Webber's stomach from a combination of nerves and excitement, but he almost lost it when he felt Tristan's hand running through his hair. He looked up and their eyes locked as Webber took Tristan into his hand and ran his tongue up and down his swollen member, never looking away. Webber could feel Tristan tense as he gently moved with Webber's attentions, giving him the courage to take the plunge. He yanked Tristan's underwear completely off and closed his mouth over the flared head, sucking gently and taking him to the back of his throat in one long movement. Tristan was smooth against Webber's tongue, and he felt the slightly smaller man shudder beneath him as he slowly moved up and down his length.

When Webber tasted the first hint of Tristan's arousal on his tongue, the sharp, spicy taste drove him wild with desire. He quickened his motions, coaxing another whimper out of Tristan, and the sweet sounds escaping his lips had Webber so aroused he hurt with need. Webber felt Tristan's hands on his shoulders so he could steady himself, and realized Tristan was probably fighting the urge to thrust up into his mouth. He looked up to make sure Tristan was all right, and when he did, he saw the unmistakable look of a man teetering on the verge of ecstasy. His head was thrown back and his lips were parted ever so slightly, allowing small, raspy whimpers to fill Webber's ears. Tristan's body suddenly tensed. "Web," he cried. "Can't hold on much longer."

Webber released Tristan from his mouth. "Let go, baby, I want to taste you on my tongue."

He again took Tristan and swallowed him while massaging the tender skin between his dick and balls. Tristan's muscles tensed and he cried out wordlessly as the first spurt hit the back of Webber's throat. Webber continued the slow, methodical movements until he'd milked every last drop from Tristan. He released him and placed gentle kisses along Tristan's body as he moved up and snuggled in next to him. Tristan lay with his eyes closed, one arm resting over his forehead, trembling slightly. Webber watched as he opened his eyes and smiled seductively. Tristan slipped his arm under Webber's shoulders and rolled them until he was looking down at Webber, then kissed him deeply before speaking. "Web, that was amazing. I'm keeping you."

Webber chuckled. "That good, huh?"

"That good," Tristan confirmed with a nod and a kiss to the forehead. "But it's time to get rid of these," he added as he played with the waistband of Webber's silk boxers.

Tristan was roughly an inch shorter than his own six-foot-three-inch frame, but they seemed to line up perfectly from their groin to their lips. Webber was still as hard as a rock, and the pressure from Tristan's groin against his was making him throb painfully. Amazingly enough, he could feel Tristan already getting hard again. *Ah youth,* he thought to himself. Then his heart sped up and his stomach rolled. Tristan was fifteen years his junior; would he be able to keep up with the younger man? Burying the slight wave of panic, he concentrated on Tristan. They would have to discuss that later, but for now, he was going to enjoy every second of the man now lying on top of him.

Tristan slid to one side, leaving a leg resting between Webber's as he began to nibble at his neck and then his earlobes, eventually finding his lips and taking his mouth in a devouring kiss. Tristan ran his hand up and down the length of Webber's body from neck to groin, lightly brushing his goose bumped skin. Webber's nerve endings were on fire with each brush of Tristan's fingers against him. Never breaking the kiss, Tristan slid his hand into Webber's boxers and wrapped his fingers around Webber and stroked him lightly. Webber abandoned himself to the sheer sensuality, relishing every touch and giving himself over to the moment. He could feel sweat beading on his temples, and he gently thrust into Tristan's hand. Tristan released him and nestled between his legs, where he leaned in to put his lips to Webber's nipple, licking, circling, and then biting ever so lightly. Webber arched his back and gasped with the pleasure of it all. With his head thrown back and his eyes closed, he felt Tristan working his way down his chest, nipping and licking as he went.

Webber tensed a little when he felt his boxers being slid down his legs and over his feet, leaving him completely naked and vulnerable. The brief moment of unease faded when Tristan's soft, warm lips encircled his shaft. He couldn't help but run his hands through Tristan's hair while he fought the urge to thrust up savagely into the perfect wet heat, trying to hold off his impending orgasm. Tristan released his cock and moved lower to lick and tease his balls. Webber shivered as Tristan ran a finger over his sensitive opening, making his cock twitch from the sheer overwhelming sensation. Tristan took him again into his mouth and began moving up and down in slow, even motions as he continued to stroke his opening. Webber tightened his grip in Tristan's hair and rode the waves of pleasure that consumed him. Webber's balls tightened and he moved his hands to Tristan's shoulders alerting him to what was soon to come. Suddenly, his muscles tensed and he arched his back and shouted as he came, his entire body seizing with the energy pulsing through it. He felt his orgasm through every cell of his being, a feeling of ecstasy that swallowed him whole. Tristan continued draining him until his nerves settled and he sighed with relief.

It took a while for him to come down from the natural high, but when he did Tristan was there, softly kissing him and holding him. When Tristan kissed him, he could taste himself on Tristan's tongue and the sensation was oddly erotic.

When the kiss ended, Webber looked Tristan in the eyes and held his gaze. "I love you," he whispered. "So much it scares me to death."

Tristan looked at him with reassuring eyes as he ran his fingers through Webber's hair. "I know what you mean. But we have the rest of our lives to reassure each other that everything is going to be just fine."

Feeling sated and suddenly sleepy, Webber reached down and pulled the covers up over them, and then snuggled into Tristan, resting his head on Tristan's chest with an arm over his stomach. Tristan pulled him tighter and they lay there in silence, the CD long over and the wee hours of the morning creeping up on them. They drifted off to sleep secure in each other's arms.

Nine

TRISTAN awoke to the sounds of birdsong filling his ears. He lazily opened his eyes and saw beams of sunlight shining through the open balcony door. He closed them tightly against the brightness of the morning and lay still, simply enjoying the happy concert taking place right outside the room. Remembering the previous day and especially the night filled his heart with a sense of joy and peace he'd never experienced.

He spent the next few minutes stretching and savoring the slow start to his day. He yawned one last time and reached over for Webber. Running his hand over cool, empty sheets, he panicked and sat up, the sheets pooling at his waist. His heart raced and once again the fear that all this had been a dream struck him like a fist to the gut. He lay back down and closed his eyes, trying to calm himself, when he heard the bedroom door open. He opened his eyes to see Webber standing there with a tray of coffee, juice, and cheese danish. He closed his eyes again and sighed, hoping Webber didn't see the fear he felt certain was etched on his face.

Webber placed the tray on the bedside table and sat down next to him on the bed. "You okay, baby? You're white as a ghost."

Tristan nodded, not looking Webber in the eye. He thought about it briefly but then decided that no matter how lame his excuse was for being upset, honesty was the best policy. "I'm sorry, Web, I woke up and you weren't here and I sort of panicked. I keep thinking this is all a dream."

Webber pulled him into his arms and held him tightly, rubbing circles on his back with one hand and stroking his hair with the other. "You know, in a way this is all a dream, but a dream that has come true, for both of us."

Tristan relaxed in Webber's embrace and chuckled, feeling a little ashamed. He leaned back and finally looked Webber in the eye. "You know, I'm not normally this skittish and insecure."

Webber laughed, brushing Tristan's bangs out of his face and kissing him on the cheek. "Tris, stop it. I know you, remember. We've been through a lot in the last couple of days. Hell, if we're being honest, I kept reaching over to touch you last night just to make sure you were really in my bed." He paused for a second then cupped Tristan's face with both his hands. "I'm here and I'm not going anywhere, so get used to it."

Tristan smiled and laid his head on Webber's shoulder, still clinging to him tightly. "Me too and... thanks," he whispered.

After a minute, Webber took him by the shoulders and held him at arm's length. "How about some coffee? Two sweeteners and lots of cream, right?"

Tristan nodded and grinned in amazement. He still couldn't get over the fact that Webber had taken the time to learn the little things about him. In their relationship at work, Tristan had always been the one who paid attention to what Webber liked. But somewhere along the line, Webber had also been watching. Webber knew his favorite music and now how he took his coffee.

"Sure," Tristan said. "And... is that cheese danish I see on that tray?"

"Looks that way, doesn't it?"

Tristan studied the delectable treats. "Amani?"

Webber nodded as he poured coffee into Tristan's cup, then his own, and then added the sweetener and cream to both. "She makes them for me every time I'm here."

Tristan accepted the hot cup of coffee from Webber, wrapped both hands around the cup, held it up to his nose, and inhaled. "God, Web, we need to take her and Kenton back to Atlanta with us."

Webber chuckled and took his first sip. "Don't think I haven't tried."

He set his coffee down, placed a danish on a plate, and offered it to Tristan. He did the same for himself then kicked off his flip-flops, crawled back into bed, and stretched out next to Tristan. Tristan set his coffee down and took a bite of the danish and moaned in pleasure. "This is so much better than we get back in Atlanta."

Webber took a bite of his. "It is, isn't it? Just like I remembered," he said, holding his hand in front of his mouth.

Tristan punched him in the arm and waited for a response.

Webber had a surprised look on his face and almost spit out what was left of his danish. "What was that for?"

"That was letting me think I'd found the best cheese danish you'd ever had back in Atlanta," Tristan said with a smirk.

Webber laughed. "I'm so busted."

"Yes, you are," Tristan said, this time with a jab to the ribs.

"All right, all right, I give up," Webber said, putting his plate back on the tray and attempting to take Tristan's. They played tug-of-war for a few seconds, Tristan not wanting to give up his breakfast, but eventually Webber won out. Tristan reluctantly released the plate and Webber placed it next to his on the tray. He turned back to Tristan and encouraged him to slide down in the bed and within seconds, Webber's lips were covering his, but this time Tristan didn't open to him. Webber stopped and pulled back in confusion, tilting his head to one side. Tristan smiled wryly. "I haven't brushed my teeth yet."

"Oh good Lord," Webber said through a smile. "Okay, go."

Tristan threw his legs over the side of the bed and started to get up. Webber stopped him.

"Better yet, how about we brush our teeth while we shower."

Tristan's face lit up. "I like that idea much better."

AN HOUR and a half later, at Amani's insistence, they were finishing up the breakfast poolside.

"God, Webber, if I keep eating like this, I won't be able to fit into any of my clothes."

Webber patted his stomach and sighed. "I know what you mean. How about we hit the gym tomorrow?"

"Will we have time this afternoon?" Tristan asked, taking his last bite of eggs Benedict, pushing the plate away, and glancing at Webber. When Webber didn't answer but only smiled, he brought his cloth napkin up and wiped the corners of his mouth, then laid the napkin on the table where his plate had just been. "Okay, Webber, what's going on?" he asked.

Webber's smile got larger, but he still didn't answer.

"Fine," Tristan said in a teasing tone. "Let's get some work done then," he quickly added. "Where should we do this?"

Suddenly Webber raised a brow and started rambling. "Work? No sir, not today. No work today, uh-uh. We have plans."

Tristan had never seen Webber this giddy. By this point, he was practically gyrating in his seat.

"Kenton!" he yelled. "Is everything ready to go?"

As usual, Kenton appeared out of nowhere and hurried in their direction. "Yes, sir, you're all set."

Webber stood, placed his napkin on the table, and brushed his hands together. "Good man, Kenton. Now if you'll excuse us, we have somewhere to be. We'll be back tomorrow by noon," he said with a wink as he held his hand out to Tristan. "Let's go, baby."

Tristan accepted his outstretched hand, shaking his head, a baffled look on his face. But he couldn't help it. *Tomorrow noon? How long can Webber keep pulling rabbits out of hats?* He opened his mouth to speak, but Webber put his hands up to stop him.

"Tristan," Webber interrupted. "Everything you need is all packed and ready to go. Just follow me."

Tristan acquiesced. He knew he would follow Webber anywhere, so why should this be any different. Excited about the fact that he was about to embark on yet another adventure, he smiled and followed Webber like a puppy dog after a chew toy.

When they rounded the corner, the golf cart was waiting for them. Webber hopped into the driver's seat with Tristan beside him and off they went. Tristan quickly figured out that they were headed down to the boat dock, but he had no idea where they would go after that. As he'd done the previous day, Webber pulled the cart onto the dock and all the way down to the boats. He stopped the cart and walked around to meet Tristan as he hopped out. He took him by the hand and led him to the catamaran with a sly smile on his face, obviously very pleased with himself. The twin engines were already running and the boat appeared to be ready to go.

Webber hopped aboard and motioned to Tristan. "Okay, baby, you get the bow and I'll get the stern." Within minutes Webber had climbed up to the helm, which was about four feet above the deck looking out over the bow, and they were backing away from the dock and heading into the wind. Webber slowed the engines, wrapped a line around one of the winches, and pressed the button that started unfurling the mainsail. The sail appeared out of the mast and luffed in the wind until it was completely visible. Webber then allowed the boat to fall off the wind just slightly; the mainsail quickly filled with wind and the boat started to move forward. As Tristan watched carefully, Webber wrapped another line around the same winch and pressed the button again, which released the jib and it started unwinding and filling up with wind as well. The boat picked up more speed and was quickly cutting through the water. Webber turned off both engines and raised his ear to the sky. "Listen, baby, this is the best part." The boat was cutting across the surface, powered only by the wind, and all you could hear were the waves as they caressed the hull.

"Very nice," Tristan agreed, looking up at Webber.

He patted the seat next to him and offered Tristan a hand. Tristan climbed up and joined him, enjoying the view but liking being next to

Webber a hell of a lot more. They tacked back and forth for several hours, enjoying the sunshine and beautiful cerulean waters, Tristan still not sure where they were going until he thought he recognized an island off in the distance. "Jost Van Dyke?" he asked, pointing to the island.

Webber smiled. "A man after my own heart," he said as he kissed his cheek.

As they approached the island, Webber started the engines, furled both sails, and motored parallel with the white sandy beach until he found a protected spot thirty feet off shore. He dropped both anchors and put the engines in reverse until the hooks dug deep into the sandy bottom. He shut the engines off and pulled Tristan in to a tight embrace, burying his face in Tristan's neck. "You smell so good, baby. I could eat you alive."

Tristan shivered with anticipation. "I'll hold you to that," he teased.

Webber fidgeted like a schoolboy. "Do you know where we are?" he asked.

Tristan looked around again. "I think we're at the Soggy Dollar Bar, aren't we?"

Webber smiled proudly, his dimples making a special appearance. "Right again. Next question," he teased. "Do you know why they call it the Soggy Dollar Bar?"

This time Tristan smiled. "Because there are no docks and you have to swim to shore, which makes for soggy dollars."

Webber howled and pulled Tristan into his arms. "Damn, you're good. I give up. You wanna go down and see what goodies Amani packed for us?"

Still tingling from the most recent embrace, Tristan hopped down from the helm. "Sure."

Tristan entered through the companionway into a very large salon with a galley, furnished with a banquette and large sectional couch. As Webber unpacked the boxes of food, Tristan gave himself a tour. To the port side, three steps down, were two cabins with private heads and to the starboard side was one very large cabin with a sitting room attached, a private head, and a third cabin with a massage table in the center. Tristan took a peek into the head and saw all of their personal toiletries were neatly arranged. In the cabin, their clothing was carefully put away in the drawers with all their hanging clothes hung in a cedar closet.

Tristan rejoined Webber in the salon and perused all their goodies. There was a case of mixed wines, appetizers, filet mignon, potatoes, asparagus, and a variety of sandwich meats and cheeses for lunch the next day. "Man, Amani is really good at this stuff."

Webber stopped unpacking and pulled Tristan into his arms. "The best, but right now all I can think about is getting you into a bathing suit for a swim and then getting you out of it later."

Tristan pressed his lips against Webber's. They had only just gotten out of bed and the shower a few hours ago, but he was already missing the closeness they shared and desperately wanted it back. He reached behind Webber and cupped his firm, round ass with two hands and held on as he kissed him passionately.

When the kiss ended, both of them were breathless and sporting well-kissed and swollen lips. Webber seemed to be the first one able to voice a coherent thought. "What do you say we swim over to the bar, have some lunch, spend a little time on the beach, and then come back and take a nap before dinner?"

Tristan leaned in and rested his forehead against Webber's. "Sounds perfect," he said in a hushed tone.

They changed into swimsuits and Webber put towels, T-shirts, flip-flops, ball caps, the boat keys, and some money into a watertight bag and threw it over his shoulder. "I think I've got everything. You ready?"

Tristan stood at attention and gave a mock salute. "Right behind you, Captain."

Webber smirked and jumped off the back of the catamaran with Tristan right behind him and they headed for the shore. They ate lunch at the Soggy Dollar Bar and wandered up to the small inn. They looked around a bit and then spent about an hour on the beach soaking in the beautiful Caribbean sunshine.

Tristan lay on his side, up on one elbow and resting his head in his hand. His eyes were fixed on Webber, who was lying on his back, propped on his elbows with his head thrown back, face pointed up to the sky. He must have sensed Tristan's gaze, because he turned his head and opened one eye.

"What can I do for you, Mr. Moreau?"

Tristan grinned bashfully. "I'm getting a little tired. You ready for that nap?" he asked with a wink.

Webber's face broke into a smile as a faint blush filled his face. "A nap, huh?" He looked up at the sky. "Yeah, I'm a little tired myself."

Tristan was up and shoving stuff in the watertight bag in the blink of an eye. "Based on the way you're moving, you don't look too tired," Webber teased.

"Exhausted," Tristan shot back with a wink. "Now get up so I can add your towel to the bag."

Webber did as he was told and minutes later they were entering the water.

"Last one back doesn't get to nap!" Webber yelled as he dove head first into the surf and swam for the boat like a barracuda.

Tristan cursed under his breath at the damn bag over his shoulder and for allowing Webber to get a head start. But he followed Webber's lead and dove right into the first wave just before it broke and gave it everything he had. Pretty evenly matched, they both cut through the water with ease, but Tristan, being the better swimmer of the two, kicked like mad and stretched his long arms out in front of him, passing Webber halfway and making it back to the boat a good body length ahead of Webber.

Out of breath and clinging to the swim ladder, he looked back at Webber with a broad smile. "What will you do while I nap?" he asked playfully.

Just as out of breath, Webber reached the swim ladder and before Tristan could react, Webber had his hand on the top of Tristan's head dunking him below the surface.

Tristan surfaced cursing, spitting saltwater in Webber's face. He threw the bag up to the swim platform and dove after Webber. They both sank below the surface fumbling and playing until Webber's lips found Tristan's and the horseplay stopped. Tristan felt Webber's mouth close over his as they'd done in the pool and allowed them to sink as they kissed passionately under the surface. When Tristan felt his ears start to pop, he kicked his feet and started to propel them to the surface. Webber did the same and they broke the surface, out of breath and full of desire. With no more horseplay on his mind, Tristan climbed up the ladder and offered his hand to Webber, pulling him up in one haul.

Tristan anxiously followed Webber through the salon and into their cabin. Halfway there, he reached out and pulled Webber's bathing suit down to his ankles and Webber stepped out of them. Passing the head, Tristan reached in, grabbed a towel and began drying Webber's back as they continued on. Tristan kicked out of his bathing suit and dried as quickly as he could before they hit the cabin. He handed Webber the towel as he dove for the bed, crossing his hands behind his head and dragging his gaze possessively up and down the long nude length of Webber's body, not trying to hide his appreciation one bit. When Webber was dry, he crawled into bed and rolled into Tristan, his body relaxed and interested. He laid his forehead against Tristan's and kissed him slowly, dragging his teeth along Tristan's lower lip. Tristan closed his arms around Webber. "You belong to me" escaped his lips before he had time to think about it. Tristan surprised himself with the sudden possessiveness he was feeling.

Webber looked into Tristan's eyes seductively. "I do belong to you. Take me."

The words "take me" were intoxicating to his ears and what they implied was enough to send him over the edge. Webber must have sensed his reaction. He ran his fingers gently down Tristan's face and whispered, "I want you inside me."

Tristan cupped Webber's face and kissed him deeply, their tongues seeking, needing, exploring, and finding everything. "We don't have any supplies," he whispered against Webber's lips.

"There's lubricant in the drawer and condoms too, if you want them."

Tristan drew back and looked at Webber. "Do we need them?"

"I don't," Webber offered. "As I told you, it's been over two years since I've been with anyone and as chairman of the board for Kincaid, I have regular physicals. The HIV test is part of the routine blood tests."

He looked at Tristan with a raised brow waiting for his response.

"Web, it's been forever for me and I already told you how many people I've been with. But I'm tested once a year during my yearly physical. I'm negative."

Webber reached up and brushed Tristan's cheek with the back of his fingers. "Then we don't need the condoms, unless you want them."

Tristan took his hand and kissed his palm. "Hell no, I don't want them. I don't want anything between us."

Webber pointed behind Tristan. "Good, the lubricant's in the drawer."

Tristan reached behind him and retrieved the unused bottle. He rolled back over, his lips barely brushing Webber's as he smiled.

"And you're smiling because?" Webber asked, amused.

"Oh, I don't know," Tristan teased. "A new bottle of lubricant and condoms just happened to be on the boat that you rarely use. Pretty sure of yourself, I think."

"Not that sure, but hoping," Webber said through a blush at the accusation. "But I guess I'm guilty as charged."

"Lucky for me," Tristan added in a soft voice as he peeled the plastic wrap off of the bottle. He placed the bottle on the bed next to them and pushed Webber onto his back, bringing their lips together again in a kiss loaded with desire and need. He ran his tongue along Webber's bottom lip and nipped at his tongue as the intensity of the kiss built. Tristan was beginning to crave Webber's touch. It was no longer simply wanting him, it was needing him, and that frightened and elated him at the same time.

Webber broke the kiss and rolled over away from Tristan, half on his side and half on his stomach, bringing his arms under his head and sliding one knee up along the cool sheets, exposing his round, muscular ass. Tristan, lying behind him, placed open-mouthed kisses on his back and shoulders as he rubbed his groin against Webber's ass. His actions were rewarded with a slow drawn-out "Trisssss." The mere mention of his name on Webber's lips with such need sent shivers up his spine.

He continued to nip and bite at Webber's shoulders while lightly running his hand down Webber's arm to his waist and then along his thigh and up to his bent knee, leaving goose bumps in his wake. Tristan ran his fingers across Webber's opening and felt him tense, then shiver, and eventually relax into the touch. Tristan opened the lubricant and squeezed some onto his fingers. He dragged one finger down Webber's cleft, leaving a trickle of lubricant in his wake. He could feel Webber shudder and tense at the meager sensation. Looking back, Webber reached over and gently cupped the back of Tristan's head, bringing him in for another kiss. While they kissed passionately, Tristan continued rubbing circles around Webber's opening, teasing and, from what he remembered, tormenting him as well. He had only bottomed a few times with Justin, but he understood the anticipation of wanting and waiting. With his tongue lodged deeply down Webber's throat, Tristan slowly slid a finger inside him, and Webber gasped against his lips, tightening around his finger. Tristan ran his fingers through Webber's hair as he gently rubbed Webber's insides.

Webber started to move, thrusting forward and back, so Tristan slipped another finger inside. Webber instantly pushed back on Tristan's fingers and pulled his knee up, exposing more of himself to Tristan. He could feel Webber accepting him and beginning to loosen up around the fingers that were now sliding in and out of him with ease. Tristan twisted his two fingers as he added a third, feeling that special place, and Webber came up off the bed, arching his back, still reaching back for Tristan. Tristan was finding it hard to keep any measure of control with Webber so close and so trusting and open. "Are you okay, baby?" he asked breathlessly.

"So good," Webber responded, turning his head back in search of Tristan's mouth. "I need you now. Please, Tris."

The sound of Tristan's name spoken with such desire and desperation was impossible to ignore. He slid his fingers out slowly as Webber arched his back in mock protest. Tristan poured more lubricant onto himself and lined up with Webber. "I'm ready, baby. You okay?"

Webber again reached back and grabbed Tristan behind the neck. "Just go slow," he whispered. "It's been a very long time."

Tristan kissed him again and then slid down between his legs in search of the right angle, finally positioning himself at Webber's opening. He slowly pushed in, then stopped and held his breath waiting for a sign from Webber. When Tristan breached him, he had heard Webber gasp and felt him reach back and dig his nails in Tristan's leg. After a moment, Webber released his grip and relaxed around him. Tristan took that as a sign to continue and he pushed in farther, rocking slowly, the warm tightness almost making him lose it right then and there. He stopped again, closing his eyes tightly, trying to ignore the emotions running through his head and attempting to get himself back under control and slow down his impending release. When he thought he was in control again, he started to move slowly, working his cock deeper and deeper into his lover. Webber threw his head back and fisted the sheets. "Yes, Tris, sooo good."

As Tristan moved in and out of Webber in long, slow strokes, Webber rolled over onto his back, throwing his left leg over Tristan's body, allowing their lips to come together. Webber pulled Tristan against him and kissed him so hard it took his breath away. Tristan gasped for breath between kisses as he felt Webber running his hands through his hair, over his face, across his chest and any other part of Tristan he could get to.

Webber whimpered and trembled as he accepted Tristan's thrusts into his welcoming body. The sounds Webber made sent shockwaves through Tristan's soul, and he had to stop again and breathe deeply before he could continue. Both their bodies were glistening with sweat and Tristan held onto Webber so tightly he was afraid he might leave bruises, but Webber didn't seem to mind and gave as good as he got. Tristan squeezed more lubricant into his hand and wrapped it around

Webber's length, stroking him in rhythm with the rigorous pounding he was taking. Webber's body tensed as he cried out wordlessly and spilled over Tristan's fingers. Tristan felt Webber's body spasm around him and his control finally broke. "I love you, Webber," was the last thing he was able to say before he gave way, coming hard and long into Webber's welcoming body.

They lay still in the sweat-soaked sheets for minutes before either one of them could actually move or speak. "I love you too," Webber said, still not moving. Tristan was the first to attempt any type of movement. He shifted slightly, and Webber winced as Tristan slipped from his body. He crawled out of bed and left the cabin, returning with a warm cloth and slowly cleaning Webber as well as himself. He threw the cloth in the direction of the head and climbed back into Webber's waiting arms. They wrapped around each other, arms and legs entwined, and without a word, drifted off to sleep.

WEBBER awoke slowly and didn't have to open his eyes to know where he was. The gentle waves lapping against the hull of the catamaran told him everything. The familiar sound always reminded him of a time shortly after his mother died when his father would take him on overnight sailing trips where sound of the waves was the only thing that gave him solace in the lonely, sleepless nights. It was like a melancholy lullaby from his childhood.

He rolled onto his back, straightening his legs, and raising his arms over his head in a restful stretch. He winced a little at the gentle reminder of the afternoon's events and smiled, bringing his fingers up to his mouth and rubbing his chafed lips. He was still wondering to himself how so much could change in such a short time. But he was so thankful for whatever good he'd done in his past to make the gods smile down on him. He had Tristan and he would move heaven and earth to keep him. He opened his eyes when he felt soft fingers running through his hair, brushing it away from his face.

"You're beautiful when you sleep," Tristan said in a lazy voice. He was lying on his side with his arm folded under his pillow, staring intently at his lover. He leaned in to kiss Webber on the tip of his nose.

Webber smiled. "Hey, handsome," he said in a sleepy voice. "What time is it?"

Tristan looked at his watch. "Almost six o'clock."

"Noooo," Webber quipped. "It can't be."

Tristan held up his watch and allowed Webber to verify his ability to tell time.

Webber blinked through sleepy eyes and looked closely at the gold watch on Tristan's wrist. "Jeez, I can't believe we slept this long."

"Just tired, I guess," Tristan replied with a wink.

There were several knocks on the side of the boat and Tristan cocked his head to one side. "What in the hell?" he asked looking confused.

"Up and at 'em," Webber said as he climbed out of bed and slipped on one of the bathrobes that were now puddled on the floor at the foot of the bed. He smiled down at Tristan, leaning in and placing a small kiss on his temple. "We have company," he said as he headed for the door.

"What are you up to now, Webber Kincaid?" Tristan asked as he threw his pillow at him. Webber stopped dead in his tracks and looked over his shoulder. "You'll pay for that later," he teased as he pulled the door closed.

Webber made his way topside and heard "Permission to come aboard, sir?"

"Permission granted, you shit," he said, smiling and offering his hand, pulling the man into a bear hug. "Good to see you, Johnny."

"You too, sir."

"What's with the *sir* crap, Johnny? We practically grew up together," Webber questioned.

Johnny looked down at his feet. "You're a big hotshot CEO now. I saw you on television ringing the opening bell at the New York Stock Exchange, not to mention the tabloids."

Webber raised a brow and looked at his childhood friend. "Hell, Johnny, we've both done pretty well for ourselves." He put his hand on Johnny's shoulder and squeezed. "It's not like we had many options. Our dads were set on us taking over the family businesses and I'm not complaining, I love my job and I'm sure you do too, but sometimes, I wish I had a job with a little less pressure."

Johnny looked up and met Webber's eyes. "I can see that."

Johnny's dad had been Webber's dad's masseuse and had a client list that paled in comparison to any A-list Hollywood party.

"Look, we're both successful, just in different fields. I don't know anyone who can give a better massage than you so don't ever sell yourself short; you're successful for a good reason."

Johnny smiled. "Thanks for saying that, man."

Webber hugged him again. "I said it because it's the truth."

Their embrace was interrupted as Tristan stepped on deck wearing the other bathrobe.

Webber smiled broadly at Tristan, genuinely happy to see him. "Johnny Carlisle, I want you to meet my—" He looked at Tristan, wondering what term they would use. "—my... life partner, Tristan Moreau."

Tristan smiled and stuck his hand out. "Nice to meet you, Johnny."

Johnny returned his handshake and gave Webber an inquisitive look.

Johnny was two years older than Webber, and when they'd met as kids, he'd been Webber's first crush. They'd been inseparable and experimented as kids do, but as they got older and Webber had spent less and less time in the Caribbean and more and more time at Kincaid, they'd drifted apart. Webber often wondered which lifestyle Johnny had chosen, but had never had the nerve to ask.

Johnny's gaze turned into a soft smile and he said, "Likewise."

"Tris, Johnny's here to give us massages and man, is he the best."

Tristan's eyes lit up and his smile broadened. "God, that sounds great," he admitted.

"Johnny, why don't you go down below and get set up and I'll send Tristan down in a few."

"Sounds like a plan," Johnny said, nodding to both men as he threw his canvas bag over his shoulder.

Webber pulled Tristan into his arms and whispered, "Surprise!" before he crushed his lips against Tristan's.

Tristan smiled against Webber's lips. "You're awfully friendly with your massage therapist," he joked. "Anything I should know?"

Webber chuckled. "Long story, but I'll tell you over dinner. Now get your fine ass down there and enjoy your massage."

Tristan turned, then stopped and looked over his shoulder. "You've got to stop with the surprises. You're the only surprise I need."

"Never," Webber responded with a wink. "Enjoy."

While Tristan was getting his massage, Webber dug Tristan's iPod out of his bag and put on more of Tristan's favorite music so that it now played softly throughout the entire boat. Webber then busied himself prepping for dinner. He went through a mental checklist. The grill was cleaned and ready. The steaks were coming up to room temperature. The potatoes were washed, wrapped in foil, and in the oven. And the asparagus was marinating in olive oil and garlic. He opened a bottle of Stags' Leap Cabernet, allowing it time to breathe, and folded his arms across his chest. *What else?* he thought. "Oh, apps," he said out loud.

Webber dug through the fridge, retrieving a hunk of smoked Gouda cheese and a peppercorn-encrusted summer sausage, which he sliced and arranged on a platter. He opened several types of crackers and sliced a baguette. He smiled when he felt warm, relaxed arms surround his waist and a kiss at his neck. He looked at his watch and turned in Tristan's embrace.

"Has it been ninety minutes already?" he inquired, surprised.

"Yes, ninety glorious minutes," Tristan shared. "Man, were you right when you said he was the best. I can't tell you the last time I felt this relaxed."

Webber chuckled. "I aim to please," he said, kissing Tristan lightly.

Tristan slapped him on the butt. "Now it's your turn. What can I do out here?"

Webber looked around the galley. "If you'll keep an eye on the potatoes and turn the grill on in about forty-five minutes, I'll do the rest," he said. "There's a bottle of red open and ready on the table and everything else is good to go." He pressed a hasty kiss to Tristan's lips. "I'll be back in the blink of an eye."

Tristan winked. "Enjoy, baby."

TRISTAN poured himself a glass of wine and moved out to the trampoline that stretched across the bow of the catamaran. It was quiet except for the sound of the music coming from the small speakers facing the bow and the Caribbean flag flapping in the light, gentle breeze. He stared at the onshore lights in the distance, reflecting against the deep blue water.

For the first time in his life, he was truly happy. He no longer felt like he was dreaming and anticipated a future with Webber, something he would have never dreamed of three days ago. They still had obstacles to overcome. How were they going to handle things at KIC? How would the board react? Not to mention the press and the tabloids. Webber was a very well-known man, as much for his philanthropy as for his business skills, and his coming out of the closet would be big news. Would Webber go public with their relationship, or would he expect Tristan to keep it hidden? He contemplated how he would feel either way, and he decided that whatever Webber wanted, he would go along with it. But he thought for now the best thing would be to keep things under wraps until they could sort through everything.

He felt a hand run through his hair and soft lips caressing the back of his neck.

A sense of panic ran through him. "Oh my God, Webber, are you already through? I haven't even turned on the grill. And the potatoes!" He tried to get up, but Webber held him down. "Web, I'm so sorry."

"No worries, it's all taken care of," Webber assured him. "The potatoes are fine and the grill's warming up nicely, so relax."

Tristan took a deep breath and raised his hand to cover Webber's, now resting on his shoulder. "I'm really sorry, Web. Time has a way of passing really quickly around here."

Webber smiled. "I know. It caught up with me earlier as well, but that's not my concern. I checked the potatoes, lit the grill, and helped Johnny cast off and you never even looked up. That only happens when you're deep in thought and concentrating really hard. What's on your mind, baby?"

Webber came around and sat cross-legged next to him. He was carrying the bottle of wine and a second glass, and after topping off Tristan's, poured himself some. He looked gorgeous and relaxed and Tristan didn't want to get into anything heavy that might ruin the mood. "You do know me, Web, mind always working. It's nothing really."

Webber put the wine bottle down and took Tristan's hand, rubbing his thumb across Tristan's knuckles. "Tris, you're going to have to trust me. You can tell me anything. I'm not going anywhere."

Tristan covered Webber's hand with his own. "I do trust you, Web. For some reason, I've trusted you from day one, when I didn't even have anything to base that trust on. I'm head over heels in love with you and I trust you with my life."

Webber leaned in and kissed him sweetly. "I feel the same way, but there's one more thing I'd like to ask of you."

Tristan cocked his head to one side, gazing curiously at Webber. "Anything, baby, you know that."

"I'd like you to promise me that you will always be honest with me, no matter what. If we're honest with each other, good or bad, nothing or no one can ever come between us."

Tristan took Webber's hand, brought it to his lips, and kissed his palm gently. "I will," he promised. "But I'll accept nothing less from you."

"Deal," Webber said, rubbing the side of Tristan's face tenderly. "So now, what had you so deep in thought?"

"Webber Kincaid," he huffed. "I do believe you just tricked me into getting what you want."

Webber smiled coyly. "Uh, I think I did."

Tristan sighed. "I was thinking about what we're going to do when we get back to Atlanta."

Webber looked at him questioningly. "I was hoping you would move in with me or we could get a place together and start our lives."

Tristan smiled and squeezed his hand. "Web, I would love that. But I was thinking more along the lines of what we would do at KIC."

This time Webber nodded and gave him a knowing look and then turned to look out over the horizon. "I've thought a lot about this over the last few days, and I've decided that I'm coming clean with the board, the shareholders, and the employees. Tris, I would never hide you away."

Tristan reached up and turned Webber's face back to his. "That means more to me then you'll ever know, but I want you to rethink that decision."

Webber frowned. "You don't want people to know about us?"

"Oh God, Webber, I want to shout it from the rooftops. I love you and want to spend the rest of my life with you, but we have your reputation to consider as well as KIC's. Let's not let our happiness influence a bad decision for KIC."

Webber looked back out over the horizon. "I don't like the idea of sneaking around with you."

Tristan moved around in front of Webber and rested his free hand on Webber's knee. "How about this, baby," he started. "Now hear me out before you stop me, okay?" Webber nodded. "At KIC, we don't sneak around. But… we don't flaunt it either," he added. "Look, the way I see it, we won't have to change a thing at the office. We spend so much time behind closed doors; no one will give it a second thought. We even spend time together at the Agency lounge, and no one's ever given us a second look. Maybe we drive to work in separate cars, which is nothing different then we do now, and we control ourselves in public. That's it. We can do that, right?"

Webber looked defeated, but he placed his hand on top of Tristan's. "I guess," he agreed hesitantly. "But just until the bidding process is over for this next round of acquisitions. There are a couple of agencies I want really badly, and a big news story could affect the outcome."

Tristan sighed. "Good, then it's settled."

"For now," Webber said. "But I don't have to like it."

"I don't like it either," Tristan acquiesced, "but right now, I think it's for the best." He raised his nose to the air. "Hey, I smell hot grill and I'm pretty damn hungry."

Webber took a sip of his wine and cupped the back of Tristan's neck with his other hand, bringing their faces so close together that Tristan could feel Webber's breath. "I love you and I want everyone to know you're mine."

"I know, Web, I feel the same way."

TRISTAN sat sipping his wine and nibbling on cheese and summer sausage while Webber grilled steaks and asparagus. Later, they ate an amazing meal, took a midnight swim, and then dozed under the moonlight. They retired to their cabin and spent the rest of the night making love, falling asleep wrapped in each other's arms, then waking up and making love all over again.

They arrived at Nectar Island by one o'clock the next afternoon and Kenton met them at the dock. Against arguments from both of them, he insisted on taking over unloading and cleaning the boat. They spent a couple of hours in the gym, had another swim and a nap, and then dressed for another one of Amani's unbelievable meals. Now they were lying hand in hand in chaise lounges watching the moon and the stars shining against the midnight-blue sky. Kenton, Amani, and Kit having long since retired, they enjoyed the solitude. The breeze lightly ruffled the palm trees and the sounds of the Caribbean frogs filled the night.

Tristan threw his feet over the side of his chair and slid over onto the end of Webber's chair. Webber turned to his side and eased over, giving him more room to slip in and stretch out. He kissed Webber sleepily. "What do you say we turn in? Tomorrow after breakfast, we start sorting through all those possible acquisitions."

"Buzzkill," Webber teased.

"Webber?"

"Yeah, baby," he answered without opening his eyes.

"These past few days have been the best days of my life."

Webber opened his eyes and looked at Tristan. "Mine too, baby, mine too."

Tristan placed a gentle kiss on Webber's lips. "I love you more than I ever thought possible."

"Tristan," Webber said in a hushed tone. "I've spent so many years building my father's legacy, trying to do some good along the way, and never really paying attention to what was missing from my life. When I met you, what was missing hit me like a ton of bricks. It was you! And... I will never go back. You're stuck with me for as long as you'll have me."

"Then it's settled, we're in this forever."

Tristan stood and offered his hand to Webber. "Let's go to bed."

THE next morning unknowingly set the agenda for the rest of the trip. They slept in, made love unhurriedly, had a late breakfast, worked on acquisitions right through lunch and spent the afternoon playing in the boat. They'd brought fifteen potential acquisitions to review and they had to get through one a day to get them all done, allowing them a couple of days off during the process. The routine seemed to work well, and it still gave them plenty of time to enjoy the Caribbean.

One day they spent the afternoon on Jost Van Dyke at Foxy's enjoying frozen drinks until sunset. The next, they had a late lunch at Willy T's, a schooner anchored in The Bight at Norman Island. They also snorkeled at a popular rock formation called the Indians, rented a Jeep and spent a lazy afternoon on St. John exploring the national forests, and shopped on Tortola. But most days, they would anchor in a secluded cove and swim and make love, simply enjoying being together.

The acquisitions possibilities were not disappointing. Each day they sorted through all the financials, studying revenues and expenses, how extensive the client lists were, any press releases or recent announcements, and any popular national ad campaigns they had under their belt. All fifteen companies they were considering were openly for sale, which meant they were accepting bids by a certain date, and the bidding process was strictly monitored by the Securities and Exchange Commission, or the SEC.

It was the morning of their last full day, and Webber decided they were going to take the power boat to Anegada, have lunch, spend the day snorkeling on Horseshoe Reef, and still be back in plenty of time for Amani's big farewell dinner. The only problem was they still had the Moniker Communications file, the last possible acquisition, to review. Tristan agreed to peruse the files while underway and determine whether Webber should take a look for himself. If it looked promising, Webber could do it on the airplane tomorrow and still have everything done by the time they got back to Atlanta.

As she'd done almost every day, Amani packed a basket of their favorite lunch items and handed it off to them on their way down to the dock. With a promise to Kenton that they would be back by dinnertime, they were gone. Tristan sat next to Webber at the helm, carefully studying the paperwork in front of him. His bare feet were on the dash and Webber's hand was resting on his knee.

After twenty minutes of flipping through files, he looked up. "Webber?" he asked with a confused look.

"Yeah, baby?"

"This file seems very familiar to me," he said flipping back and forth between papers. "Do you remember when you started mentoring me and you gave me a stack of older acquisitions to review to help me learn?"

Webber looked back and forth between Tristan and the water, keeping an eye on the traffic. "Sure, I thought it would help you grasp the process."

"I may be crazy, but this one looks so familiar," he added shaking his head. "It's like I've seen these financials before, and the client list, I swear I've seen this client list before."

"Put it aside for a little while and when we get to Anegada, I'll take a quick look and see if it seems familiar to me as well."

Tristan used his index finger and motioned for Webber to bring his face in closer. When he did, he kissed him on the cheek. "Thanks, Web."

"Hell, if that's all it takes to get a kiss, I'll look at anything you want me to."

Tristan raised his eyebrows. "Anything?"

"Anything," Webber said through a smile.

Safely anchored at Anegada, Webber opened two Coronas and Tristan shoved lime wedges into the longneck bottles. He raised his beer to Webber in a toast. "To our last day in the Caribbean."

Webber held up his bottle. "And to the next time."

"Cheers," Tristan said, tapping their bottles together.

Webber opened the six-inch-thick folder and started scanning the files. He went straight to the financials and then the client list. After studying the information, he closed the file and looked at Tristan.

"You're right, baby. There's something about these financials that feels familiar, and I've definitely seen this client list before too. You've got a very good eye, darlin'."

"So what do we do now?"

Webber thought for a moment. "Well, if you think you recognized some of the information from a previous acquisition, when we return to Atlanta, we should go back and pull the files and compare notes."

"Then that's what I'll do. I'll bet I can put my hands on it pretty easy."

Webber slapped the file closed. "We're officially done. Let's go have some fun."

"A man after my own heart," Tristan proclaimed.

"Hey, I thought I already had your heart," Webber retorted.

Tristan dropped the smile and took Webber's face in his hands. "Heart and soul," he said, kissing Webber softly.

Webber beamed with apparent joy and Tristan couldn't help but beam along with him. Tristan jumped off the seat and stood in the companionway door. "Last one in makes lunch."

"Damn," Webber cursed playfully. But instead of heading in Tristan's direction, he ran to the back of the boat and jumped in, fully clothed.

Tristan howled with laughter, running to the back of the boat to make sure he was okay.

Webber surfaced and treaded water for a few minutes, smiling like he'd won the lottery. "I'll have turkey on rye with cheddar, lettuce, tomato, and mayo."

"Fine," Tristan said folding his arms over his chest. "I'll make lunch."

"And chips," Webber said as he threw his wet Vans on the back of the boat and started up the swim ladder.

Tristan offered him a hand and when Webber was almost up the ladder, Tristan tried to let go, sending him back into the water, but

Webber was quicker and grabbed him with his other hand and tugged, sending them both into the water. Tristan surfaced and spit water in Webber's direction. He swam over and threw himself on top of Webber, sending him under the surface. They played tit for tat, dunking one another over and over and swearing to call a truce, each time the other making one last attempt to win the contest. Webber eventually surrendered and proclaimed Tristan the winner and Tristan cupped both hands together and raised them over his head in triumph. "You wanna get the snorkel gear now?" he asked a little out of breath.

"Sure and maybe put our swimsuits on?"

"Or maybe not," Tristan teased. "Maybe we should snorkel nude."

"I don't know," Webber chuckled. "This reef is known for its barracuda, and what's dangling, the fish might eat."

"Good point," Tristan agreed. "The suits stay on."

Ten

THE Kincaid jet sat on the runway in Tortola waiting to take off with Tristan and Webber seated side by side. Webber's fingers were laced tightly through Tristan's as he thumbed through a magazine. Out of the corner of his eye, he could see Tristan wearily staring out of the window. He'd noticed Tristan had been fairly quiet and subdued since they boarded the helicopter at the villa and was a little concerned.

When they'd said their good-byes to Kenton, Amani, and Kit, Tristan had looked genuinely sad to leave them. These people were the closest thing Webber had to family, and the fact that they accepted Tristan and Tristan honestly cared about them warmed him to his core.

He was shaken out of his thoughts as the engines whined and the plane shook gently as it picked up speed and started down the runway. Webber turned to Tristan, who was still peering out of the window, and saw his reflection in the glass showing a furrowed brow and concern written all over his face. He wondered what was bothering him, but knowing Tristan, he would fess up soon enough. Webber had learned over the couple of years they'd worked together that Tristan was the analytical type and needed time to process things before he was able to put words to his thoughts.

About twenty minutes into the flight, true to form, Tristan sighed and placed his other hand over their laced fingers, but didn't say anything.

"Do you want to talk about it yet?" Webber asked, his concern growing.

Tristan laid his head back in his seat and closed his eyes. "I don't know where to start," he said in a shaky voice.

"Tris, you're starting to worry me," Webber said, beginning to fidget in his seat. "Did I do something wrong?"

"Oh God, no, Web, it's not you at all. It's just, well... the last three weeks feels like we've been locked in a fairy tale, and now the story is ending. I'm so worried about what's going to happen when we get back to the real world."

Webber sighed and tried to soften his expression. "Nothing is going to happen to us, baby. I love you. We're in this together. And our fairy tale is just starting."

Tristan's concern didn't waver. "But, Web, your world is so much different than mine. You know how much money I make. And what are we going to do about living arrangements? We've spent the last three weeks together day and night, and I don't want that to change. I don't want to be without you, but I don't know how to be in your world."

"Whoa, whoa, baby. Slow down," Webber said, trying to soothe his lover. "You are my world now and you're coming home with me. I don't want to be without you either."

Tristan seemed to relax a little, but his face still betrayed the concern he was feeling. "Okay, but what next?" he asked as a single tear slid down his cheek. "Web, I don't want to be a kept man and I can't afford your lifestyle. Hell, I haven't even been to your house, but I'm sure it's *way* out of my price range."

"Trisss," Webber drawled, wiping the tear from his cheek and pulling him into a tight embrace. "If it's that important for you to contribute, we'll sell my house and buy one that you can afford, or we'll live in yours. I don't care where I live as long as we're together."

Webber felt a little more of Tristan's tension ebb and he pulled back to look him in the eyes. "If you don't want to live with me, we'll go by my house, get some things, and we can stay at yours until we decide. I really don't care. And for the record, I've not seen your house either."

Tristan grunted, smiled, and seemed to relax a little more. "I'm sure it's nothing compared to yours."

Webber chuckled. "Come on, Tris, I hope you know that kind of stuff doesn't matter to me."

"I'm sorry, you're right," Tristan offered. "It's just so easy to be happy and have everything perfect when you're on a secluded island for three weeks with no outside distractions and people waiting on you hand and foot. I'm so afraid things are going to be different when we get home."

"I'm sure some things will be a little different, but not the things that count. We'll still love one another and we'll still be together. Sure, there might be some outside forces involved, but I think we're strong enough to handle it. Don't you?"

Tristan nodded.

"Do you remember the promise we made to one another about always being honest? If we are completely honest with each other and never keep secrets, no matter how difficult, no one or nothing can ever come between us."

"I remember," Tristan acknowledged.

"Tris, we'll take this one day at a time. Things are going to come up, but we'll handle them and we'll be stronger for it. I love you. Never forget that."

"I love you too, Web. Thanks."

Tristan turned to look out of the window again.

"Well?" Webber asked smiling mischievously.

Tristan turned back to face him. "Well what?"

"Where are we going to live?"

Tristan cocked his head to one side, obviously contemplating the question. "Well, I live in Midtown, twenty minutes from the office, and you live on West Paces Ferry, which is not that much farther. I have a one bedroom condo with limited closet space and you have, I'm assuming a mansion, with lots of closet space. You probably have a full staff and I have a housekeeper that comes twice a month." He smiled. "Hmm, what to do, what to do."

Webber chuckled and dug into his pocket. "The only fair thing is to flip a coin."

"Good idea," Tristan agreed.

"Okay," Webber said. "Heads your place, tails mine. And this is just until we decide where *we* want to live."

He threw the coin in the air with his left hand, caught it with his right and slapped it on his left forearm. He slowly uncovered it and shoved his arm in Tristan's direction. "You look," he said, chuckling. "I can't bear the thought of no servants."

Tristan smacked him before looking at the coin. "Tails, you win. I guess 'I'm moving on up.'"

"Wow, that's a relief," Webber teased. "The thought of me doing laundry sent chills down my spine, and not in a good way," he added.

Tristan smacked him again.

THE flight was uneventful and Tristan was delighted when they landed to a glorious afternoon in Atlanta. Their driver was waiting for them on the tarmac, and it only took them a few minutes to get their bags loaded and get on the road. KIC's car service assigned a pool of cars and drivers exclusively to KIC management, which meant the same drivers taxied all the executives around. Webber had told him that over the years, he'd learned more about his executives and their whereabouts from their drivers than he ever could through any private investigators. So Tristan made sure to be on his best behavior.

They settled in next to each other comfortably but didn't dare touch in any way. Webber pressed a button, which raised the soundproof glass between them and the driver, and looked at Tristan with something that couldn't be mistaken for anything but longing and frustration. It warmed Tristan to his toes, because he was feeling the exact same way.

For the last three weeks, they'd been free to touch and kiss and show their affection for one another without fear of prying eyes, but not being able to touch at will was going to really be hard.

"This behaving ourselves is going to be tougher than I thought," Webber confessed.

Tristan scooted his foot over and rested it against Webber's. "I know what you mean. Is this okay?"

"No, it's not okay," Webber said as he sighed deeply. "But I guess it's all we have for now." He moved his foot against Tristan's. "Remember, Tris, it was your idea to keep our relationship quiet for a while."

"Stupid me," Tristan mumbled under his breath.

Webber laughed. "I heard that."

"Yeah, well, it's for the best," Tristan added. "Just until you close the next round of acquisitions. Then we bust out of this jail cell."

"All I know is you better damn well love me, 'cause we're going to be spending a lot of time at home, alone, behind closed doors."

"Sounds perfect to me," Tristan responded. "Are we there yet?"

Their laughter was interrupted by the buzz of the intercom. Webber pressed the intercom button. "Yes, Mac?" he said.

"To the office, Mr. Kincaid?" the driver asked.

"Yes, please," Webber replied, frowning at Tristan and releasing the button. "I hate this."

Tristan discreetly moved his foot back and forth against Webber's, trying to make any contact he could. "I know, Web."

Webber looked out the tinted window and back at Tristan. "When we get our cars, what do you say if we head to my house and drop one of the cars off and then go over to your place and get your things?"

Tristan nodded. "Good idea. I'd say skip my place altogether, but I have nothing to wear to work tomorrow, unless you want me to wear my tuxedo and white dinner jacket?"

"That *would* be hot. But it would probably get us in serious trouble. I don't think I could keep my hands off of you."

THE limo pulled into the KIC parking lot and dropped them off at their cars. Tristan rounded the curve in his Volkswagen Passat and saw Webber waiting for him at the bottom of the ramp in his black Mercedes CL65. He followed Webber through the streets of downtown Atlanta, up Peachtree Street, and through Buckhead to Paces Ferry, which eventually turned into West Paces Ferry. West Paces Ferry was an incredibly beautiful street with enormous houses sitting way back off the road with winding driveways and security gates. When Webber put his blinker on, Tristan realized that Webber's house was no different. He followed Webber up the bricked driveway to the security gate where Webber punched in a code and the black wrought iron gate slowly opened, allowing them passage.

The house began to appear in the distance and Tristan gripped the steering wheel tightly with anticipation as it came into full view. It was a stunningly beautiful French country estate, painted a buttery Tuscan yellow with dark wood beams and lots of stonework. The gardens surrounding it were full, lush, and very well manicured. Tristan pulled up next to Webber and nervously got out of his car. Webber was waiting for him with his head cocked to the side, apprehensively shifting from one foot to the other, obviously waiting for some type of response.

"It's breathtaking," Tristan offered.

"Thanks," Webber said in a relieved tone. "And welcome home by the way," he added, pointing to the rear of the house. "There are four garages around the back if you prefer your car to be covered."

Tristan glanced at his car nervously. "I'm sure it will be fine here for now."

Webber held up his arm, gesturing to the front door. "Let's go in, and I'll show you around."

Tristan was in awe, his head turning from side to side taking everything in as he moved toward the entrance with Webber right behind him. The massive wooden front door was flanked by two large leaded glass sidelights that even in daylight sparkled from the glow of the two copper gas lanterns hanging next to them.

Webber slipped his key in the lock, pressed down on the handle with his thumb, and pushed the heavy door open. He and Tristan stepped in and Webber closed the door behind them. Before Tristan could look around or even say a word, Webber pinned him against the door, his hands on either side of Tristan's head, Webber's lips solidly covering his in a crushing kiss. When the kiss ended, Webber stepped back and smiled. "I've been dying to do that since we got into the limo."

Tristan brought his fingers up to his lips and savored the lingering kiss. He was definitely overwhelmed by the situation, and Webber trying to make it feel, well, for a lack of a better word, normal, made him relax a little. He ran his fingers through Webber's hair and cupped his cheek. "Thanks for understanding how overwhelming this is for me."

Webber smiled again and took him by the hand. "Come on, I'll show you around."

Directly in front of the foyer was a formal living room with an enormous fireplace, grand piano in the corner, and four sets of French doors leading to the terrace. "This is a room I use about twice a year, if you don't count passing by it to get to the bedroom," Webber joked. "But it was here so I kept it."

Tristan nodded, still holding his hand tightly.

Off the foyer, immediately to the left, Webber took him into a mahogany-paneled study with built-in bookcases lining the walls, a large desk, and two leather wingback chairs flanking a fireplace. "This is where I work when I work from home."

The room was warm and inviting. The combination of the wood with the deep red walls and leather made it very masculine, handsome even. "I can easily see you working here. This room is as handsome as you are."

Webber stole a kiss as he dragged him across the foyer to the formal dining room. Tristan counted and it sat at least twelve. Off the dining room was a hall he assumed led to the kitchen. "And here's the kitchen, a room I rarely used in the past, but one I look forward to using more now that you're here." Tristan looked around and took everything in. A chef's kitchen was not a good enough description. It was massive, with a center island, eight-burner stove, two full-size refrigerators and two full-size freezers, and a pantry as big as Tristan's bedroom. Webber walked him through the room that led to a small informal dining area and a comfortable den with a stone fireplace and more built-ins. Continuing on, they passed a wet bar and then they were back out in the foyer.

"And here's my new favorite room," Webber explained. "The bedroom." He led Tristan through the foyer to an entry hall that opened to a beautiful master bedroom with a trey ceiling, a king-size canopied four-poster bed, a couple of club chairs in front of a fireplace, and, of course, more built-ins, and French doors leading to the same terrace.

Tristan looked around in amazement. "It's beautiful, Web," he said. "Masculine but stylish and very well done. It reflects your personality perfectly."

"You can thank my decorator for that," Webber teased. "And here's the bathroom."

A large room done in hunter greens with a garden tub in the center, a large glass-enclosed shower to one side, and double sinks on the other. There were his and hers—or in their case, his and his—water closets, and beyond that were two gigantic wardrobe closets. Webber was sort of a clotheshorse, but he also knew Tristan was as well. "This is where you'll put your clothes," Webber teased.

"Are you serious?" Tristan asked. "This is almost as big as my entire condo. I'll just live in here."

Webber laughed, wrapped his arms tightly around the other man, and buried his face in Tristan's neck. "I love you and I want you to be happy here."

"How can I not be happy here," Tristan asked. "This place is magnificent, Web, really. What's upstairs?"

"Six more bedrooms that I never use," Webber admitted. "I can show you those later, but let me take you downstairs first."

Tristan stopped him. "Can I ask you something first?"

"Anything."

"Why did you buy such a big place if you never use it?"

"I didn't," Webber said with a hint of melancholy in his voice. "My mom and dad bought this place a year before my mother died, and when my dad died, he left it to me free and clear. I sold my condo on Peachtree and moved in. Of course I redid the entire place, but it makes me feel closer to them, so I just stayed here."

"Then it's settled. This is where we're going to live."

A warm smile spread across Webber's face and he took both of Tristan's hands in his. "Thank you for saying that, baby. But look, I didn't have anyone in my life and keeping this place made me feel like I did, but now that I have you, we can make our own memories. Let's not decide right now, okay?"

Tristan squeezed Webber's hands. "Whatever you want is fine with me."

"Shall we move on?"

"Lead the way," Tristan teased.

Webber took him down a set of stairs that led to another foyer with a wine cellar off to the right. "This is my pride and joy," he admitted. "I have so many vintages I haven't even tried them all yet." He looked at Tristan warmly. "I don't know, but I've always felt like I was waiting for someone to enjoy this with and"—his voice cracked—"now you're here."

Tristan's eyes started to fill up, and he took Webber into his arms and held him tightly. "I am here," he whispered. "And I love you."

"It just feels so damn good finally having you here after wanting you for the last two years. I'm such a sap." Webber stepped back and pounded his chest. "I am manly. Manly, I tell you," he added with a chuckle.

"Manly, right," Tristan said, popping him in the chest. "What else is down here?"

Webber led him to a very large ballroom with a bar area and tons of entertaining space. Beyond that were a guest suite, a home theater, and a game room, all with French doors accessing the lower terrace. Webber opened one of the French doors and pointed down to the kidney-shaped pool and hot tub with blue stone decking, a tennis court, and a gazebo with two hammocks hanging within.

"Wow," Tristan said. "This must be great in the summer."

"It is pretty nice, but again, I don't entertain that much," Webber shared. "Hopefully that will change. I mean, if you want it to, that is."

"I think I'll keep you to myself for some time to come," Tristan teased. "But maybe in a few years or so we can talk about it."

Walking back though the house, Tristan remembered wondering if the Agency lounge was a reflection of Webber's taste and ultimately his home, and now he knew the answer was yes. His style was unmistakable: masculine, traditional, classic, and extremely Webber. He was going to love living here.

Tristan drove them back to Midtown to get some of his things, and while he had Webber captive and on his turf, he decided that now was as good a time as any to have the finance talk. After much deliberation, Webber agreed reluctantly to allow Tristan to pay half of the expenses to run the household, but not until he sold or sublet his condo. Tristan agreed, knowing he wouldn't be able to afford it any other way, but he would contribute what he could until that time.

"Tris, do you know how much money I have?" Webber asked.

"I have no idea and I don't want to know," Tristan protested.

"Why not? Half of it's going to be yours, and of course, if anything happens to me, it will all be yours."

Tristan pulled over and put the car in park. He turned to Webber. "Because I don't want your money, I want you."

"I know that," Webber huffed. "But please hear me out. I need you to know a few things."

Tristan rolled his eyes, starting to feel sorry he'd brought this up.

Webber continued. "First of all, I have a lot. More than we can ever spend in our lifetime. Secondly, I need you to know I didn't earn hardly any of it. The bulk of it came from my father's estate. And thirdly, what I've made on my own, I made when we took Kincaid public and most of that is in Kincaid stock."

Tristan simply stared at Webber. "Is this supposed to make me think you're a useless slug?"

"No," Webber said, his voice now lower. "That's not what I want you to think at all."

"Good," Tristan said. "Because I would never think that. Webber, you work damn hard and you are good at what you do. Don't sell yourself short, ever."

Webber sighed. "I don't, Tris, but I'm trying to make a point here. Can you give me a minute?"

Tristan placed a hand on Webber's shoulder and squeezed. "I'm sorry, but all this talk about money and something happening to you is scaring me. My God, Web, I just got you, please don't talk about dying."

Webber reached up and covered Tristan's hand with his own, leaned his head back, and closed his eyes. "I'm sorry too, Tris," he said softly. "I didn't mean to be morose. I just need to say something, and I'm having trouble putting it into the kind of words that don't make me sound like an asshole."

"Web, just say what you need to say, I would never think you're an asshole."

"Okay, I don't want to work for the rest of my life. I don't know about you, but I want us to travel, see the world, and enjoy the finer things in life. But… what I don't want is for you to say we can't do the things we want to do because you feel like you have to pay your own way and you can't afford it. Baby, we can't take our money with us when we die, so why not enjoy it." He looked at Tristan with concern in his eyes. "Am I making any sense?"

Tristan sighed. "It's making sense, but it's hard for me to wrap my head around all of this, and I don't like it. This lifestyle is going to take a lot of getting used to."

"I know, baby," Webber assured him, turning to gaze out of the window. "I had the same problem when my dad died. I felt guilty for having the money he and my mother spent their lives accumulating. They both died way too soon and never got a chance to enjoy the fruits of their labors. I don't want the same thing to happen to us."

When Webber turned back there were tears streaming down his face, and it broke Tristan's heart. Tristan raised a hand and wiped Webber's tears away with his thumb. "Okay, Web, you win. I can't take it when you cry." He leaned in and brushed his lips against Webber's, put the car in drive, and pulled onto the road, contemplating everything Webber had said.

TRISTAN'S condo was on the corner of 10th Street and Juniper Avenue with spectacular views of Piedmont Park and midtown Atlanta. It was a one bedroom, one-and-a-half bath with formal living and dining rooms and a den/study, and it took Tristan about five minutes to give Webber the full tour. The condo was much smaller than Webber's estate, but just as impressive in its own right. It was meticulously neat and very warm and welcoming. Webber had tried many times over the last couple of years to imagine what Tristan's home would be like, but he never imagined their tastes would be so similar.

While Tristan was debating over what clothing to take with him now and what to leave until later, Webber wandered through the condo admiring the furnishings Tristan had accumulated. The condo was beautifully appointed, and everything was of exceptionally good quality and fit perfectly in their surroundings. While admiring Tristan's things, he realized all of their pieces would meld beautifully together when they actually decided where they were going to live.

Standing in the formal living room, he ran his hand along the camelback divan and tried to imagine Tristan at home here. He could almost picture him across the room on the chaise reading a book on a lazy Sunday afternoon, legs crossed at the ankles, brows furrowed in concentration, and the thought made him realize something. From the moment he walked through the front door, he'd felt comfortable here. *I could live here with Tristan and be very happy.*

He felt certain Tristan had a mortgage on the place, and he decided that first thing tomorrow morning, after he called his attorney to make changes to his last will and testament to include Tristan, he would look into paying off this place. Then a thought hit him. Tristan must have worked very hard to buy his home, and Webber didn't want to take away the sense of pride and accomplishment he must surely feel. No, he would to wait until they decided where they would live and then he would approach the subject.

He was shaken out of his thoughts by long, muscular arms circling his waist. "Everything all right?" Tristan asked. "You looked like you were pretty deep in thought."

Webber turned his head and kissed Tristan's cheek. "I'm good, baby. I was just imagining you living here. I really like this place and I think I could be very happy here with you."

"Haven't we already decided that we're going to live at your place?" Tristan asked.

"Well, you did, but we're a team, remember? We decide everything together, and I'm just not convinced yet."

"Yeah, but Web, I never want to take you away from a place that makes you feel close to your parents."

"And I love you for that," Webber admitted. "But I have enough fond memories of my parents to last a lifetime and I don't need that house to keep those memories alive. I have you now and it's time we start making our own memories."

Tristan turned Webber around in his arms and kissed him deeply. When the kiss ended, Tristan took him by the hand. "Let's get my things so I can get you home and in bed. And don't expect to see anything but the inside of your—no wait, our bedroom, until the sun comes up tomorrow morning. Got it?"

"I got it," Webber said, sounding as happy as Tristan had ever remembered.

THE next morning, knowing these last stolen moments would have to last them the rest of the day, Tristan and Webber kissed passionately just inside the front door of their temporary—or permanent, depending on which one of them you talked to—home. Tristan knew Webber still wasn't convinced they should live there, but after his first night, he realized he felt very comfortable there. It was Webber's house and all of Webber's things and, well, it was simply Webber. How could he not love it? Last evening when they returned home, he'd wandered around and familiarized himself with the large estate and recognized places where he could add his touches and his things, and that was really all he needed to see. He was already convinced they should live there. Now he just had to convince Webber.

After they'd made love for the last time and were wrapped in each other's arms, comfortable and sated, in the middle of the king-size bed, Tristan claimed victory. Just before Webber had fallen off to sleep, Tristan had finally bugged him enough and he conceded and offered a compromise. They would look at houses together and if they didn't find one they liked, they would stay and make this their home. Tristan knew how much this home meant to Webber, and the fact that he was willing to give it up for him was all he needed to know. He, too, had given in to sleep, with Webber locked tightly in his arms, knowing this *would* be their home.

Tristan stepped into the elevator carrying his Coach bag and a cardboard file box with the results of his and Webber's due diligence over the last few weeks. He smiled when he recognized the faint smell of Webber's cologne. Was it still lingering on him from their earlier embrace, or had Webber taken the same elevator just before he did? Either way, he inhaled deeply and savored the spicy scent. Before the elevator doors could close completely, a hand appeared between them, causing them to open once again. Nathan Bridges stepped into the elevator, wearing his usual scowl.

"Don't we look happy and tanned?" Nathan said sarcastically. "Looks like you played more than you worked."

"Good morning, Nathan," Tristan said with an even tone to his voice.

He could feel Nathan's stare. "I guess I don't have to ask how your trip went," he said, looking Tristan up and down.

Tristan was looking up, watching the floor numbers go by as the elevator quickly climbed to the top floor, trying his best to ignore his elevator mate. "We got a lot done."

"So what did Webber decide in the Caribbean," Nathan asked in a nicer tone, obviously trying to get information out of him.

"You should probably talk to Webber about that," Tristan answered, smiling inwardly, knowing his answer would really piss Nathan off. "I'm not really at liberty to say."

The elevator dinged and came to a stop. "I'll just do that," Nathan said as the doors opened and he huffed out. Tristan grinned widely, knowing he shouldn't torment Nathan, but it sure was fun. He walked down the hall toward his office, stopping every now and then to chat with a coworker or just say good morning.

When he reached his office, he put the file box down on the chair in front of his desk and flipped on the lights. He looked at his desk and sighed deeply. Three weeks of his and Webber's mail and God only knows what else covered the surface. He hit the button on his CD player and the sounds of Lena Horne singing "Stormy Weather" filled his office. Knowing Webber was already here, he walked over to the break room to get their coffee and found his boss being cross-examined by Nathan.

When Tristan appeared in the doorway, Nathan stopped talking and glared at him for the second time in one day. "Am I interrupting something?" Tristan asked, already knowing the answer.

"Morning, Tristan," Webber said, seeming happy for the distraction.

"Morning, Web," Tristan said nonchalantly, ignoring Nathan's glare. "I was just coming to get your coffee, but it looks like you beat me to it."

"Thanks," Webber offered. "I was trying to sneak in, grab a cup, then sneak out, but the coffee pot was empty, so I had to brew a new pot. And then ole Nathan here showed up."

Tristan saw the twinkle in Webber's eyes. He enjoyed tormenting Nathan as much as Tristan did. "And you brewed a new pot all by yourself?" Tristan asked in a teasing tone.

"Barely," Webber said. "You know I'm not good at domestic things."

Tristan chuckled. "Why don't you head back to your office and I'll meet you there as soon as the coffee's finished. Don't forget you have a conference call in ten minutes."

"I didn't forget, but thanks for reminding me," Webber said. "I'll see you in my office then. Nathan, we'll catch up in the staff meeting later today."

Nathan nodded. "I'll be there."

While Tristan waited for the coffee to brew, he leaned on the counter with his arms folded across his chest and his legs crossed at the ankles. Again Nathan glared at him. "I'll just come back," he said.

"See ya later," Tristan offered with a slight wave.

When the coffee was ready, he poured two cups, added cream and sweetener, and headed down to Webber's office.

When he reached the doorway, Webber was already entrenched in paperwork and didn't hear him come in. Tristan saw him jump when he kicked the door closed with his foot and it slammed a little harder then he'd planned. "Sorry, I guess I don't know my own strength."

Webber chuckled as he leaned back in his chair and folded his arms over his chest. Tristan set the coffee cups down on the corner of the desk, holding his gaze and watching as Webber cocked a brow and smiled. Tristan then walked over and closed the boardroom door and picked up the two coffee cups and handed one to Webber. "Good morning again," he said as he leaned in and stole a small kiss before moving around the desk and taking a seat.

Webber licked his lips. "Good morning again to you too. I could really get used to this."

"Get used to what?" Tristan teased. "I've brought you your coffee almost every morning for the last two years."

"Yeah, but this is the first time it came with a good morning kiss."

Tristan smiled. "True… and I suspect it won't be the last."

"I'm counting on that," Webber replied, leaning in and taking a sip of his coffee. "So what's on your agenda today?"

Tristan tipped forward and whispered, "Besides squashing the desire to bend you over your desk and have my way with you?"

Webber choked and almost spit coffee all over his desk. "Yeah, besides that," he said with a slight blush, clearing his throat and wiping the coffee running down his chin.

"Oh, the usual," Tristan retorted, loving the fact that he could make Webber blush at will. "My desk is covered with three weeks' worth of mail and who knows what else, so I'm gonna sort through all of that and then I want to head down to Finance and see if I can find that acquisition file we talked about at Anegada."

Webber smiled seductively as he took another sip of his coffee. "That sounds so boring. I prefer the idea of me being bent over the desk a hell of a lot better."

"You sure as hell aren't the only one," Tristan whined. "But my boss is a real ass, and if he catches us having sex on his desk, he might blow a gasket."

"Or blow something else," Webber said with a chuckle.

Tristan shifted in his chair trying to ignore the stirring in his groin. "Okay, we need to stop this or I won't be able to leave until the tent disappears in my pants."

"Party pooper," Webber joshed.

Tristan smirked. "In all seriousness, Web, you don't happen to remember the names of the files you gave me to review back then, do you?"

Webber leaned back in his chair and linked his fingers, laying them on his stomach. "That was so long ago. I seem to remember one of them being Creative Magic, that firm out of Philly, and maybe Marquis Advertising out of Paris? But that's all I've got."

"I guess that'll have to do. Oh, by the way, earlier in the break room, I assume Nathan was prying for information about our trip."

Webber smirked. "You got that right. Why?"

"He caught me in the elevator and was pumping me as well."

"What did you tell him?"

"I told him he'd have to talk to you."

"Good boy," Webber said. "I did tell him you would be bringing the potential acquisitions over this morning and I wanted him to get his team started on them ASAP."

"How did he react to that?" Tristan asked.

"The same ole same ole. He was pissed that you had any part of it, said you could be a security risk, etc. etc. etc. But when I told him I trusted you implicitly, that pissed him off even more. I just don't get him, Tris."

"I think it's just a power struggle," Tristan surmised. "I certainly realize why he keeps this stuff tightly under wraps, but he goes way beyond just keeping things quiet and is borderline secretive."

"I know, right?" Webber added. "It's almost as though he thinks he's more valuable and indispensible if only he and his team know what's going on. Does he think I'm so trusting that I wouldn't stay in the loop? I'm the one at risk if he does something underhanded or makes a stupid mistake that no one catches."

"I just don't know about him, Web. Something about the way he does business bothers me. Please keep an eye on him."

"I will and thanks for caring."

"I've always cared, Web, even before we went away," Tristan added with a wink as he downed the last of his coffee. "Oh and thanks for the info on the acquisitions. At least I have somewhere to start. I know I made notes, but I'll have to see if I still have them."

Tristan walked around Webber's desk and reached down to the throw his empty cup in the trash. When he bent down, he suddenly found himself on his back in Webber's lap with Webber's lips crushing his. He went with the assault and gave as good as he got, enjoying Webber's arms wrapped tightly around him. When the kiss ended, Webber lifted him up and off his lap and he stood unable to move, blushing with his fingers caressing his puffy lips. "Now who's blushing," Webber taunted. "That'll have to hold you until we get home, big boy."

"Maybe, maybe not," was all Tristan said as he made his way through the boardroom and back to his office, leaving Webber with his mouth hanging open.

The morning flew by in a flash. Webber had a lunch meeting downtown, so Tristan saw no need to stop working. Between eight and lunchtime, he'd waded through his and Webber's voicemails, returning the important calls, addressing the others, and deleting what was left. He then tackled their mail, leaving the things that needed Webber's attention on his desk and handling everything else. He remembered that he had to take the acquisition files down to Nathan, so he opened the file box and removed the file in question, put the cover back on the box and headed down to Finance. He was very happy when Nathan's assistant told him Nathan was at lunch, and she allowed him to drop the files on Nathan's desk. He added a brief note and was out of there in no time. He went back up to his office and started sorting through all the paperwork on his desk, organizing everything into categories and eliminating each category until everything was back in order.

He was digging through a file drawer when he heard the clearing of a throat. He looked up to see Webber standing in his doorway with his hands behind his back.

"Don't tell me you worked through lunch again?"

Tristan frowned, taking the opportunity to stretch. "Guilty as charged," he said, stifling a yawn. "What time is it?"

Webber looked down at his watch. "It's two forty-five."

"It can't be. You just left."

"Come on, Tris," Webber pleaded. "I left at twelve fifteen."

Tristan laughed. "Web, I swear I don't know where the time went. Don't worry, I'll go downstairs and grab a cup of soup in a minute. I'm still trying to find my notes on those acquisitions."

Webber sighed and walked into Tristan's office and placed a white paper bag on his desk. "Here's a turkey sandwich. I figured you'd work through lunch, so I thought I'd save you the trouble of going downstairs."

Tristan couldn't help the smile that rapidly spread across his face. He looked down at the white bag then up at Webber. "Thanks, Web."

Webber winked and looked around nervously. "Don't take too much time eating if you have a lot of work to do, because we're leaving on time today. You've got until five o'clock to get your work done or I'm leaving without you."

Tristan raised his eyebrows incredulously. "You wouldn't leave me behind, would you?"

Mocking Tristan's words earlier in the day, Webber said with a coy smile, "Maybe, maybe not," as he turned and headed for his office.

"Touché," Tristan yelled while laughing hysterically. *God I love that man!*

"EUREKA," Tristan bellowed when he found the notes he'd been looking for most of the afternoon. He glanced down at his watch. *Three fifty-five. That gives me an hour to go down to Finance and get what I need so Webber and I can go over the files tonight.*

Tristan went down to the Finance department and asked one of the clerks to show him where they kept the previous acquisition files. She apologized, but told Tristan those were confidential files and she couldn't give him access to them without Nathan's approval. Tristan knew it wasn't her fault, so he didn't give her a hard time; instead he headed to Nathan's office to get the permission he needed, prepared to take the crap Nathan would surely give. When he got there, though, Nathan's assistant told him Nathan had an off-site meeting and was gone for the day. He headed back up to Webber's office to have him make the call.

Webber was on the phone but winked and smiled at Tristan when he came in. He plopped down in the chair opposite Webber's desk, sulking somewhat that he had to play the "Webber" card to get things done, but since Nathan was gone for the day, he had no other choice.

Webber hung up the phone and looked at him with concern. "Before I forget, that was Deanna and she sends her love. She's going to be in town for a shoot next week for "A Pea in a Pod," and I invited her to stay with us. I hope you don't mind."

"Of course I don't mind. I'd love to see her," Tristan said in a monotone voice.

"What's wrong, Tris?"

Tristan sighed. "Nothing really except I found my notes with the files we wanted to review, and I went down to Finance to get them and they won't allow me access without Nathan's permission, and Nathan's gone for the day."

"And you want me to call down there?"

"Would you mind?" Tristan asked. Before Webber could answer, he added, "I thought if we got the files today, we could go over them tonight, and I could give Nathan the final acquisition candidates tomorrow morning. You know me and my checklists."

Webber leaned in and whispered, "One of the perks of sleeping with your boss is that he'll do pretty much anything you ask him to."

Tristan smiled. "I think I'm gonna like this relationship. A lot!"

Webber chuckled. "Who do I need to call?"

Tristan gave Webber the extension and minutes later he was headed back down to Finance with the power of Webber Kincaid behind him. When he got there, the clerk reluctantly unlocked the file room and took his list, attempting to locate the files he needed. She found the first three immediately, but the last two, ironically the two that Webber had remembered, were not where they were supposed to be. "These two aren't here," she said, pointing to the list. She walked over to the door and looked through a book sitting on a small table. "And they haven't been checked out either. This is very odd."

"You mean people can check these files out anytime they want?" Tristan asked.

"Of course not," the clerk said. "But there is a small list of people from Finance, Legal, and Business Development that are authorized to check these files out if they need them."

"Interesting," he said more to himself than to the clerk. "So what do we do now?"

"I'll look around to see if they are misfiled. But if I don't find them, I'll have to check with Nathan. He may have them."

"Does he not have to check them out like everyone else?"

"Anyone who takes files out of this room is supposed to check them out."

Tristan learned they only kept transactions that took place in the past five years on-site, so it wouldn't take long to go through each of the files to see if they had been misfiled. The clerk started in the Zs and Tristan in the As. Tristan found the Creative Marketing file in the F section, filed under its code name "Fender," and eventually the clerk found Marquis Advertising filed in the Ts under its code name "Tower."

"Do you normally file them away under their code names?" Tristan asked.

"Never," the clerk promised. "Code names are something we use to keep the potential acquisitions confidential until the announcement is made. We—"

Tristan cut her off. "I know all about code names and why we use them," he assured her. "What do I need to do to check these files out?"

"Just write the file name, the date, your name and department, and sign on the right."

Tristan filled in the paperwork, looked down at his watch, and cursed under his breath. "Quarter past five." *Damn, I'm coming, Web.*

He thanked the clerk and then hurried to the elevator, balancing the heavy file box on his shoulder. When he reached his office, he found Webber sitting at his desk with his feet propped up. He looked down at his watch and then up to Tristan. Tristan smiled weakly. "Sorry, Web, but we couldn't find all the files."

"What do you mean you couldn't find the files?"

"I'll tell you all about it when we get home. Let's go. And by the way, I guess the answer's 'maybe not'."

Webber looked at him with a questioning look. "What answer?"

"When I asked if you'd really leave me this afternoon, you said 'maybe, maybe not.' I guess the answer's 'maybe not'."

Webber smirked, knowing Tristan had called his bluff, and stood and took the file box from Tristan, a smile forming on his lips. "Get your bag and let's get out of here."

"Is it okay that we walk out together?"

"How many times have we walked out together and never thought a thing about it?"

Tristan thought about that. "You're right. Let's go," he said.

They stepped into the elevator and Webber leaned against the wall and propped his foot up, balancing the file box on one knee. Tristan hit the button indicating the ground floor.

Tristan eyed Webber up and down. "Please give me that, Web," he said, reaching for the file box. "It looks like you're carrying my books to the bus stop."

"I'd carry your books to the bus stop if we were courting," Webber joked, relinquishing the box of paperwork. "But I've already won your heart, so there's really no need."

Concerned, Tristan looked up at the security camera on the corner of the elevator. "Do you think they record the conversations in the elevators?"

"Nope, only video."

"In that case, do you think I'm that easy, Mr. Kincaid?" Tristan asked with a slight smile. "Because if you do, you don't know me as well as you think."

"We'll see," Webber said in a self-assured tone as the elevator doors opened and they were greeted with an out-of-breath and frantic-looking Nathan Bridges.

"Nathan," Webber said. "Is everything all right? You look a little panicked."

Nathan smoothed his hair back, brushed the front of his suit coat, and took a deep breath, obviously trying to catch his breath.

"Ah, yeah," he replied. "I'm fine, just forgot something and I'm running a little late for an early dinner date."

Tristan eyed him suspiciously. "Your assistant said you were at an off-site meeting and wouldn't be back in the office until tomorrow."

"Oh right, yeah," Nathan said, then he paused like he was thinking about what he was about to say. "I… uh… forgot some paperwork I wanted to work on at home tonight, so I thought I'd run back by and pick it up."

"Ooookay then, have a good evening Nathan," Tristan said as he motioned for Webber to go ahead of him.

"Someone else looks like they're taking work home as well," Nathan said, stepping in front of him, blocking his way, and referring to the file box in Tristan's arms. "I don't think you're authorized to remove those files from the building, or even view them for that matter."

Before Tristan could answer, Webber stopped midstep and turned around when he heard the tone of Nathan's voice. "He's carrying those files for me," he said protectively.

"Oh?" Nathan said. "My file clerk said Tristan checked out some highly confidential files, and unfortunately, he's not authorized to do so."

Webber took the file box from Tristan. "He checked those files out on my behalf, and I know you're not questioning my authority, are you, Nathan?"

"Of course not, Webber," Nathan replied. "But next time, for security purposes, I would appreciate you checking them out yourself, or call me and I'll do it for you."

The hair stood up on the back of Tristan's neck and he straightened his back and stood tall. "For security purposes? Really?"

Webber stepped in. "Nathan, I'll remind you one more time that Tristan is my assistant and therefore an extension of me. And... when I ask him to do something on my behalf, I do not expect his motives to be questioned. Got it?"

"Sure, Webber," Nathan said. "I'm only trying to protect your interests."

Tristan saw the blood rushing to Webber's face and he felt the tension building. "Tristan, you go on home, I have a few things to talk to Nathan about. I'll see you tomorrow."

Tristan looked at Webber with a raised eyebrow. "Are you sure?"

"I'm sure," Webber assured him. "See you in the morning."

Tristan walked past them both and headed for the parking garage.

WEBBER waited for Tristan to round the corner to the parking garage before he let Nathan have it. "Protecting my interest?" he questioned. "That's bullshit, Nathan. From the moment Tristan turned down your job offer to work in Finance, you've been giving him as much shit as you can and frankly I've had enough of it. This is where it ends."

Nathan turned as white as a sheet and stepped back. "That's not true—"

"Just save it, Nathan," Webber interrupted. "We both know that anyone that questions you or shows loyalty to anyone other than you gets treated like shit. You know it, I know it, and, most importantly, Tristan knows it, and it stops here."

Nathan opened his mouth again to speak and Webber put up his hand. "I'm not through yet," he huffed. "How do you think he feels, being treated like this when he's shown nothing but loyalty to me and to this company? Let me make this very clear. The next time I send my assistant to Finance to get something for me, you better hand it to him on a silver platter or heads are going to roll. You got it? And you better pass this bit of information along to your little patsies as well."

"Webber, I—"

"Good night, Nathan."

Webber turned on his heels and headed for the parking garage, finding Tristan leaning against his Passat with his arms crossed over his chest and a worried look on his face. He put the file box on the roof and turned to Tristan. "You okay?" he asked.

Tristan nodded. "But more importantly, are you okay?"

"Yeah." He leaned in and whispered, "Let's go home and we can talk about it over a glass of wine."

"That's sounds good to me," Tristan agreed. "And Web... I don't know what you said back there, but I feel like I need to say thank you."

"No thanks needed, Tris. I only said what needed saying. I'll see you at home," Webber said, opening Tristan's car door.

Tristan turned to him and looked him in the eye. "Please drive safely," he said.

Webber looked around the garage and seeing it was empty for the moment, stole a quick kiss. "You too."

He lifted the file box from Tristan's roof and walked the ten spaces down to this car, put the box in the backseat, got in the car, and drove off.

Neither Tristan nor Webber saw Nathan lurking near the stairwell watching them.

Eleven

WEBBER pulled into the driveway and entered the code into the automatic gate. He looked in his rearview mirror as he'd done every few minutes sine they'd left the office and Tristan was still right behind him. He sighed with relief when the gate closed, cutting them off from the rest of the world. *Why am I so jittery?* After his encounter with Nathan, he'd had an uneasy feeling that'd nagged him all the way home. Nathan had always been an asshole, but something about the way he acted today was beyond his normal assholeness. He'd looked downright frantic when the elevator doors opened and he and Tristan were walking out with those files. And he was so determined to keep those files from leaving the office. But why?

Webber didn't know Nathan that well outside the office. But what he did know, he really didn't like very much, and he was certainly not the type of person Webber would hang out with. He felt certain that Nathan despised him as much as he despised Nathan, so they did their jobs, worked together when necessary, and went their separate ways at the end of the day. But Webber had kept him on at KIC out of a sense of loyalty because his father had hired him a long time ago and must have trusted him. So far, he'd done nothing, besides being an asshole, that would give Webber reason to distrust him. But something just wasn't right with the whole situation earlier. *Why am I suddenly questioning his loyalty?*

Webber was in deep thought and jumped when Tristan tapped on his window. "Are you going to get out or spend the night in there?"

Webber smiled and opened the door. "Sorry, I was thinking about Nathan and that whole scene in the lobby. What crap!" he added.

"Tell me about it," Tristan began. "I thought about little else all the way home."

Webber grabbed the file box off of the backseat, and they walked to the door.

"Whose car is that next to yours?"

Webber was slipping the key in the door and before he had a chance to answer, the door opened and a short, round, older lady with silver-blue hair and a purse like Queen Elizabeth's on her arm squealed and almost fell into his arms. He dropped the file box and grabbed her by the elbow to steady her.

"Oh, Mr. Kincaid, you scared the heck out of me."

"Sorry, Sophie, are you okay?"

Sophie smoothed the front of her black dress, straightened her white apron, and patted her hair. "Yes, sir, just a little startled is all."

"Sophie, do you have a minute before you leave?" Webber asked.

Tristan picked up the file box, moved past them, and dropped it on the foyer floor.

Sophie looked a little nervous as she stepped back inside. "Is everything okay?"

"Oh, everything's perfect; I just want to meet my partner, Tristan Moreau. He'll be living here with me from now on."

"Will he now?" she asked, looking him up and down. She batted her eyelashes and smiled at Tristan.

Tristan immediately smiled back and stuck his hand out. "Pleased to meet you, Sophie."

Sophie bowed her head just a little and took his hand. "The pleasure's all mine, Mr. Moreau."

"And you must call me Tristan."

Webber laughed. "Good luck with that. I've been trying to get her to call me Webber since she stopped changing my diapers. At least she doesn't call me Master Kincaid anymore."

Sophie swatted Webber on the arm, obviously very comfortable around him. "He teases me all the time," she said with a wink. "He thinks he's too big for me to throw over my knee, but I'm gonna surprise him one day."

Tristan laughed out loud. "Oh, please make sure I'm here to see that."

Webber put his arm around Tristan and squeezed. "I just wanted you two to have a proper introduction."

"Thank you, Master Kincaid," Tristan teased.

Sophie's face lit up at Tristan's ribbing. "I think I'm gonna like you."

Webber frowned. "It looks like I'll need to keep you two apart."

"Come on, Mr. Kincaid, walk an old lady to her car?"

He placed a kiss on Tristan's cheek. "I'll be right back."

He stuck his bended arm out and Sophie took it and followed him out of the door. When they reached her car he said, "Okay, I'm waiting."

"Waiting for what?" she asked.

"For you to give me the third degree."

She squeezed his arms. "Oh, Mr. Kincaid. Like I would…. Are you happy, honey?"

"The happiest I've been in my entire life," Webber openly admitted.

"Then I love him and I'm very happy for you. He sure is a looker."

"That he is," Webber agreed.

"I did notice some extra things in the bathroom and the closets, but I wasn't going to say anything. I must admit, I had my fingers crossed though," she added, opening her car door. "Now give an old woman a hug and get back in there and take care of your man."

He threw his arms around and squeezed. "I love you, Sophie."

"I love you too, honey. Now go. I'll see you tomorrow."

Webber kissed her on the cheek, closed her car door, and watched her drive down the long driveway, smiling broadly.

He wandered back inside and found Tristan in the den, collar open and shoes off, sitting on the couch with his feet propped up on the ottoman and his head resting on the back of the couch. Webber walked over behind the couch and covered Tristan's lips with his own. His tongue ran along the other man's teeth and he bit Tristan's lower lip lightly. Tristan moaned and opened for him and he tasted his lover for the first time since they stole that quick kiss while sharing coffee at the office. "Hi," Webber said, taking off his tie and loosening his collar. He toed out of his shoes and walked around and hopped onto the couch, his head landing in Tristan's lap.

Tristan smiled down at him. "That's what I call a hello."

"Thank you."

"Is Sophie okay?"

"She's fine and it looks like you made a great impression," Webber boasted proudly.

"She's sweet as she can be," Tristan said.

"Yeah, she and Amani are the closest thing I've had to a mother since my real mother passed away."

Tristan stroked Webber's hair fondly. "You still miss your mother, don't you?"

"Every day," Webber admitted.

Tristan bent his head down and brushed Webber's lips lightly. When he lifted his head again his face had taken on a more serious look.

"Will you tell me what happened with Nathan?"

"Of course I will," Webber said, taking Tristan's hands and resting them on his chest. "I set him straight about you and threatened his job if he pulled any crap like this again."

Tristan sighed. "Don't you find it odd that he reacted so strangely to me taking those files out of the building?"

"Something's not right, Tris. I can't put my finger on it, but I—we'll find out what it is. What do you say we change, open a bottle of wine, and dig into those files? I'm suddenly very interested in what's in that box."

"Me too," Tristan said.

Thirty minutes later they were comfortably piled on the couch in sweats and T-shirts. Webber'd ordered Italian food for dinner and they were leaning against one another sorting through piles of paperwork, looking for anything that resembled the Moniker Communications file. The buzzer sounded, indicating the arrival of dinner, and Webber got up to open the electronic gate. Tristan looked up when Webber yelled, "Soup's on." He walked back in carrying a huge brown paper bag that looked like it contained enough food for ten people.

Tristan took one last glance at the paperwork in his hand before getting up to help Webber. Halfway to his feet, he yelled, "I knew it! Here it is." He took a second look at the name on the file. "Marquis Advertising."

Webber walked over and sat next to Tristan, now back on the couch. "Let me see that?" he asked, holding out his hand. He studied the file for a second. "I remember this acquisition very well. Nathan and I fought until the bitter end on this one. I didn't think it was worth the asking price, but Nathan eventually convinced me that they had the right client list and contracts to support the price. But in the end I was right. We bought them in"—he glanced at the date on the contract—"2005 and divested them two years later because of poor performance. They consistently missed their target revenue every quarter for the two years we owned them. So now they're headquartered in Sydney and go under the name Moniker Communications, huh?"

"Look, Web," Tristan pointed out. "The client list is virtually the same, a few more international clients added to Moniker's list, but almost exact."

"Can I see the financials?" Webber asked.

Tristan handed over the folder and watched as Webber scanned the profit and loss summary comparing Moniker to Marquis. "I don't understand how Moniker could have gone from this to this in three years," he said, holding up the two different financial reports. "Very unrealistic."

Tristan refilled Webber's wine glass. "What do we do?"

"First, we eat," Webber suggested. "And then we review and compare the detailed profit and loss statements to determine where the difference in the bottom line is coming from. Then, I'm sure as hell going to find out why Nathan is pushing an acquisition we bought and sold once already without disclosing that information to me."

They spent the next couple of hours painstakingly reviewing the financials line by line, noting apparent differences between the two sets of reports. Webber explained to Tristan why certain numbers stood out, while others were harder to quantify and needed to be further researched. Webber decided that they'd done as much as they could with what they had, and first thing tomorrow morning, he was going to request the documents from when KIC divested Marquis Advertising and throw those numbers into the mix. Once he had all the information he needed, he was going to confront Nathan and see what he had to say for himself.

With their work done for the evening, Tristan put all the files back in the file box and sat at Webber's feet. "You look concerned, Web. What do you think of all this?"

"It just doesn't feel right," he replied. "We both know firsthand that Nathan can be an asshole, but I never suspected that he could do anything unethical."

"Well," Tristan said, the word drawn out, "maybe he didn't and he can explain all this away."

"I sure hope so," Webber said with some degree of skepticism in his voice. "We're a public company, Tris. If he did anything unethical, my signature is all over those documents, and I would be held liable."

Tristan rose up and rested on his knees between Webber's legs. "Even if you didn't know anything about it?"

"It doesn't matter if I knew about it or not. I signed off on it, and that's all they need," he tried to explain.

"By 'they' you mean the Security and Exchange Commission, right?"

Webber nodded. "If I even suspect Nathan did anything out of line, I'll call the SEC and tell them what I believe. They'll probably open an investigation on the down low, find out all they can from the principals at Marquis, and hopefully come back to me with what they know."

"Web," Tristan said, trying to keep the fear out of his voice. "Let's go back to the office and look for the other Marquis file. The one from when you divested the company."

Webber looked at Tristan incredulously. "It's late, baby, it'll wait until the morning."

Tristan's rested his head in Webber's lap. "It's not like I'm gonna sleep tonight anyway."

"Besides, I don't think they keep files on-site past five years," Webber shared. "We're going to have to call it back from the storage company and that will take a day or so."

Suddenly Tristan was feeling very insecure and needy, a feeling that he'd never experienced before. He stood up and started pacing. "Hell, Webber, I'll go over there and get the file myself if I have to, but I'm not waiting a day to two to get it. I just got you; I'm not letting you go down for something Nathan might have done."

Webber stood and took Tristan into his arms, looking him in the eyes. "Baby, nothing's going to happen to me. I won't leave you."

"Promise me," Tristan said as he burrowed his head in Webber's chest.

Webber leaned his chin on Tristan's head. "I promise."

Tristan lifted his head and looked at Webber with a slight smile. "I think I know what a parent feels like."

"What do you mean?" Webber asked, returning the smile.

"Because I never knew that loving someone as much as I love you could absolutely petrify me," he admitted. "Web, I'm not a violent person, but I think I could kill anyone that tried to hurt you."

Webber took Tristan in his arms again and held him tight. "I feel the same way, baby."

"Can we go to bed?" Tristan asked before burrowing his head back in Webber's chest. "I need to be close to you."

Webber kissed the top of Tristan's head, took him by the hand, and led him to their bedroom.

Standing at the foot of their bed, Tristan felt his T-shirt being slowly pulled over his head and watched it hit the floor. Gentle fingers lightly caressed his chest, bringing goose bumps to his flesh, while soft kisses covered his neck and shoulders. Webber kissed his way down Tristan's long, ripped torso, hooking his fingers in Tristan's sweats and underwear and pulling them down as he fell to his knees. Tristan stepped out of the pile of clothing at his feet, hands resting on Webber's shoulders for balance. When Webber took him in, swallowing his length, Tristan sucked in a breath as the warmth of Webber's mouth surrounded him. Tristan lightly caressed Webber's hair, hoping the mere touch of his fingertips was enough to convey the love, desire, and now desperation he was feeling.

His knees started to tremble as Webber moved up and down his length, stopping only to tease and taunt him by licking in the most sensitive of places. Webber's finger ran lightly along Tristan's underside, tormenting that little patch of skin just past his balls and Tristan hissed when Webber's warm, moist hand reached his opening, circled its perimeter several times, and the finger gently entered him. No one but Justin had ever been where Webber's finger was now tantalizing him, bringing more goose bumps to his already chilled skin. Tristan swayed while he rode the waves of pleasure coursing through his body. He whimpered and almost buckled when Webber's finger brushed across that all too sensitive bump just inside him.

Tristan's knees were no longer just trembling; they were now weak with desire and threatening to betray him as his pulse skyrocketed from Webber's pleasurable assault. Obviously sensing Tristan's pending collapse, Webber retreated and guided him to the bed. Tristan's nerve endings were still on fire, and he felt like he was about to combust as he watched Webber slowly peel out of his clothing. Webber moved Tristan's legs around and urged him to the center of the bed. Webber joined him there, wrapping his body in warmth and protection. His lips covered Tristan's in a crushing kiss that, when it ended, left them both gasping for air. Tristan stared up into Webber's dreamy blue eyes and saw into Webber's soul. The rush of emotion was enough to send him over the edge right now, but he wanted more. He suddenly knew he wanted more. He wanted Webber inside him. No... he needed Webber inside him. He suddenly craved that intimate connection and wanted Webber's seed to fill him and bond them together forever. "Web," he said, dragging the name out in a pleading tone. "I need you inside me, please."

Tristan saw the look of concern in Webber's eyes. "Are you sure, baby?" he asked. "You don't need to do this."

"I do need to do this, Web, but not for you, for me."

He hoped Webber saw the need and desire in his eyes because there was no way he could put what he was feeling into words.

Webber must have sensed it because Tristan felt the bed shift and Webber was leaning to one side, opening a drawer and retrieving a small bottle of lubricant.

When he was back and again lying on top of Tristan, he looked caringly into his eyes. "How do you want me, Tris?" he asked, almost in a whisper.

Tristan threw his arms around Webber's neck. "Just like this, I want to see your face, feel your lips on mine. Please, Web," Tristan begged.

Webber kissed him again, long and hard. "Anything," was all he said.

He shifted down and opened the lubricant, coating his fingers as he took Tristan into his mouth again. As he slid up and down Tristan, he massaged his opening with the lubricant and gently entered him again. Tristan fisted the sheets and moved his head from side to side. Again, every one of his nerve endings was tingling as Webber moved up and down his shaft and in and out of him. The sensation of both actions at one time was almost more than he could bear. He began to shift under Webber's onslaught, almost gyrating with the pure feelings of the most natural high there was, Webber James Kincaid.

Webber slipped a second finger inside him, taking his time to stretch the tight muscle. He then added a third, until Tristan was full and relaxed around his fingers. Webber could hear himself making unidentifiable sounds, but it was as though he no longer had control of his own body.

Webber lifted Tristan's legs and rested them on his shoulders. Tristan watched as Webber liberally coated himself with lubricant and then applied more to Tristan, positioning himself at Tristan's opening. Tristan felt Webber against him and dropped his legs to Webber's waist and locked his ankles behind him. As Webber began to slowly press into him, Tristan rose up and cupped his arms behind Webber's neck and brought him closer. He needed to feel Webber's lips on his. He wanted nothing, not even air, between them when he and Webber became one.

When Webber finally breached him, their lips were pressed against each other's in a gloriously warm kiss. Tristan dug his nails into Webber's back and gasped into his mouth when Webber pushed in farther and past his ring of muscle. Tristan held on when Webber stopped to allow him time to adjust to the intrusion. Tristan forced himself to relax around Webber and felt the jolt of pain start to recede. He suddenly needed more and pushed against Webber as Webber slipped farther inside him. When Tristan felt like he was about to explode from the fullness of his lover inside him, Webber started whispering words of encouragement, which eased his nervousness and allowed him to further relax around Webber's length.

Tristan literally saw stars when Webber started to slowly move in and out of him. The sensation of Webber's actions, his skin brushing against Tristan's insides, was driving him insane. He clutched at Webber frantically, pulling him closer and trying to disappear into him, making their bodies one. Their lips met again, teeth grinding against one another's as their tongues roamed freely, desperately searching for another level of closeness.

The friction of their bodies rubbing together with Tristan's hardness trapped between them, along with the steady pummeling he was getting from Webber, was bringing him to a climax much sooner than he'd hoped. He wanted to tell Webber to slow down, but he couldn't form any words. He was floating somewhere between heaven and earth and he couldn't imagine anything in his life ever measuring up to this moment in time. "Web!" was all he was able to say as his entire body clenched around Webber, jolting with the force of his climax. Not a second later, Webber called his name through their hot, frenzied kisses. Tristan felt Webber's warm seed fill him as his own seed flowed between them. They rode out the waves of pleasure until they both had no energy left. Webber collapsed on top of Tristan and they lay there with no words needing to be said. Tristan wiped the sweat off Webber's brow and brushed his hair out of his face. When Tristan was finally able to form coherent words, he looked at his lover with amazement. "My God, Web, that was the most intense thing I've ever done in my life. I didn't think I was going to survive the pleasure. You were amazing."

Webber rested his forehead against Tristan's. "Baby, I love you so much. I never knew it could be like this."

Tristan knew it was the adrenaline release, but suddenly he was on the verge of tears. His bottom lip quivered and he wanted desperately to tell Webber he loved him, but his voice cracked and left him before he could get the words out. Tears spilled down his cheeks as he caressed Webber's face. At this point, the best he could hope for was that Webber saw in Tristan's eyes what was overflowing from his heart.

Twelve

THE next morning on the drive in to work, Webber was still reeling from the emotional bond that he and Tristan had cemented the night before. He'd fallen in love with Tristan almost from the get-go, but he hadn't realized how deep his love went until last night. After their intense lovemaking, Tristan had fallen asleep with Webber's head resting on his chest.

Not being able to sleep, Webber'd eased out of the bed and into the bathroom to have a drink of water. He stood at the sink and stared at himself in the mirror. Before he knew it, tears were freely flowing down his cheeks. Images of Tristan's teary face as he lay sated and so full of love and trust captured his heart. And then images of his mother and father entered his mind. He missed them terribly, but he also missed the idea of belonging to someone, a family. His mind went back to Tristan. Webber realized now that he belonged to Tristan and Tristan to him. Tristan was all the family he needed. He'd gone back to bed and burrowed into Tristan's arms and fell asleep the happiest he'd ever been.

But as good as he felt personally, the thought of Nathan Bridges was slowly starting to put a damper on his happiness.

During his drive in, Webber'd called the file clerk in Finance and instructed her to call the storage company and retrieve the file for the divestiture of Marquis Advertising and have it on his desk by noon today.

"But sir," she tried to explain. "It takes them at least twenty-four hours to locate the file and have it sent over."

"I don't care if you have to go there and find the file yourself," Webber insisted. "I want it on my desk by noon."

Webber sighed as he pressed the button on his steering wheel, disconnecting the hands-free call. *What in the hell are you up to, Nathan?*

When he reached his office, Tristan was already there with his coffee and a tray of hot cheese danish. Webber closed his office door behind him and took Tristan into a quick embrace. "Good morning again."

Tristan smiled. "I picked up your favorite breakfast on the way in this morning."

Webber looked at the tray of danish. "That was very sweet of you."

"Well, what would it look like if I stopped spoiling you just because we were lovers?"

"Not right," Webber replied. "Not right."

They were sharing danish and coffee while they went over the agenda for the day when there was a knock on Webber's office door. Tristan got up to answer the door, and much to his surprise, Nathan Bridges stood on the other side.

He looked around Tristan, obviously trying to see if Webber was at his desk.

"Am I interrupting something?" he said with a hint of sarcasm. "I need to see Webber. In private."

Tristan looked at Webber and Webber nodded his approval. Tristan stepped to the side and Nathan walked past him and sat in the chair Tristan had been occupying. Tristan gathered his coffee cup and plate of danish, leaving the tray on the credenza, and headed for the door. He stopped, turned around, and looked at Webber. "I'll be in my office if you need me."

"He won't need you," Nathan spewed.

Webber watched as Nathan's gaze followed Tristan to the door, obviously waiting for him to close it before he spoke. While Nathan was preoccupied with Tristan, Webber took the opportunity to reach into his desk drawer and switch on the digital recorder he frequently used for dictation. He removed his hand and left the drawer open.

"What can I do for you, Nathan?" Webber asked.

Nathan shifted in his chair and crossed his leg at the knee. "I've been told that you requested the file for the divestiture of Marquis Advertising."

Webber nodded. "That's right."

"May I ask why?" Nathan said with a tilt of his head.

"I'm doing a little research," Webber offered.

"Come on, Webber, we've known each other too long to play games."

"I'm not playing games," Webber said calmly. "I'm just trying to do my job."

"Really? First, you held back the Moniker Communications file when you turned over all of the other potential acquisitions to Finance, then you checked out the acquisition file for Marquis Advertising, and then you requested the file for the divestiture of Marquis. I'm not stupid, Webber, that's a very strange coincidence."

Webber held his gaze but didn't offer any more information.

"We're adults here," Nathan said. "Let's put all our cards on the table and be honest."

Webber still didn't offer an explanation.

"Okay. I'll go first," Nathan said. "How did you find out?"

"Find out what?" Webber asked without expression.

Nathan leaned forward and slammed his fist down on Webber's desk. "You know exactly what I'm talking about, and I want to know what you're going to do about it."

Webber never flinched. He leaned back calmly in his chair. "How did you do it?"

"Oh, it was simple actually," Nathan explained. "I merely convinced the owner of Marquis to inflate the asking price, supply me with a list of bogus contracts to support that price, and we'd split the difference. Clean and simple."

Still showing no expression, Webber got up and poured himself a glass of water from the credenza. "But why risk everything? You make a good living here."

"I needed money," Nathan admitted. "I was in the middle of divorce, being taken for everything, and my girlfriend wanted more and more."

"And you might have gotten away with it if you hadn't gone back for a second round," Webber concluded. "Did you really think I wouldn't put two and two together?"

Nathan shifted in his chair again. "Hey, can't blame a guy for trying," he said with a wink. "I'm curious though, how did you find me out?"

"Actually Tristan did, but only because he looked at the Moniker files before I had a chance to. It turns out that when I was mentoring him on evaluating acquisitions, I gave him a handful of KIC's previous acquisitions to review and Marquis happened to be one of them. So when he was reviewing the files for Moniker, he recognized the client list and financials."

"I'm impressed," Nathan admitted. "I didn't give the twit enough credit."

Webber laughed. "You're calling him a twit? But I must admit, you seem awfully calm for a man about to be in very big trouble."

"Oh, I don't think I'm in that much trouble," Nathan said with confidence in his voice.

Webber tilted his head to the side. "Really, why not?"

"Well, because if I go down, you go down right along with me," Nathan warned. "You signed off on the transaction, remember."

"I remember the argument we had over this transaction and you producing a series of contracts supporting the purchase price," Webber confessed. "But… I had no idea those contracts were fabricated and worth nothing."

Nathan smiled. "It's your word against mine now, isn't it. Come on, Webber," Nathan continued. "That transaction was a long time ago. If you keep your mouth shut, no one will ever be the wiser."

"I'm afraid I can't do that," Webber replied.

Nathan got up and stood behind his chair. "I'm sorry to hear that, because that leaves me no choice but to out you and that twit back there," Nathan said, glancing over his shoulder to Tristan's office.

Webber did his best to hold on to his poker face, but his mind was whirling. "What are you talking about, Nathan?"

Nathan's knuckles went white as he dug his nails into the back of the leather chair. "There you go playing games with me again, Webber," he said through closed teeth. "I think the board will be happy to learn that you've been cavorting around the Caribbean on company resources with an employee of yours, doing who knows what," he threatened. "I've always suspected you two had something going on. I could just tell by the way you looked at each other, but I didn't know for sure until your little display of affection in the parking lot yesterday. Thanks for giving me some leverage."

Webber was quietly trying to decide how to handle this. The digital recorder was still recording and he didn't want to be caught in a lie, so he fessed up. "What Tristan and I do behind closed doors is no concern of yours, or the board's."

Nathan smiled incredulously. "You're quite right, but what you're forgetting is when you use corporate resources to fund your little rendezvous, that becomes a very different story."

"Nathan, you know perfectly well we were on a legitimate business trip," Webber insisted. "We evaluated fifteen potential acquisitions in a quarter of the time it would have taken your business development department to do it."

"Oh, Webber, you disappoint me sometimes. The reasons why have nothing to do with it," Nathan said. "You took a personal trip on a company-owned jet with an employee with whom you were romantically involved. That doesn't bode well in your favor at all."

Webber simply shook his head. Although he'd not been stupid enough to use company funds to pay for his trip, he had used the KIC jet. He knew why he'd taken that trip, and although part of it was for work, the majority of it was to try to see if there was anything between him and Tristan. Nathan had him hands down and he would have to pay the piper for that mistake. No, it wasn't a mistake. He'd gotten Tristan out of it and he would never be sorry for that.

Nathan smiled victoriously. "You just think about it for a little while and we'll talk again before the end of the day. I'm sure when you think this through, you'll agree it's better for everyone if we both keep our mouths shut and forget this ever happened."

Nathan turned and walked out of the office, slamming the door behind him.

WEBBER reached into his drawer and turned off the digital recorder, leaned back in his chair, and closed his eyes. He opened them to a knock on the door as Tristan walked in.

"Web, is everything okay?"

"Not really, but come here."

Tristan walked toward the desk as Webber stood and pulled him into a tight embrace. "I love you."

Webber held on tightly, trying to find the courage to do what he knew he had to do. He closed his eyes and inhaled Tristan's strong scent and relaxed into the embrace.

Tristan released him and held him at bay by the shoulders. "Tell me what happened, Web, you're scaring me."

Webber sighed and gestured for Tristan to take his normal chair. Then he sat back down and pressed play on the digital recorder.

Webber kept his eyes on Tristan as he listened intently. He was a little afraid that Tristan would somehow blame himself and that was the last thing he wanted. And of course he was right. The first thing Tristan said when the recording ended was, "This is all my fault."

"Tristan, look at me," Webber ordered. "This is not your fault. I'm the one who invited you to join me in the Caribbean. I don't regret a second and I would the same thing all over again if it meant I'd get you in the end."

"But Web, I knew if I got involved with you, it was going to hurt you in some way. That's one of the reasons I would never let my feelings show."

Webber felt a stab of panic. "Tris, we'll get through this. You can't leave."

"No! Webber, I would never leave you. We will get through it, but I can't help but feel responsible."

Webber stood and walked around his desk and stood in front of Tristan and offered his hands. Tristan accepted them and stood. They embraced again and held on for a long time.

When the embrace finally ended, Webber asked Tristan to call the board members and set up an emergency board meeting for the next morning. Webber sat back down in his seat and picked up his phone. His first call was to his attorney, who came over immediately, and together, they called the SEC and the Justice Department.

Thirteen

WEBBER and Tristan watched from outside Nathan's office door as he was escorted down the hall to the elevator, handcuffed and probably humiliated. He continued his threats, getting angrier by the second, until the elevator doors opened and he was forced inside. This is not the way Webber had wanted this to play out, but it seemed that there was no other way. The SEC and the Justice Department were now involved, and they had their own way of doing things.

Webber rested his arm on Tristan's shoulders. "Webber!" Tristan said through closed teeth, not wanting to bring any more attention to them. "There are employees watching."

Webber tightened his hold. "I know," he admitted. "Do you not think they all heard Nathan calling us queer and threatening to out us?"

"Threats are one thing, but confirming it for them is a little different."

Webber sighed. "Can we talk about this at home?" he asked. "This has been a really long day."

Tristan conceded and smiled warmly. "Sure, let's get you home."

They left Webber's car at the office and rode home together. On the way, Webber explained that because of the recording, it was no longer Nathan's word against his and his attorney told him that information would really help his defense. But they did have a legitimate concern about using the corporate jet for personal reasons, even though Webber had personally paid for the fuel.

The fact that Nathan's confession had been recorded was the reason he'd been arrested so quickly. He would make bail and be out of jail in a few hours, but at least they had charges against him. For Webber, if they decided to do more than fine him, it would be a while before they could build a case and press any charges. But they agreed that they would get through whatever came at them together. No running, no blaming, no guilt, just together.

Webber slipped his key in the lock and they stepped into the foyer. Tristan inhaled deeply and his mouth began to water from the wonderful aroma simmering through the house. He turned to Webber. "What smells so delicious?"

Webber smiled. "I had Sophie make us a special dinner," he explained. "And if I know Sophie, that delectable aroma is her famous braised leg of lamb."

"Whatever it is, it smells divine."

Tristan glanced into the formal dining room and saw the table was set for two. "Wow, she went all out."

"Yep, only the best for my man. Sophie, we're home!" Webber yelled through the house.

"In here, Mr. Kincaid," Sophie said as she walked down the hall from the kitchen.

"Hey, Soph," Tristan said with a chuckle.

"Hi, Tristan, honey."

"Tristan!" Webber stammered. "How come he gets Tristan and I still get Mr. Kincaid?"

Sophie blushed and winked at Tristan. "Oh, I don't know, I guess 'cause I never changed his diaper. It's easier to be a little more casual when you haven't seen a man's winkie."

Tristan and Webber howled with laughter and before long, Sophie was joining right in.

She smacked Tristan on the arm. "Dinner will be ready in about thirty minutes. You boys go get cleaned up."

"Some things never change," Webber said.

Sophie kissed him on the cheek and smacked his shoulder as he and Tristan walked toward the bedroom hand in hand.

After a quickie in the shower, they were fifteen minutes late for dinner and Sophie was standing in the hallway with her hands on her hips. "I hope you're late for a good reason?"

They both smiled and blushed a little.

"Good, then take a seat," she instructed, heading toward the kitchen. "Your first course, gentlemen," she said as she returned, "will be fried green tomatoes topped with pimento cheese and bacon." She placed the plates down and disappeared down the hall.

Tristan took a bite and hummed with delight. "This is scrumptious."

"They are pretty good," Webber agreed. "But it's hard to mess something up that's fried and topped with pimento cheese."

"You're right about that, but don't tell Sophie," Tristan teased.

"Never," Webber agreed.

"Hey, Tris, can I ask you something?" Webber said while they munched.

"Anything, you know that."

"What are your long-term career goals? I mean if you weren't at KIC?"

Tristan gave him a funny look. "Am I getting fired?"

"Of course not. Go on."

"I don't know, I've always been drawn to business development, but I would have never left my position as your assistant, so I didn't think much farther than that," Tristan tried to explain. "Why do you ask?"

Before Webber could answer, Sophie came back to clear the first course before she dropped the second. "I'll be right back, boys," she promised.

Webber picked up where they'd left off. "I guess I've been feeling a little restless at KIC for the last year or so," he confessed. "I knew when my job became more about being with you than working, something had changed. I mean, before I met you, KIC was my life, but now you're in my life and I suddenly want to live it. With you!"

Sophie returned with two plates. "For your second course, I've prepared a freshly marinated beet salad over mesclun greens with a balsamic vinaigrette dressing. Enjoy."

"Thanks, Soph," Webber and Tristan said in unison, looking at each other and smiling.

Sophie again smacked Tristan on the arm. "Now look what you've started, Tristan."

But they could hear her chuckling under her breath as she walked away.

"So," Tristan asked. "You're thinking of retiring?"

"Only if you'll retire with me," Webber said sheepishly.

Tristan raised an eyebrow. "Web, I can't afford to retire. I need an income, and more importantly, I need a retirement plan."

"What if you had all that already?" Webber asked. "Would you retire then?"

Tristan thought about the answer. "Yeah, I guess I would."

"Sophie!" Webber yelled.

Sophie appeared with a silver platter holding a large white envelope. She placed it on the table next to Webber and excused herself again.

Webber picked up the envelope and handed it to Tristan. "This is for you."

Tristan took the envelope and opened it. Inside were two documents. He scanned the first and his heart almost stopped. It was a trust set up in his name for an ungodly amount of money. He forced himself to read the second document, which was a confirmation of a wire transfer into his bank account.

He closed his eyes for a second, took a deep breath, and slipped the documents back into the envelope and handed it to Webber. "I can't accept this, Webber."

Weber pushed his hand away. "There's nothing to accept, Tristan. It's already done," he explained. "The trust is formed, and as you can see, I already transferred a large sum of money into your account for you to do with as you please. So now you have an income and a retirement plan. And lastly, I've changed my last will and testament and you are the major beneficiary of my estate."

"But—"

"No buts, Tris. If and when we retire, I want you to have complete independence. No matter what happens to you, me, or us, this is your money and I won't take no for an answer."

Tristan's mouth hung open and he didn't know what to say. "Web, I'm speechless."

"Just say 'thank you, Webber'."

"Thank you, Webber."

Tristan watched as Webber folded his cloth napkin, laid it on the table, and stood. "I was going to wait until after dinner, but I can't wait any longer," Webber announced.

He dug into his pocket and dropped to his knee next to Tristan's chair. He opened a black velvet box and held it up to Tristan. "Tristan Paul Moreau, I am more in love with you than I thought humanly possible. I love you more than life itself. Will you spend the rest of your life with me? Marry me, Tris."

Tristan's heart skipped several beats and he started to tremble. He stared at the emerald and diamond-encrusted band, mesmerized by the light reflecting from the chandelier above the table. When he finally found the courage to speak, he took Webber's face in his hands. "It's beautiful, Web, and so are you. I love you. Yes! Yes, I'll marry you."

SCOTTY CADE left Corporate America and twenty-five years of marketing and public relations behind to buy an inn & restaurant on the island of Martha's Vineyard with his partner of fourteen years.

He started writing stories as soon as he could read, but only recently for publication. When not at the inn, you can find him on the bow of his boat writing male/male romance novels with his Shetland sheepdog Mavis at his side. Being from the South and a lover of commitment and fidelity, most of his characters find their way to long, healthy relationships, however long it takes them to get there. He believes that in the end, the boy should always get the boy.

Scotty and his partner are avid boaters and live aboard their boat, spending the summers on Martha's Vineyard and winters in Charleston, SC, and Savannah, GA.

Visit Scotty at http://www.scottycade.com and Facebook. You can contact him at Scotty@scottycade.com.

Also from SCOTTY CADE

FINAL ENCORE

Scotty Cade

http://www.dreamspinnerpress.com

Also from SCOTTY CADE

Foundation *of* Love

SCOTTY CADE
AND Z.B. MARSHALL

http://www.dreamspinnerpress.com

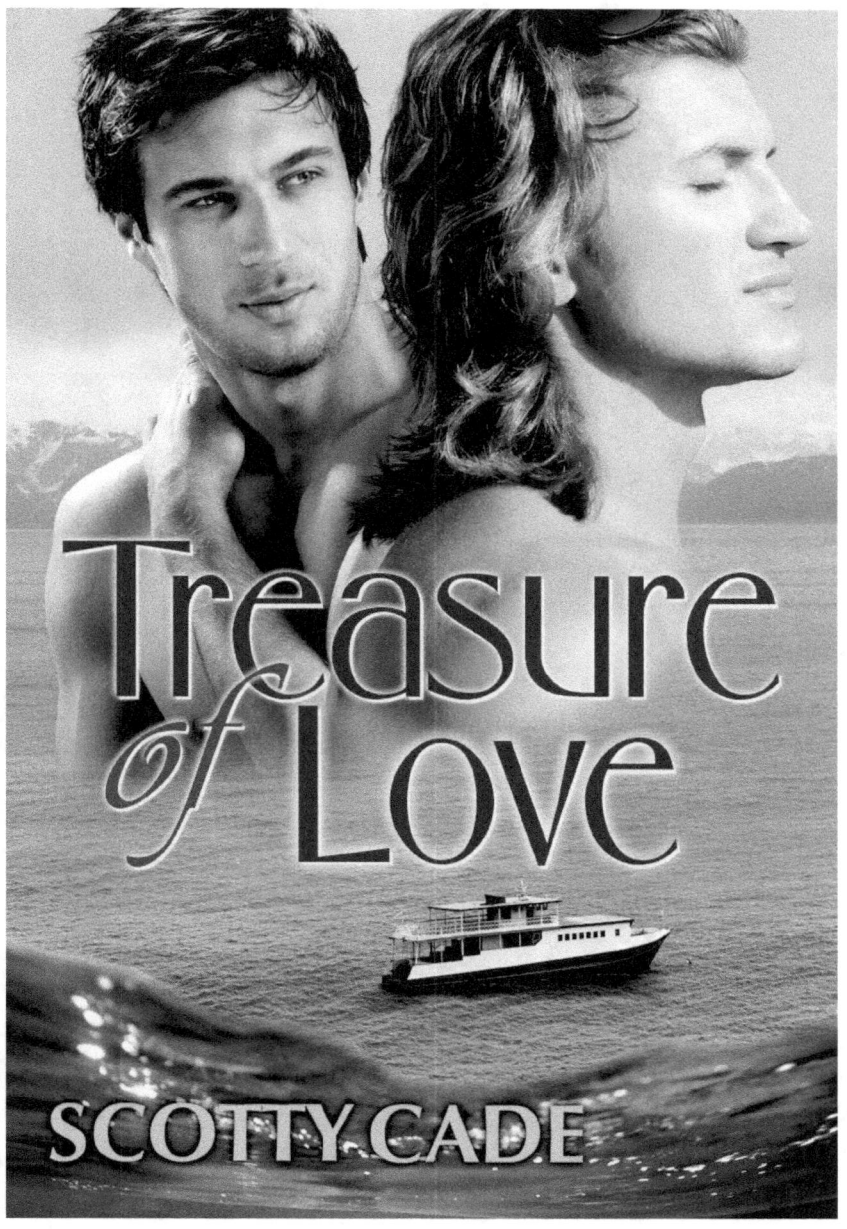

Treasure
of Love

SCOTTY CADE

Also from SCOTTY CADE

http://www.dreamspinnerpress.com